# A Mile in My Flip-Flops

Melody Carlson

a novel

# A Mile in My Flip-Flops

WATERBROOK
PRESS

A Mile in My Flip-Flops
Published by WaterBrook Press
12265 Oracle Boulevard, Suite 200
Colorado Springs, Colorado 80921
*A division of Random House Inc.*

The characters and events in this book are fictional, and any resemblance to actual persons or events is coincidental.

ISBN-13: 978-0-7394-9992-4



Printed in the United States of America

# 1

I'm not the kind of girl who wants anyone to feel sorry for her. So after my fiancé jilted me less than four weeks before our wedding date, and since the invitations had already been sent, my only recourse was to lie low and wait for everyone to simply forget. Consequently, I became a recluse. If I wasn't at work, teaching a delightful class of five-year-olds, who couldn't care less about my shattered love life, I could be found holed up in my apartment, escaping all unnecessary interaction with "sympathetic" friends. And that is how I became addicted to HGTV and ice cream.

Okay, that probably calls for some explanation. HGTV stands for Home and Garden TV, a network that runs 24/7 and is what I consider the highest form of comfort TV. It is habit forming, albeit slightly mind numbing. And ice cream obviously needs no explanation. Other than the fact that my dad, bless his heart, had seven quart-sized cartons of Ben & Jerry's delivered to my apartment the day after Collin dumped me. Appropriately enough, dear old Dad (who knows me better than anyone on the planet) selected a flavor called Chocolate Therapy, a product worthy of its name and just as addictive as HGTV.

But now, eighteen months and twenty-two pounds later, I seem to be in a rut. And apparently I'm not the only one who thinks so.

*"Come on,* Gretchen," urges my best friend, Holly, from her end of the phone line. "Just come with us—*please!"*

"Right…," I mutter as I lick my spoon and dip it back into a freshly opened carton of Chunky Monkey—also appropriately named, but let's not go there. Anyway, not only had I moved on to new ice cream flavors, but I also had given up using bowls. "Like I want to tag along with the newlyweds. Thanks, but no thanks."

"Like I keep telling you, we're not newlyweds anymore," she insists. "We've been married three months now."

"Yeah…well…"

"And it's Cinco de Mayo," she persists, using that little girl voice that I first heard when we became best friends back in third grade. "We *always* go together."

I consider this. I want to point out that Holly and I *used* to always go to the Cinco de Mayo celebration together—as in *past* tense. And despite her pity for me, or perhaps it's just some sort of misplaced guilt because she's married and I am not, I think the days of hanging with my best friend are pretty much over now. The image of Holly and Justin, both good looking enough to be models, strolling around holding hands with frumpy, dumpy me tagging along behind them like their poor, single, reject friend just doesn't work for me.

"Thanks anyway," I tell her. "But I'm kind of busy today."

"So what are you doing then?" I hear the challenge in her voice, like she thinks I don't have anything to do on a Saturday.

I slump back into the sofa and look over to the muted TV, which is tuned, of course, to HGTV, where my favorite show, *House Flippers,* is about to begin, and I don't want to miss a minute of it. "I'm, uh...I've got lesson plans to do," I say quickly. This is actually true, although I don't usually do them until Sunday evening.

She snickers. "Yeah, that's a good one, Gretch. I'll bet you're vegging out in front of HGTV with a carton of Chocolate Fudge Brownie."

"Wrong." Okay, Holly is only partially wrong. Fortunately, I haven't told her about my latest flavor.

"Come on," she tries again. "It'll be fun. You can bring Riley along. He'd probably like to stretch his legs."

I glance over to where my usually hyper, chocolate Lab mixed breed is snoozing on his LL Bean doggy bed with a chewed-up and slightly soggy Cole Haan loafer tucked under his muzzle. "Riley's napping," I say. "He doesn't want to be disturbed."

"Like he wouldn't want to go out and get some fresh air and sunshine?"

"We already had our walk today."

Holly laughs. "You mean that little shuffle you do over to the itty-bitty park across the street from your apartment complex? What's that take? Like seven and a half minutes for the whole round trip? That's not enough exercise for a growing dog like Riley."

"I threw a ball for him to chase."

"So there's nothing I can do or say to change your mind?"

*House Flippers* is just starting. "Nope," I say, trying to end this conversation. "But thanks for thinking of me."

"Want me to bring you back an empanada?"

"Sure," I say quickly. "You guys have fun!" Then I hang up and, taking the TV off mute, I lean back into the soft chenille sofa and lose myself while watching a hapless couple from Florida renovate a seriously run-down split-level into something they hope to sell for a profit. Unfortunately, neither of them is terribly clever when it comes to remodeling basics. And their taste in interior design is sadly lacking too. The woman's favorite color is rose, which she uses liberally throughout the house, and she actually thinks that buyers will appreciate the dated brown tiles and bathroom fixtures in the powder room. By the time the show ends, not only is the house still on the market despite the reduced price and open house, but the couple's marriage seems to be in real trouble as well.

"Too bad," I say out loud as I mute the TV for commercials.

Riley's head jerks up, and he looks at me with expectant eyes.

"You just keep being a good boy," I tell him in a soothing tone. Hopefully, he'll stretch out this midday nap a bit longer. Because once Riley starts moving, my tiny apartment seems to shrink, first by inches and then by feet.

My hope for an elongated nap crumbles when his tail begins to beat rhythmically on the floor, almost like a warning—*thump, thump, thump*—and the next thing I know, he's up and prowling around the cluttered living room. Riley isn't even full grown yet, and he's already way too much dog for my apartment. Holly warned me that his breed needed room to romp and play. She tried to talk me into a little dog, like a Yorkie or Chihuahua, but I had fallen for those liquid amber eyes...and did I mention that he's part *chocolate* Lab? Since when have I been able to resist chocolate? Besides, he reminded me of a cuddly brown teddy bear. But I hardly considered the fact that he would get bigger.

After he climbed into my lap that day, licking my face and smelling of puppy breath and other things that I knew could be shampooed away, there was no way I could leave him behind at the Humane Society. I already knew that he'd been rejected as a Christmas present. Some dimwitted father had gotten him for toddler twins without consulting Mommy first. Even so, Holly tried to convince me that a good-looking puppy like that would quickly find another home.

But it was too late. I knew Riley was meant for me, and that was that. And I had grandiose ideas of taking him for long walks on the beach. "He'll help me get in shape," I assured Holly. She'd long since given up on me going to the fitness club with her, so I think she bought into the whole exercise theory. She also bought Riley his LL Bean deluxe doggy bed, which I could barely wedge into my already crowded apartment and now takes up most of the dining area, even though it's partially tucked beneath a gorgeous craftsman-style Ethan Allen dining room set. Although it's hard to tell that it's gorgeous since it's pushed up against a wall and covered with boxes of Pottery Barn kitchen items that won't fit into my limited cabinet space.

"This place is way too small for us," I say to Riley as I shove the half-full ice cream carton back into the freezer. As if to confirm this, his wagging tail whacks an oversized dried arrangement in a large bronze vase, sending seedpods, leaves, and twigs flying across the carpet and adding to the general atmosphere of chaos and confusion. My decorating style? Contemporary clutter with a little eclectic disorder thrown in for special effect.

Although, to be fair, that's not the real me. I'm sure the *real* me could make a *real* place look like a million bucks. That is, if I had a real place…or a million bucks.

I let out a long sigh as I stand amid my clutter and survey my crowded apartment. It's been like this for almost two years now. Overly filled with all the stuff I purchased shortly after Collin proposed to me more than two years ago. Using my meager teacher's salary and skimpy savings, I started planning the interior décor for our new home. I couldn't wait to put it all together after the wedding.

"Have you ever heard of wedding presents?" Holly asked me when she first realized what I was doing.

"Of course," I assured her. "But I can't expect the guests to provide everything for our home. I figured I might as well get started myself. Look at this great set of espresso cups that I got at Crate & Barrel last weekend for thirty percent off."

"Well, at least you have good taste," she admitted as she stooped to admire a hand-tied wool area rug I'd just gotten on sale. Of course, she gasped when she saw the price tag still on it. "Expensive taste too!"

"It'll last a lifetime," I assured her, just like the Karastan salesman had assured me. Of course, as it turned out, my entire relationship with Collin didn't even last two years. Now I'm stuck with a rug that's too big to fit in this crummy little one-bedroom apartment—the same apartment I'd given Mr. Yamamoto notice on two months before my wedding. It was so humiliating to have to beg to keep it after the wedding was cancelled, but I didn't know what else to do.

And now, a year and a half later, I'm still here. Stuck. It's like everyone else has moved on with their lives except me. It wouldn't be so bad if I had enough room to make myself at home or enough room for Riley to wag his tail without causing mass destruction…or enough room to simply breathe. Maybe I should rent a storage unit for all this stuff. Or maybe I should move myself into a storage unit since it would probably be bigger than this apartment.

As I pick up Riley's newest mess, I decide the bottom line is that I need to make a decision. Get rid of some things—whether by storage, a yard sale, or charity—or else get more space. I vote for more space. Not that I can afford more space. I'm already strapped as it is. Kindergarten teachers don't make a whole lot. I feel like I've created a prison for myself. What used to be a convenient hideout now feels like a trap, and these thin walls seem to be closing in on me daily.

Feeling hopeless, I flop back onto the couch and ponder my limited options. Then I consider forgetting the whole thing and escaping back into HGTV, which might call for some more ice cream. But that's when I look down and notice my thighs spreading out like two very large slabs of ham. Very pale ham, I might add as I tug at my snug shorts to help cover what I don't want to see, but it's not working. I stare at my flabby legs in horror. When did this happen?

I stand up now, trying to erase that frightening image of enormous, white thunder thighs. I pace around my apartment a bit before I finally go and stand in front of an oversized mirror that's leaning against the wall near the front door. This is a beautiful mirror I got half price at World Market, but it belongs in a large home, possibly over a fireplace or in a lovely foyer. And it will probably be broken by Riley's antics if it remains against this wall much longer. But instead of admiring the heavy bronze frame of the mirror like I usually do, I actually look *into* the mirror and am slightly stunned at what I see. Who is that frumpy girl? And who let her into my apartment? I actually used to think I was sort of good looking. Not a babe, mind you, but okay. Today I see a faded girl with disappointed eyes.

Some people, probably encouraged by Holly, a long-legged

dazzling brunette, used to say I resembled Nicole Kidman. Although they probably were thinking of when Nicole was heavier and I was lighter. Now it's a pretty big stretch to see any similarities. To add insult to injury, Nicole has already hit the big "four *o,*" whereas I am only thirty-two. Her forties might be yesterday's twenties, but my thirties look more like someone else's fifties. And I used to take better care of myself. Okay, I was never thin, but I did eat right and got exercise from jogging and rollerblading. Compared to now, I was in great shape. And my long strawberry blond hair, which I thought was my best asset, was usually wavy and fresh looking, although you wouldn't know that now. It's unwashed and pulled tightly into a shabby-looking ponytail, which accentuates my pudgy face and pale skin. Even my freckles have faded. It doesn't help matters that my worn T-shirt (with a peeling logo that proclaims "My Teacher Gets an A+") is saggy and baggy, and my Old Navy khaki shorts, as I've just observed, are too tight, and my rubber flip-flops look like they belong on a homeless person—although I could easily be mistaken for one if I was pushing a shopping cart down the street.

Then, in the midst of this pathetic personal inventory, my focus shifts to all the junk that's piled behind me—the boxes, the myriad of stuff lining the short, narrow hallway and even spilling into the open door of my tiny bedroom, which can barely contain the queen-size bed and bronze bedframe still in the packing box behind it. If it wasn't so depressing, it would almost be funny. I just shake my head. And then I notice Riley standing strangely still behind me and looking almost as confused as I feel. With his head slightly cocked to one side, he watches me curiously, as if he, too, is afraid to move. This is nuts. Totally certifiable. A girl, or even a dog, could seriously lose it living like this. Or maybe I already have. They say you're always the last to know that you've lost your marbles.

"It's time for a change," I announce to Riley. He wags his tail happily now, as if he wholeheartedly agrees. Or maybe he simply thinks I'm offering to take him on a nice, long walk. "We need a *real* house," I continue, gathering steam now. "And we need a *real* yard for you to run and play in." Of course, this only excites him more. And that's when he begins to run about the apartment like a possessed thing, bumping into boxes and furnishings until I finally open the sliding door and send him out to the tiny deck to calm himself. After he settles down, I go and join him. It's pretty hot out here, and I notice that the seedling sunflower plants, ones we'd started in the classroom and I'd brought home to nurture along, are now hanging limp and lifeless, tortured by the hot afternoon sun that bakes this little patio. Just one more thing I hate about this place.

So much for my attempt at terrace gardening. I'd seen a show on HGTV that inspired me to turn this little square of cement deck into a real oasis. But in reality it's simply a barren desert that will only get worse as the summer gets hotter. I feel like I'm on the verge of tears now. It's hopeless.

*This is all wrong.* On so many levels. This is not where I was supposed to be at this stage of the game. This is not the life I had planned. I feel like I've been robbed or tricked or like someone ripped the rug out from under me. And sometimes in moments like this, I even resent God and question my faith in him. I wonder why he allows things like this to happen. Why does he let innocent people get hurt by the selfishness of others? It just doesn't make sense. And it's not fair.

Oh, I've tried to convince myself I'm over the fact that my ex-fiancé, Collin Fairfield, was a total jerk. And I try not to blame him for being swept away when his high school sweetheart decided, after fifteen years of being apart, that she was truly in love with him. I heard that the revelation came to Selena at the same time she received our engraved wedding invitation, which I did not send to her. She wasn't even on my list. And I actually believe that I've mostly forgiven Collin…and that sneaky Selena too. And I wish them well, although I didn't attend their wedding last fall. A girl has to draw the line somewhere.

But all that aside, this is still so wrong. I do not belong in this stuffy little apartment that's cluttered with my pretty household goods. I belong in a *real* house. A house with a white picket fence and a lawn and fruit trees in the backyard. And being single shouldn't mean that I don't get to have that. There must be some way I can afford a home.

Of course, I'm fully aware that real estate isn't cheap in El Ocaso. It's on the news regularly. Our town's prices certainly aren't as outrageous as some of the suburbs around San Diego, but they're not exactly affordable on a teacher's salary. I try not to remember how much I had in my savings account back before I got engaged and got carried away with spending on my wedding and my home. That pretty much depleted what might've gone toward a small down payment on what probably would've been a very small house. But, hey, even a small house would be better than this prison-cell apartment.

And that's when it hits me. And it's so totally obvious I can't believe I didn't think of it sooner. I will become a house flipper! Just like the people on my favorite HGTV show, I will figure out a way to secure a short-term loan, purchase a fixer-upper house, and do the repairs and decorating myself—with my dad's expert help, of course! And then, maybe as early as midsummer, I will sell this beautifully renovated house for enough profit to make a good-sized down payment on another house just for me...and Riley. Even if the second house is a fixer-upper too, I can take my time with it, making it just the way I want it. And it'll be so much better than where I live now. I'm surprised I didn't come up with this idea months ago. It's so totally simple. Totally perfect. And totally me!

"We are going house hunting," I announce to Riley as I shove open the sliding door and march back inside the apartment. His whole body is wagging with doggy joy as I quickly exchange my too-tight shorts for jeans and then reach for his leather leash and my Dolce & Gabbana knockoff bag—the one I bought to carry on my honeymoon, the honeymoon that never was. I avoid looking at my image in the big mirror as we make a hasty exit.

"Come on, boy," I say as I hook the leash to his collar at the top of the stairs. "This is going to be fun!" And since this outing is in the spirit of fun, I even put down the top on my VW Bug, something I haven't done in ages. Riley looks like he's died and gone to doggy heaven as he rides joyfully in the backseat, his ears flapping in the breeze. Who knows, maybe we'll find a house for sale on the beach. Okay, it'd have to be a run-down, ramshackle sort of place that no one but me can see the hidden value in, but it could happen. And while I renovate my soon-to-be wonder house, Riley can be king of the beach. The possibilities seem limitless. And when I stop at the grocery store to pick up real-estate papers, I am impressed with how many listings there are. But I can't read and drive, so I decide to focus on driving. And since I know this town like the back of my hand, this should be easy.

But thanks to the Cinco de Mayo celebration, the downtown area is crowded, so I start my search on the south end of town, trying to avoid traffic jams. I'm aware that this area is a little pricey for me, but you never know. First, I pull over into a parking lot and read the fliers. I read about several houses for sale, but the prices are staggering. Even more than I imagined. Also, based on the descriptions and photos, these houses already seem to be in great shape. No fixer-uppers here. Then I notice some condo units for sale, and I can imagine finding a run-down unit in need of a little TLC, but it's the same situation. According to the fliers, they're in tiptop, turnkey shape—recently remodeled with granite counters and cherry hardwood floors and new carpeting and prices so high I can't imagine doing anything that could push them a penny higher. My profit margin and spirits are steadily sinking. Maybe my idea to flip a house has already flopped. Just like the rest of my life.

# 2

After several hours of driving around town, complete with doggy pit stops, and finding not one single fixer-upper house, I begin to feel seriously discouraged. Maybe this isn't going to be as easy-breezy as I thought. Finally, feeling totally dismayed and in need of a little encouragement, I stop by my dad's beach condo on the north end of town and dismally knock on the door.

"Hello, Gretchen," says Betty, my dad's girlfriend. She smiles brightly as she opens the carved wooden door wider. "Come on in. We were about to sit down to dinner. You're just in time."

I glance at my watch. "Oh, I didn't realize it was dinnertime already." I also didn't remember that it's Saturday, a day Betty and Dad usually spend alone together. "I don't want to intrude."

"You're not an intrusion, Gretchen," Dad calls from somewhere inside. "I've been barbecuing a pile of ribs all afternoon. Come on in and join us."

"I don't know..." I glance over my shoulder trying to think of an excuse to get out of here. It's not that I don't like Betty, but I just wanted to see my dad.

He appears at the front door now, wearing a big smile. He's attired in a loud Hawaiian shirt, khaki golf shorts, and a red chef's apron that says "Real Men Don't Use Recipes" tied snugly over his rounded midsection. "I actually tried to call you about an hour ago," he says with a curious expression. "But no one answered. Everything okay?"

"I was out…and my cell phone was off." I remain in the hallway with Riley tugging eagerly at my leash, trying to get inside. I'm sure Dad's wondering why I wasn't holed up at home as usual.

"Come on in, Gretchen," urges Dad, taking me by the hand and pulling me.

"I've got Riley."

"I can see that. Bring him on in," he commands.

"What about your cats?"

"It's okay. They can take care of themselves, or they can hide in the spare bedroom if they want."

When I was growing up, my dad always claimed that he hated cats. But shortly after Mom died, when I was thirteen, I rescued a little black kitten in the middle of a busy street. It had been a particularly rough day in middle school, and the warm, furry kitten seemed like a real find. But once I got it home, Dad did not agree. He immediately put an ad in the local paper and some "found cat" signs in the neighborhood. When no one claimed my prize, I insisted on keeping her. Jasmine turned out to be a delightful cat, and later when I went to college, Dad pretty much adopted her and never did give her back. She had a good long life, and when she died a couple of years ago, it was Dad who decided to replace her. But instead of buying just one cat, he got three. He fell in love with three tiger kitties from the same litter, brought them all home, and named them Mowzer, Wowzer, and Bowzer. My dad's never been terribly clever with names, and even now he can't seem to tell them apart.

The cats are not the only reason I keep Riley on his leash. I've only brought him here once before, and he knocked over a potted palm that sat right next to the door. Fortunately that plant is now tucked safely away in a corner.

"Come outside with me, Riley," says my dad as he takes the leash from my hand and leads Riley out with him. Dad's first-floor condo has a nice walled-in area with a patio and a patch of grass. Not really big enough for a dog to run, but much nicer than my tiny sunbaked deck. "Check out my ribs, boy," Dad says to my dog. "You like meat?"

I chuckle to myself and think what a wonderful grandpa my dad would make. Not that it's likely to happen anytime soon...if ever.

"Want a soda or some iced tea?" offers Betty.

"Iced tea sounds good." I follow her into the kitchen, noticing how neat she looks in her crisp white Capri pants and blue and white striped top. Unlike me in my grungy jeans and a T-shirt with a shoulder that's still soggy from dog slobber, Betty always keeps herself up. I figure it's because she used to have her own real-estate brokerage and just never stopped looking professional. But like my dad, she recently retired. A divorcée of about ten years, she's independently wealthy and travels a lot. She calls herself a liberated woman, which makes me wonder if she thinks the rest of us aren't.

They've been dating for about six months, and I still don't know what I think about her. She's a few years younger than Dad, although her platinum blond hair makes her seem more youthful. And she's nice enough, but it's strange seeing my dad dating someone this regularly. It took him ten years after Mom died to decide to date anyone. And then it was only sporadically, thanks to the demands of his contracting business. As a result, this is the most serious relationship he's been in. And I can tell he likes her a lot, but I'm not so sure about Betty's intentions. Sometimes she seems slightly aloof, and I'm not sure that she's into him like he's into her. I guess I just don't want to see him get hurt.

"Did you go to Cinco de Mayo?" Betty asks as she hands me a tall glass complete with a generous lemon wedge.

"No…Holly tried to talk me into going with her and Justin…but I had other things to do…" I refrain from admitting how I didn't want to be a fifth wheel, which is sort of what I feel like right now.

"Other things?" I can tell she's skeptical. It seems that everyone is concerned about my hermit ways. So as we head out to join Dad and Riley, I stupidly blurt out in my defense that I went house hunting.

She pauses in the living room, turning to peer curiously at me. Her narrow arched brows lift slightly. "House hunting?"

Without answering, I continue outside, watching my dad as he uses a long set of tongs to carefully turn the ribs. The smell is almost intoxicating, and Riley sits like a dog statue at Dad's feet with long strings of slobber hanging from his gaping mouth. Then, just as Betty hands Dad a soda, Riley comes to life and starts running around the tiny square of lawn, turning round and round in tight circles like he's gone crazy.

"Stop it," I tell him, embarrassed by his neurotic behavior. "Be good, Riley!"

"Oh, it's okay." Dad chuckles as he closes the barbecue. "He just needs to stretch his legs. Poor thing's cooped up in your apartment day in, day out. I'd be running in circles too."

"Gretchen says she's been house hunting," says Betty.

"House hunting?" My dad turns and looks at me like I have just sprouted a second head. "Why are you doing that?"

So, hesitant but nonetheless excited, I explain to them about my house-flipping plan. I go into all the details of how it's done, the short-term financing, how I'd be really good at it, how I'll have extra time once school's out next month, and how I already have a lot of furnishings and things that I can "stage" it with when it's time for the open house.

"You've obviously given this a lot of thought," says Betty. But I can tell she's still not convinced.

"It's a really great way to make money," I say. "And I can use my profits from the flip for a down payment on a house for me."

"Sounds like you have it all figured out," says Dad. But I sense a slightly sarcastic tone. He looks even less on board than Betty.

"Well, I don't have it *all* figured out," I admit. "But I think it's something I could do...I might even be good at it. Maybe I could do one every summer as a way to supplement my income."

"Real estate is pretty spendy around here," Betty points out. Thank you, Captain Obvious.

"Yes. But that's one reason it makes sense," I counter. "People are willing to pay high prices. I just need to find a run-down piece of property—something that nobody wants—and then transform it into something wonderful...and sell it."

"Sort of a get-rich-quick scheme?" Dad's furry brows draw together, and I notice how white they've gotten. They used to be sort of a reddish blond, like mine. Sometimes I forget that he's getting old.

"No," I insist, "it's not a get-rich-quick scheme. It's an honest way to make money. And I'm fully aware it will involve a lot of hard work, but I do know a thing or two about construction." I wink at him. "After all, I grew up watching you do it. I know how to use a circular saw and how to swing a hammer."

He grins and pats my head. "That you do. But remodeling isn't the same as new construction, sweetie. It's a whole different can of worms."

"And depending on the age of the home, you could run into all kinds of problems," warns Betty. "Plumbing, electrical—"

"Look," I say, knowing it's rude to interrupt but feeling too frustrated to let her continue. "I *want* to do this. If you guys think it's stupid or foolish, I just won't bother you with the—"

"Don't get upset," says Dad. "We just care about you, Gretchen. We don't want you to get in over your head. Remodeling is serious business."

"I know that already." I stubbornly fold my arms across my chest and suddenly feel like I'm the same age as the kids in my class.

"*How* do you know that?" asks Dad.

"I watch *House Flippers* on HGTV," I say, then instantly wish I hadn't, because I know it sounds ridiculous. And I can tell they're trying not to laugh at me. And who could blame them?

"Is that some kind of educational channel?" asks Dad, who watches only sports or news and thinks cable is a waste of time and money. Consequently, I've tried to keep my HGTV addiction a secret. I don't think he'd understand.

"It's a home-improvement network," Betty informs him. "And it's actually somewhat educational, although I don't know that they can cover everything, especially when it comes to remodeling. It's just trickier than what can be explained in a one-hour segment."

"I'll say," agrees Dad. "I've tried to stay away from doing remodels over the years. I'd rather tear down a house and rebuild it from the ground up." He peers at me. "You sure you're up for something like this? Just from watching television?"

"Okay, I know it probably sounds silly to you," I admit. "But I've actually learned a lot watching those shows. Enough to know that it's possible." I don't mention the show I saw today where the house flip didn't go so well. "And I've seen people on the show make good money on house flips. People who know less about construction than I do."

Dad still looks skeptical. So I playfully sidle up to him and slip my arm around his thick waist. "Besides, I'm lucky. I have a dad who's an expert. Most of the people on that show don't have an experienced contractor in their back pocket."

He chuckles. "You think you've got me in your back pocket?"

"And now that you're retired, you have more time, Daddy. You'll be just the person to advise me."

This almost seems to do the trick because Dad starts to get a dreamy look in his eyes, like he's really considering the possibilities and liking them. "I suppose it could be interesting…"

"And fun," I add.

"And you know that I'd love to see you get into a house of your own. I just wish I had enough cash to help you out, but you know how that last job set me back some…" He turns away from me now, focusing his attention on the barbecue again as he applies a fresh coat of sauce to the already dripping ribs.

Saddened that I've made him remember this, I exchange an uncomfortable glance with Betty. This is a painful topic that we try to avoid. For Dad's sake, we just don't go there. Most of the town is aware that he was horribly taken advantage of in his final construction job. After a lengthy hotel project was finally completed, the stingy out-of-state investor had the audacity to accuse Dad of doing unsatisfactory work. My dad, who had worked in Southern California for decades with nothing but happy customers. To add insult to injury, this tightwad jerk not only refused to pay Dad but filed a claim against him with the state contractor's board and withheld payment to Dad's subcontractors as well.

As it turned out, that good-for-nothing investor was flat broke and ended up filing for bankruptcy himself, but that didn't help anything on Dad's end. He wound up paying his subcontractors from his own pocket and hiring a lawyer to go after the investor. In the midst of this, Dad's health went seriously downhill, and at his doctor's insistence, he decided it was time to retire. The attorney, who's gone pro bono, still thinks there's a chance the lawsuit will pay off, but at the rate it's going, Dad might be a hundred years old before he sees a dime of settlement. Fortunately his condo is paid for, and he seems to get by fairly well on his Social Security.

"I don't want you to feel like you'd have to do much in the way of helping me…I mean, as far as physical labor," I say quickly to Dad. "I'll mostly need your expertise and advice, because I know that your health is—"

"Nonsense," he says. "I'm fit as a fiddle. My blood pressure has gone down considerably, and that new cholesterol medicine is working so well that I can eat like a king now."

I point to the ribs. "So that's what this is about?"

Betty frowns with concern. "I told Hank it wouldn't hurt him to continue some of the healthy eating habits he's established."

"I'm sick and tired of vegetables and whole grains," he says as he licks barbecue sauce from a finger. "And if I never eat anything to do with soy again, I'll be a happy man. Besides, what's the point in being alive if you can't enjoy your life a little?"

"With moderation," injects Betty. "Which reminds me…I brought a bottle of Merlot."

"You drink wine now?" I ask Dad as Betty goes back into the house.

"Betty says it's good for me—just a glass at dinnertime for my cholesterol and heart. I didn't like it much at first, but I can't argue that I've been feeling better."

Betty returns with the bottle and corkscrew and hands them over to Dad. "The wine needs to breathe a little," she tells me.

"Betty's right about moderation," I say to Dad as he fiddles with the corkscrew. "Moderation is a very good thing for someone with high blood pressure and high cholesterol and ancestors with a history of heart disease."

"I agree with you about moderation." He winks at me as he pops the cork, then hands the bottle back to Betty. "And I think these ribs are *moderately* done now—that means medium and just exactly how I like 'em. You girls ready to indulge in some fine red meat, or would you rather go chew on a celery stick somewhere?"

No one argues as he stacks the delicious-smelling ribs on a platter. But I do have to question his sensibility when we sit down at the patio table, where Betty has just set out the side dishes, which don't look any healthier. "Your dad made these," she says, almost in self-defense.

I look at the creamy potato salad, which is loaded with eggs and bacon bits, and then the second bowl, which I recognize as his famous "southern" coleslaw. I'm thinking there must be about a gallon of mayonnaise between these two large bowls.

"You think you got enough cholesterol on this table?" I ask Dad as he pours us each a glass of wine.

He chuckles as he sets a glass in front of me. "If it makes you feel any better, I used *light* mayonnaise."

I bite my tongue as I wait for Dad to say grace. Maybe there's no point in nagging the poor man. I take a deep breath, noticing the nice cooling breeze coming straight off the Pacific. And I realize it's actually sort of nice sitting outside and sharing a meal with Dad and Betty. I feel guilty for having been such a hermit for so long, but maybe things are starting to change for me now. And maybe I'll become more social when I finally have a place of my own. I imagine a house with a yard where I can set up a table and a barbecue like Dad's. Then as he prays his usual blessing and I hear Riley happily chewing on a bone beneath my feet, I think that life seems to hold some promise now. Things are about to change.

Dad says, "Amen" and passes me the bowl of coleslaw, but as I put a cautious serving on my plate, I see that it's literally dripping in dressing. "You're sure this is *light* mayo, Dad?"

He clears his throat as a slight smirk appears on his face. "Here's the deal, Gretchen Girl. You lay off my dietary decisions, and I won't get on your case regarding your remodeling abilities or lack thereof."

"Meaning you're going to help me flip a house?"

He picks up a big rib. "Yep. I'm thinking it sounds like fun." He winks at me with those blue gray eyes that are just a couple of shades lighter than my own, then smacks his lips and takes a bite.

"It could be fun," adds Betty, "as long as your flip doesn't go flop."

I try not to scowl at her. "Of course, it won't be a flop," I say with confidence. "Dad and I will make a great house-flipping team. He'll be the brains, and I'll be the brawn."

They laugh, and Dad questions my current physique, and I try not to take offense. I also try not to obsess over how I suddenly feel like a misfit. But the two of them look like such a couple—laughing at each other's jokes, looking into each other's eyes. And then here I am...alone. It's not that I think Collin should be sitting next to me. I don't. In fact, most of the time I think I'm over him. Or nearly. Still, it's not easy being the single one when I'm with couples. It's not the way I thought I would be. But I guess I need to get over it.

# 3

"I think I've found something with potential," Betty tells me over the phone. I'm just walking through the parking lot at the end of a long workday, heading to my car, which has been baking in the sun. I wish I'd put the top down this morning.

It's been exactly eleven days since I decided to flip a house. I did what felt like an exhaustive search for fixer-uppers in our area and came up with nothing. Then Betty stepped in and offered her scrvices. On Monday she contacted all her real-estate associates and even did some looking on her own. She's turned up a couple of options, but so far nothing has been quite right. "Quite right" as in cheap enough for my budget.

Even with Dad cosigning the loan for me, which he offered to do, and even with using his condo as collateral, which makes me nervous, I can borrow only $500,000. And although that sounds like a nice chunk of change to me, it will not go very far in El Ocaso. Plus, I'll probably need to hold back about fifty grand for renovations as well as for reserves in case the house doesn't sell at the end of six weeks, when the loan payments become due. Needless to say, this greatly reduces my buying power.

Still, I've been optimistic. And I've even been praying, something I hadn't done for quite some time...like about eighteen months.

On the Sunday after I made my decision to flip a house, I went to church and actually listened. Pastor Briggs preached about expecting God to do the impossible. I like that. And I think it fit nicely with my flipping plans. So I've been clinging to that idea. Especially since, as days have gone by, finding the right house has begun to seem unlikely and fairly impossible. So I've been trying to trust God. Hoping for the impossible to materialize. On the bright side, and as Dad pointed out, this waiting period has given me time to work out the financing and get preapproved so I'll be ready to jump when the opportunity arises. Maybe it's today.

"So, where's the house?" I ask Betty, feeling unexpectedly hopeful as I unlock my car, open it up, and stand outside for a moment, waiting for the interior to cool off. It's been a long day. The kids know that the school year's nearly over, so they're getting antsy. For the last couple of hours, all I've wanted to do was go home, kick off my shoes, and dive into a new carton of B&J's Chocolate Fudge Brownie yogurt. Yes, I'm talking about frozen yogurt, *not* ice cream. After harping on Dad about his dietary choices and after witnessing the shape of my thighs, I decided it was time to cut back on some fat and carbs myself. As a result, I've been eating frozen yogurt for more than a week now, and I'm almost getting used to it. At least it's chocolate, and it's cool and refreshing. Okay, I still watch HGTV when I'm not out hunting for a house. But now I consider it a research resource, a form of education, like Remodeling 101. But suddenly the lure of chocolate frozen yogurt and TV pales in comparison to seeing this house.

"It's on the east side," says Betty.

"East side..." I consider this. It's the least desirable section of town, but it's also the cheapest. "What's the house like?"

"I haven't seen it yet, but the price is in your ballpark."

"Which part of the ballpark?"

"It's just been listed at $479,000. But my real-estate friend Judy says she's sure they'll have to come down. Apparently it's been a rental for quite some time...and it sounds like it's not in very good shape."

"That's what I'm looking for." I get in my car now, turn on the engine, and crank up the air conditioning.

"Anyway, I have the key if you want to stop by and get it from me. I'd offer to go with you to check out the house, but I need to get to my hair appointment in a few minutes. I thought maybe you could meet me in town."

"I have to run home and take care of Riley first," I tell her. "He'll need some exercise. But then I could swing by your place and pick it up if that's okay. When do you think you'll be finished at the hair place?"

"I expect it'll be a couple of hours. After my hair, I'm getting a manicure and pedicure. You know I'm going on that European trip with my sister, and I have to get myself all fixed up before we leave." She laughs lightly.

"When do you go?"

"Friday morning."

"And you really plan to be gone for two whole months?"

"Yes. Louise and I will start with a two-week Mediterranean cruise, just to relax and catch up. And after that, we'll tour around France, Austria, Germany, and Switzerland in a rental car. We want to take it at a leisurely pace, lingering in certain places and basically just soaking it all in."

"Sounds wonderful. Dad's really going to miss you."

"Well, I have a feeling you'll be keeping him pretty busy with your house-flipping project while I'm gone."

"I hope so."

"Gretchen, just don't let him overdo it, okay?" I hear warmth in her voice now, like she might care for him more than I realized. For Dad's sake, I hope that's the case.

"Of course not. He's simply going to be my consultant."

"Great."

"Now what about the key? I'm dying to see this house!"

"How about if I leave it, along with the address and Judy's card, with the receptionist at Simi's Salon?"

"Sounds perfect."

"And if I don't see you before I leave, good luck with your project."

"Thanks. And you have a great trip."

"Oh yes, I intend to. Louise and I have been planning this for years."

"Make sure you take lots of photos," I say.

"Yes. And you too. I want to see how things go with your house. Too bad you couldn't be on that *House Flippers* show so I could watch the whole thing. Have you considered actually looking into that?"

I laugh. "I'm not sure I want the whole world to see my first house flip."

"Maybe next time then."

"Maybe."

As I hang up, I feel somewhat relieved that Betty will be out of the picture for a couple of months. It's not that I don't like her, but I have a feeling that, having worked in real estate, she'd have her own opinions about how things should be done. And I'm not sure I want someone looking over my shoulder. Plus, and selfishly, her absence will allow Dad more free time to spend with me...and my house. It feels like a win-win to me.

I go home and take Riley to the park to get some fresh air and to do his business. As usual, I have several plastic baggies handy for removing his doo-doo piles. I'm not sure I'd do this if there weren't a fee for leaving them. I deposit the filled baggies in the trash can, then throw a ball for Riley. But after only ten minutes, I tell him that's it. I know he's disappointed as we head back to the apartment, where I quickly change my clothes. When I come out of my room, Riley is waiting expectantly by the door, tail thumping in happy anticipation.

"Sorry, boy," I tell him. "But I think it might be considered bad etiquette to bring a dog to look at someone else's house." I pat his head. "And I can't exactly trust you alone in my car yet." I probably won't trust him with much of anything until he gets out of this chewing stage, which the vet assured me should end soon. In the meantime it's driving me nuts. Yesterday he devoured one of my LL Bean sandals. When I found it in his bed, it looked like someone had put it in the food processor on high. Of course, the other sandal is still in perfect condition to remind me that they used to be a pair. I wish Riley didn't have such good taste in shoes. Why can't he go for those cheap pumps from Target? Or even my old flip-flops. But no, he has to sink his teeth into pricey LL Bean and Cole Haan. Note to self: put all expensive shoes on top shelf of closet ASAP.

"Be good," I tell him as I grab my purse. "If you can keep from destroying anything, I'll take you for another run when I get back." Then I hurry down to my car and quickly drive downtown and park behind Simi's, a very nice salon I wouldn't mind going to someday—if I could afford it.

When I pick up the envelope containing my precious key, I spy Betty not too far off in a comfortable-looking chair with a young woman hovering over her and doing something with her hair. I consider waving and saying hello, but she looks so relaxed I don't want to disturb her. Besides, I'm eager to see this house. As I hurry back to my car, I think that Betty's got the life. And I suppose I sort of envy her. Okay, it's not like I want to be in my sixties, but if I could remain my present age, I would love to be in her shoes. I'd love to be getting my hair done, then having a pedicure and manicure before I left on a two-week cruise, followed by six more weeks to "leisurely" explore Europe.

I sigh as I get into the car. Well, who knows? If this real-estate venture goes well, I might become a regular house flipper. Even if I only turned over one house a year, it could add up. Maybe in thirty years I could be sitting pretty too.

I read Betty's note with the address and directions. The Realtor's business card is paper-clipped to it—and there is the key. I hold the brass key in the sunlight, seeing it as if it were a precious jewel. Then I drive east until I reach an older subdivision called Paradise. Well, the name might be a bit of a stretch, but maybe it seemed like paradise back in its day, which I'm guessing was about fifty years ago. It's a tract-home subdivision with what I'd estimate to be about a hundred ranch-style homes. Some houses look fairly well maintained with landscaped yards. But many are not. And when I get to Lilac Lane, the street where "my" house is located, I am decidedly unimpressed. My guess is that most of the houses along here are rentals. And all are lacking in curb appeal. But when I get to the house with the For Sale sign in front, I can find only one thing that's right about it: it's the saddest looking house on the street.

"The best investment opportunity," Betty told me last weekend, "is to buy the worst house in a good neighborhood."

Well, I'm not so sure about the neighborhood, but this is clearly the worst house in the entire subdivision. I park my car on the street and just sit there looking at this pathetic house. I'm not even sure I want to go inside. The paint is peeling. A screen door is hanging on its hinges. The front picture window is cracked. The yard is brown, and what once might've been flower beds are overgrown with weeds. But then I realize that these are all fixable things. And, really, not terribly expensive either. Good grief, what am I thinking? This is perfect!

"Come on," I say to myself. "This is just what you're looking for."

Feeling confident, I go up the cracked cement walkway and onto the porch, where I unlock the front door and give it a push. But I notice the house isn't empty. There are things inside. So without entering, I cautiously call out, "Anybody home?" Then I stick my head inside and am nearly knocked over by the smell. I don't know if it's from pets or a decaying corpse in the bathtub, but this place totally reeks. I blink and step away from the door, gasping for fresh air and wondering if foul air could seriously harm someone. I remember stories of archaeologists who dropped dead when they breathed the toxic air inside the pyramids. Could this be anything like that?

I stand on the front steps and stare at the neglected yard. The house may be perfect for my project, but it's nothing like what I had hoped for. I'd imagined a charming bungalow in need of some TLC. Or maybe even a neglected beach house. Something with some personality. This is a boring old ranch house that smells like an outhouse. Or worse. No way can I go inside there, even to just look around. And to work in a place like that? I'd have to be insane. Only a complete idiot would take on a nasty place like this. I'm convinced it's probably a health hazard. Not only does the place reek, but there's all that junk I saw on the mud-colored carpeting. For all I know someone might still be living here. Maybe it's an ax murderer with dozens of dead bodies rotting away beneath the floorboards.

I go back to my car but then realize I didn't lock the front door. In fact I didn't even close it. Not that anyone with any sense would dare to go inside. Suddenly I feel mad. What kind of a Realtor sends a poor, unsuspecting home buyer to a place like this? I dig the business card from my purse and dial the listing Realtor's number. Her smiling photo gives the impression that she might be a decent person, but I imagine devil horns poking out of her sleek brunette hair. When Judy answers, I tell her who I am and immediately launch into a quick but candid description of the house of horrors she's trying to sell.

"Betty told me you wanted a fixer-upper," she finally says in an obvious tone, like the giant litter box I'm staring at is an answer to prayer.

"Have you even *seen* it?"

"Of course. I wouldn't list something unseen. And yes, it's in bad shape. But Betty said you wanted a house to flip—you can't deny that this one has lots of room for improvement—and the price is quite a bit below what other homes have recently sold for in that same subdivision."

"I should hope so."

"So I don't see the problem."

"The problem is that it totally stinks. And it looks like someone might still be living there—or something inside might even be dead."

"The house is vacant. But the renters did leave some things behind. This isn't uncommon in eviction situations. And that's one of the reasons the house is priced as low as it is."

"Well, yes, but this is pretty extreme."

"Fine," she says in a sharp business tone. "Just bring the key back to my office. I think I already have a buyer for it anyway."

"You have a buyer?"

"Yes. I have someone who regularly flips properties coming by here first thing in the morning. He has essentially told me he'll be making an offer tomorrow."

"An offer? Tomorrow?"

"Yes. Like I said, this guy is a pro at flipping houses. He's done dozens of them. And trust me, he knows real-estate potential when he sees it."

"And he's *seen* this place?"

"Not the inside, but he did a drive-by just an hour ago, and he's very interested."

"But it reeks!"

She actually laughs now. "Have you ever done this before?" she asks me. "Flipped a house?"

"Well, no…"

"It's possible that you're not cut out for it then. Some people just don't like to get their hands dirty."

Now, I resent this. She doesn't even know me. "I'm not afraid to get my hands dirty," I say defensively.

"Well, renovations are extremely hard work. If you don't believe me, I can give you the name of the contractor who wants to buy that ranch house. I'm sure he could tell you a thing or two about—"

"My dad's a contractor," I snap. "And I happen to know a thing or two about renovations." There's a brief pause, and I wonder if I've offended her.

"Yes…I understand that," she says calmly. Almost the same tone of voice I might use with a cranky five-year-old who just doesn't get it. "But this would be your first house flip, Gretchen. Perhaps you need a house that's in better shape. Come to think of it, there's a cute little cottage on the west side that needs some work. It's listed at $550,000, but it could probably go for more than six if it was fixed up a little."

"That's out of my price range."

"Oh…well, then maybe you should consider a condo. I've got a nice unit in Parker Place for sale, and it's listed for just a little more than the Lilac Lane house."

"No thanks," I tell her. I don't mention that my ex fiancé and his wife live in Parker Place and that you couldn't pay me to buy a condo there. I'm looking at the neglected ranch house again, thinking that perhaps I've been too hasty in my judgment. Maybe it just needs a little TLC. Okay, a lot of TLC. But really, am I nuts to let a bad smell drive me away? And what if that other buyer snatches it out from under me, fixes it up, and sells it for big profit? Then how would I feel?

"You're sure the tenants have moved out?"

"Yes. They were evicted several weeks ago."

"And you have actually been inside the house yourself?" I ask.

"Yes. And it wasn't exactly a walk in the park. But there's definitely potential. Have you seen the backyard yet?"

"Well, no…"

"I suggest you go have a look. Before you do that, maybe you should open up the doors and let some fresh air flow through the house. After that, take a quick walk-through, try to ignore the messes, and see if you don't discover the possibilities."

"Okay…"

"Then get that key back to the office. It's the only one I have. We just listed the house and haven't even made copies yet. I only let Betty have it as a personal favor."

"Sure…yeah, I'll do that."

"And don't feel bad if it doesn't work for you. House flipping isn't for everyone. Sometimes it's better to leave things like this to the pros."

So I thank her, hang up, and then go around to the backyard. To my surprise, it is pretty nice. Although like the front, the grass is brown and dry and the flower beds are filled with weeds, it does have some mature trees and is fairly good sized. Unfortunately, though, there are as many dog-poop piles as there are weeds. No one used baggies to pick up around here. It's like walking through a minefield just to make my way to the back door. But then again, there's a covered deck that could provide a shady place to sit if it wasn't piled high with filled trash bags and various pieces of junk, including about twenty old tires stacked like a privacy fence and a bunch of broken yard toys.

I unlock and open the back door, hoping that Judy's theory of air flow will work. But the smell that comes out from this end seems even worse than the front. I'm seriously considering my ax murderer theory again. There could be a whole pile of rotting corpses inside. I don't think I've seen anything like that on *House Flippers* yet, but it would probably raise their ratings some.

Moving carefully through the land mines, I walk all around the outside perimeter of the house, checking it out. More peeling paint, more broken windows, missing screens, junk, and garbage. But even as I continue to find more flaws with this house, something in me seems to be coming around. I'm starting to envision the house with a fresh coat of paint in an inviting color, maybe an earthy sage green with tan trim, some new windows, some landscaping... That really could transform the place. Maybe all this house needs is someone who cares.

I try to imagine the original owners of this house, probably back in the early sixties. Maybe they were a young couple with two kids. I'll bet the kids were dressed all nice and neat. The house was probably squeaky clean. The furniture might've been that sixties modern-contemporary style that's considered retro now. And for all I know, there might still be hardwood floors underneath that nasty carpet.

I dig in my faux D&G bag until I find a small sample of Poison cologne that a Macy's salesgirl practically forced on me when I shopped for my dad's birthday present last month. I apply this strong-smelling scent generously to my wrists and my neck, using every drop so that it's overpowering as I stand in the front yard, mentally preparing myself to do this walk-through. I wish I had a scarf to tie over my nose and mouth like a bandit, but maybe I can hold my breath. I take several long, deep breaths, psyching myself into this. And then, feeling strong and confident, I march up to the front door and go inside.

The perfume trick works for about ten seconds, and then it's futile. Since no one's around to witness, I pull my T-shirt up over my nose, revealing my not-so-slender midsection and part of my bra. Then I literally run from room to room throughout the house. I quickly take in what appear to be three good-sized bedrooms, also piled with trash and junk, two full but filthy bathrooms, a smallish, dark living room, and a barely there family room, or maybe it's a dining room off the small kitchen.

And finally, thinking I'm about to die and wondering how long it will take for someone to find me expired on the dirt-encrusted floor of the disgusting kitchen, I explode out the back door and run across the deck, where I stand hunched over at the edge of the backyard right next to several piles of old doggy doo-doo and brace myself to throw up. I think it would be a relief to hurl just now, a way to purge the foul things I just inhaled. But the fresh air slowly revives me, and I think perhaps I'm overreacting.

I find an old plastic lawn chair that's only moderately filthy and carry it over to a semicleared corner of the deck, where I sit down and consider this whole crazy house-flipping plan. Did I expect it to be easy? No. Did I think I'd get a house that was "nice and neat"? No. Am I too much of wimp to do this? No. Am I ready to give up? No.

Perhaps a smarter woman would turn and run just now. But something inside me seems to be standing up and saying, *I can do this.* Maybe it's that image of the freshly scrubbed family moving into their "modern" sixties home that's encouraging me, telling me that there's hope for this house. Or maybe the house itself is calling to me, saying, "Help me!" Saying it wants to be restored...it wants to be clean and decent again...it wants to be a welcoming place—a place to come home to.

During my whirlwind tour, I did notice that one of the bedrooms had a hardwood floor. Okay, it was in pretty bad shape, but it's a good sign that more hardwood floors might be lying dormant beneath that horrible carpeting, which I've decided must be the source of that disgusting stench. My guess is that pets used that nasty brown carpet for their toilet.

But once the carpets are removed and taken far from this place, and once the wood floor is properly cleaned, most of that ghastly smell should be eradicated. Then with fresh paint and new surfaces, it will be nothing more than a bad memory. Then I'll do updates and upgrades to the kitchen and baths, replace the light fixtures, windows, and doors, and before long—hopefully by the end of the six weeks my loan allows me to flip this place—the worst house on Lilac Lane should be restored and ready to go on the market. Easy as pie.

I tiptoe my way around the dog piles again, this time so I can peek over the wobbly backyard fence to see that the yards on all three sides seem to be in much better shape than this one. That's a good sign. Then I walk back to the front yard and check out the surrounding houses on both sides of the street. Certainly, they're not in pristine condition, and quite possibly are rentals, but they are not anything like this place. And, who knows? Maybe if I fix up this eyesore, others will be inspired to follow suit. It's possible that some day this street will be one of the nicest parts of Paradise...and I will have been a part of it. That's a nice feeling.

I go back to my car and call my dad now. But he's not home, and his answering machine must be turned off again. My dad hates technology. He refuses to own a computer and only got a cell phone because, as a contractor, he needed it. But now that he's retired, he just leaves it in his desk, where it probably has a dead battery anyway. For all I know he might've cancelled service on it long ago.

I try Betty's number, but she must still be getting beautified. Finally I try Holly, who answers her cell phone on her way home from work.

"I think I've found a house," I tell her. She knows about my house-flipping plan and has even offered to help me when she can.

"Good for you," she says.

"But I want a second opinion," I tell her. "Any chance you could stop by?"

"Oh man, I'd love to see it, Gretch, but I promised to meet Justin at his mom's place. It's his dad's birthday, and—"

"That's okay," I interrupt. "I understand."

"How about tomorrow?" she offers. "After work?"

"Maybe...but I might have to make a decision before that."

"*Before* tomorrow?"

"Well, there's another guy interested. And this house just came on the market, and you know how hard it's been to find a fixer in the right price range."

"Are you sure the Realtor's not just feeding you a line for an easy sell?"

"She's a friend of Betty's…and I'm pretty sure she's legit."

"So maybe you should jump on it."

"That's what I'm thinking."

"Has your dad seen it yet?"

"No. He's not home."

"Oh…"

"Well, I don't want to keep you on the phone while you're driving, Hol."

"Yeah, I just promised Justin that I wouldn't talk on my cell on the road. He thinks it might be dangerous." She sort of laughs. "But let me know how it goes, okay?"

"Yeah."

"And if it seems right, maybe you should just go for it, Gretch. Pray about it and listen to your gut."

I tell her I'll do that and then say good-bye and hang up. Okay, I know that I need to be more understanding of Holly. I realize she's still a newlywed and her allegiance needs to be to Justin. But the little girl inside me is screaming, *What about me? You used to be my best friend, and now what am I to you, chopped liver?* I know that's incredibly immature and selfish, but it's how I honestly feel. Well, that and a bit jealous. Oh, I'm happy for Holly. But how is it that she found Mr. Perfect and I'm still single?

After a few minutes I realize this juvenile temper tantrum is getting me nowhere. So as I sit in my car, I play back her advice. And then I actually take it. I close my eyes, and I pray about the situation. When I open my eyes, I look at the house, and once again I picture how nice it could be—what a transformation. It would be almost like a miracle. And that's when I know that I want to be part of this miracle. I want to take something that seems nasty and worthless and turn it into something wonderful.

I imagine the open house I'll have only six weeks from now, after all the hard work is done, when the house and the yard are picture perfect. I envision the excited Realtors, maybe even Judy, coming and patting me on the back, saying what an amazing job I did. I can just see the pride in Dad's eyes as he brags to his building buddies about how his "little girl" flipped a house. And I imagine myself later on down the line, perhaps before the school year begins, with Riley proudly beside me as I buy my very own home. Maybe it will be something similar to this one, a house that needs TLC but with solid potential. And suddenly I know that I'm going to do this: I'm going to buy this house.

# 4

"So did you decide to look for something else?" asks Judy as I hand her the key. It's five thirty now, and she's ready to go home. "Something less challenging?"

"No..." I shake my head. "Not exactly."

"Does that mean you're interested?"

"I actually am."

Her eyes brighten. "So you see the potential?"

"Yes. That smell was disgusting, but if that was gone, I think I could handle the rest of it just fine."

She nods. "I totally understand. Certain aromas can really get to me too. But in my line of work, you see and smell all kinds of things in people's homes." She chuckles. "It's funny how people don't even realize what their own homes smell like—whether it's cooking odors or pets..." Then she gets an odd look. "Sort of like women who wear too much perfume."

I have to laugh. "You must mean me. I had to douse myself with a sample of Poison just to get through that house. I must smell like a perfume counter."

She smiles. "It's a little strong."

"Sorry."

"No problem. So, do you want to make an offer?"

I consider this. "An offer?"

"On the house. Like I said, I'm pretty sure that I'll get an offer on it tomorrow. Do you want to make one first?"

"Is there an advantage to making one first?"

Her brow creases. "Sometimes. Especially if the seller is eager."

"Is the seller eager?"

"Actually, he is. He and his wife just moved down to Mexico, and he told me he wants the property off his hands as soon as possible."

"But I've never done this before," I admit. "I don't have a clue."

"That's where I come in, Gretchen."

"Right...but I should talk to my dad first. I mean, he hasn't even seen it."

"Want to come back into my office and give him a call?"

So I follow her back inside, dialing Dad from my cell phone as we go, and this time he answers. I quickly explain the situation and how there's another interested party who might make an offer tomorrow. "Can you come and look at it right now?"

"I wish I could, honey, but it's the church elder dinner tonight. I was just getting dressed to go."

"Oh..."

"Why don't you tell me about it? Like, how old is the house, and what kind of shape is it in?"

"Well, it smells horrible. It was a rental."

He laughs. "That's not the kind of information I mean, sweetie."

"Right." I put on my business hat now. "It was built in the sixties. It's a three-bedroom, two-bath ranch house. It has a big yard with mature trees. A covered deck. Oh yeah, it's in a subdivision called Paradise."

"Paradise?" he says with interest. "Those used to be considered some really nice homes back in the day. Your mother and I even looked to buy there once, but they were out of our price range, so we built our own house."

It's hard to imagine a house like I looked at today being too expensive for my parents. "Well, Dad, the house you built for us was much nicer than the one I'm considering," I admit.

"Thanks. But those houses in Paradise were well built. Sturdy and with good materials."

I remember running through the house now. At least I didn't fall through any floorboards, and I didn't notice any shaking going on. "Yes, the house did seem sturdy enough."

"And good bones?"

"How do you mean?"

"The basic structure, the lay of the rooms—did that seem okay?"

"Yeah. I mean, I might want to open the family room and living room into one great room, but the rest of it was good. And I think it has hardwood floors too."

"What's the square footage?" he asks. I relay this to Judy, and she slips some paperwork in front of me, pointing to various lines.

"It's 2,145 square feet," I tell him. "And it was built in 1962."

"Sounds nice and spacious. And is it within your price range?"

I tell him the listing price. "But Betty thought I could offer less."

"Did Betty see the house?" he asks hopefully.

"No, but she sort of found it for me."

"Well, then..." He pauses, and I can imagine him doing some quick calculating. "Why don't you go ahead and make the offer, Gretchen."

"Without you seeing it?"

"Based on what you told me, I think it should be fine. I'm guessing the only changes you'll make to the house will be cosmetic. A lot of elbow grease and cleaning, some fresh paint, new countertops, fixtures..."

"Exactly!"

"Go for it," he says.

"Really?"

"If you think that's the right house."

"I do, Dad. I mean, I wasn't sure at first, but I think I was just reacting to the smell."

He laughs. "We'll get a crew in there to rip out that old carpeting, and I'm guessing the smell will be gone by the end of the day."

"So how much should I offer?"

"You say someone else is interested?"

"Yes."

"Then you don't want to lowball them too much. How about $455,000? That will leave you at least $45,000 to fix up the place, and based on the age of the house and the fact you won't be changing the footprint—"

"Footprint?"

"You know, like where the bathrooms and kitchen are. You don't plan on moving a bathroom, do you?"

"Oh no, not at all. But I would like to take out a wall or two, to open it up."

"As long as it's not a bearing wall. Or if it is, we'll put in a beam. But if you're not moving toilets or sinks or anything like that, it shouldn't be too costly. Fifty grand ought to do it—just as long as you stick to a budget and don't get carried away shopping for upgrades. You won't, will you?"

I laugh. "I quit my shopaholic ways ages ago, Dad." I don't mention that I gave it up right after Collin gave me up.

"Then you should be just fine. Go ahead and make the offer, and see how it goes."

"You're sure?"

"Are *you* sure?" he asks.

I take in a deep breath. "Yes."

"Then go for it."

"You really trust my judgment on this?"

"I do."

"Okay then. Thanks. I'll let you know how it goes. Hey, why don't you turn your answering machine on so I can leave a message?"

"Will do."

I close my phone and turn to Judy. "Okay. Let's write up an offer."

She nods happily as she pulls out a form and begins to fill it in. It's just a little past six by the time she finishes. "The seller has a fax. Let me give him a call and tell him to watch for it. If we're lucky, he may have an answer for us sometime this evening."

"Really? That soon?"

"It's possible."

"So, do I just go home and wait then?"

She smiles. "Yes, just go about your business, but keep your cell phone on. I'll let you know as soon as I hear something."

I am flushed with excitement as I drive home. I wonder if this is sort of how it would feel to be pregnant—this happy expectation of something that could change your life. But then I figure that's probably carrying it too far. Still, I feel like I'm on the edge of my seat, just waiting for the phone to ring.

I keep my phone with me and turned on while I take Riley for the promised walk. And then, after a quick dinner, I load Riley into my car and, with the top down, drive back over to what I'm now thinking of as my house. I'm surprised by how much better the house looks in the dusky light. I try to imagine what it would look like all fixed up, with lights glowing cozily from the inside. I consider getting out and walking around, but the idea of Riley, my baby, in a yard so strewn with doggy-doo and who knows what else makes me decide to wait until the place is cleaned up.

~ ~ ~

It's after nine when my phone finally rings. I anxiously pick it up, but it's just my dad wanting to know how it went.

"I made the offer," I say. "Just like you said. And the Realtor thought we might even hear back tonight."

"Well, I'll get off the line in case she's trying to call."

"Thanks, Dad."

"And I was praying about this," he tells me, "while driving home. I prayed that if it wasn't the right thing, God would close the door."

"Oh…" I don't like the idea of God closing this door, but I don't say so.

"I wouldn't want you to get into something that was over your head."

"I know. But I think this is the right house. I really do."

"Good. Let me know how it goes…but not tonight, sweetie. I

played eighteen holes of golf today, then that dinner meeting... I think I'll call it a night."

"Okay. I'll call you tomorrow with updates."

About five minutes after I hang up, the phone rings again. This time it is Judy. "Sorry to call so late, but it's an hour earlier in Baja," she says.

"That's okay," I say quickly. "Have you heard from the seller?"

"He just called...but he countered your offer."

I feel a flood of disappointment washing over me as my house seems to vanish in a puff of smoke right before my mind's eye. "What's his counter?"

"Four hundred sixty-nine thousand dollars."

"Right..."

"You can either accept his counter, or you can raise your offer to somewhere between the two figures."

Okay, I feel like I'm getting in over my head now, and I want to call Dad, but I know he's tired...maybe already in bed. So I grab a pen and write down the numbers: the asking price, what I offered, and what he said he would take. And I just stare at them.

"Are you still there?" asks Judy.

"Yeah...I was just thinking."

"Do you want to wait until tomorrow?"

"No," I say quickly. "How about if I offer him $460,000?"

"I can give it a try."

"Is that too low?"

"You never know."

"It's just that I need to have enough money left to fix up the place and keep my head above water if, heaven forbid, it doesn't sell for as much as it needs to when I'm done with it," I explain. "So I don't think I could pay any more than that."

"I understand."

"Can you tell him that I *really* want the house," I say feebly, "that I *really* care about it and that I'll make it look *really* nice?"

She laughs now. "I can tell him that, but I don't know that it'll make any difference."

I feel embarrassed now. "Right. I mean, I realize it's business."

"Do you have a fax machine?"

"No."

"I really should get your initials on the new offer," she says. "But since he's out of the country, maybe we can bend the rules. If he's interested, I'll have you pop in first thing in the morning, and we'll do it right."

"Do you think he'll be interested?"

"I don't know."

"So, you'll let me know what he says?"

"As soon as I know, I'll let you know. But that might not be until morning."

"Okay."

So I go to bed feeling a mixture of emotions. I'm trying to be hopeful, trying to believe that the impossible is possible, but I feel anxious and worried. Finally I remember what Dad said about God closing a door. I think that might be what's happening. Maybe this is not going to happen. Maybe I was never meant to be a house flipper. Maybe all I will ever be is a single kindergarten teacher, living in a tiny apartment with an oversized dog who likes to chew on expensive shoes.

# 5

After a restless and nearly sleepless night, it's finally morning, and I'm walking from the parking lot toward the elementary school with a feeling of dejection, not to mention exhaustion. I'm guessing that my offer has been refused and that the other buyer will probably get the house today. That's what I get for dreaming too big. Maybe I just need to learn to be content with my lot in life. What made me think I could pull off something like this anyway? Just then my cell phone rings, and it's Judy.

"He accepted your offer!" she says happily.

"No way!" It's honestly the last thing I expected to hear.

"Yes. Ron just called. I actually told him what you said last night about loving the house, and it must've gotten to him. He said that he and his wife bought that house in the late seventies and did some upgrades, like carpeting and whatnot, and that they really did love the house and felt bad that it had been so abused by the renters. He said that his wife wanted the buyer to be someone who cared about it."

"Really?"

"So if you can pop in and sign this new offer, we should be good to go."

"How about if I come during my lunch break?"

"Great. I'll have the paperwork all ready for you."

"Thanks!" As I close my phone, I feel like I just won the lottery.

Needless to say, I am completely distracted during the morning session of school. But I also feel happy, and my kindergarten kids, just like little mirrors, reflect that happiness back at me. When we gather on the carpet for circle time, they look bright and expectant. When we sing our songs and do our rhymes, their voices are lilting and full of joy. Just how I feel.

And it occurs to me, not for the first time, that I really do love my job. I love these little kids, and despite wanting to teach a higher grade level when I got my degree, I feel completely at home with five-year-olds now. I'm not sure I'll ever want to switch. This reminds me of my mom and one of the ways we are alike. She loved little kids too. When I started fourth grade, Mom took a job teaching at a nearby preschool. Her training had been in art, but she loved being around small children, and I think since she was unable to have more after me, the preschool kids filled that spot in her life. I can even remember feeling jealous at first, worried that she liked those "other" kids better than me. But after a while I got used to it. I realized that I was still her number one girl. And I enjoyed helping her put crafts and things together at home for her to use at preschool. Sometimes, when I'm teaching my class, I almost get the sense that she's checking in on me…and smiling.

But by noon I am so eager to get to the Realtor's office that you'd think I was on my way to a party. The new offer is quickly signed, and Judy shakes my hand. I tell her that I've already called Dad and he's meeting this afternoon with his lenders—the same company he's worked with for years on his own contracting projects.

"He assured me that the loan's already approved," I explain. "Just a matter of signing some papers."

"The final paperwork should be ready by Friday," she tells me. "It really simplifies the sale when you and your father have the financing all worked out. The sellers were hugely relieved that it was a cash offer. So much time is saved that way. It won't be long until you'll be the proud new owner of your first home."

I consider this. In some ways it's true, and I do feel a certain sense of ownership already, but I'm also fully aware that this is an *investment* deal. The house is not really going to be mine, not in the long run. It's being financed by a short-term loan—a loan that must be paid back in six weeks or it cuts into the profits. The interest rate will rise, and we'll incur severe penalties if we default. I know this. Also, Dad's credit rating will suffer. A lot is at stake here.

I thank Judy and head back to school, getting into gear for my afternoon kids. Fortunately my aide, Claire, is already there, providing good insurance if there are any early birds. I count off the days until summer break. I can't believe there are only eleven, not including today. Because kindergarten starts a week earlier than the rest of the grades so the young children have a chance to acclimate to the school environment before it gets too busy and overwhelming, it gets out a week early as well. A nice little dividend, I think.

The afternoon kids, as usual, are more subdued than my morning class. They're more worn out by this time of day, and it hasn't been too long since these little ones were having their naps. Plus the classroom is always warmer in the afternoon, especially this time of year. Snack time is surprisingly quiet, although they do liven up for recess.

Finally the day is done, and as soon as the last stragglers of the day have gone home, I call Dad to see how the financing is going.

"I signed the final loan papers about an hour ago," he tells me. "And I told them you'd come by after work and sign them too."

"No problem. Did you see the house yet?"

"Not the inside. But I drove by it on my way home."

"What did you think?" I ask eagerly.

"It looks pretty much the way you described it. It needs work, but it has good potential."

"Do you think we need an inspection?" I ask cautiously. Holly mentioned this to me the other day. She said Justin thought it would be wise. And now I'm starting to wonder if they could be right.

"I'll admit things are moving quickly," he says. "But Betty said a house at that price wouldn't last another day on the market. I'm hoping I can get in there before the three-day cancellation rule expires."

"What's that?"

"We have three business days to change our minds and cancel the loan if we need to. Since today is Thursday, that gives us until Monday to rescind."

"Oh..." Now this should be a comforting thought, but I really hope it's not necessary. I so want this house.

"I'm sorry I'm not more help just now," he says. "But this is Betty's last day before her big trip. I spent most of the day with her. Took her to the mall to pick up some last-minute things. And now she's here at my place, and we're about to head out. I wanted to drive up the coast and take her out for a nice seafood dinner."

"Sounds lovely."

He chuckles. "Well, I want to give her something special to remember me by when she's over there with all those fancy schmancy continentals in Europe."

I have to laugh at this. But then I realize that my dad might be even more smitten with Betty than I'd suspected. "Well, you guys have a good time, and tell her bon voyage for me."

"Will do."

"And tell her thanks for connecting me to Judy and helping to find that house. I owe her one."

"She's thrilled that it worked out for you. She said she can't wait to see it when you're done. And she said to remind you to take photos. Did you tell Betty about your photography, Gretchen?"

"No...I don't really do it much anymore, Dad."

"Well, you should. You're an excellent photographer."

"Thanks, Dad." Then we say good-bye, and I wonder about that last comment. It was sweet, but Dad never really seemed to be that into my photography before. Not that he ever said anything negative about it; he just never really seemed to notice. In fact, other than Holly, the perennial optimist, no one has ever given me much encouragement about my photography. And the last time I did much with it I was engaged to Collin... I suppose that was one reason I gave it up. A couple of insensitive comments from him sort of shut me down. I filed my photos away and stuck my camera in a drawer somewhere. I'm not even sure where, but I suppose I should dig it out if I'm going to get some good "before" pics of the house.

The thought of dusting off my camera is kind of exciting. Like perhaps I'm finally returning to who I used to be...or maybe someone even better. And I've been wanting to get some shots of Riley before he's full grown. I should also take some end-of-the-year photos of my class at the kindergarten picnic. It's something I've done every year, except for last year. I was disengaged then—literally—and it was all I could do to make it to the last day of school. Looking back, it seems like I was in a deep fog… I can barely remember my students now. That makes me sad.

But as I park my car, I realize that things are changing for me. Now I'm starting to feel this fresh sense of newness and anticipation, like doing this house flip is some sort of personal awakening for me too. I think this is the first time I've felt this kind of hope since Collin dumped me. And it feels good.

~ ~ ~

It takes what feels like a year to sign all the loan papers, but I know that Dad's done the bulk of the work. And I'm well aware that the equity in his fully-paid-off condo is backing this loan. All I'm doing is putting my name below his, as well as today's date in a few places.

"Who knew my autograph was so valuable?" I joke to the loan officer when I finally hand back the stacks of papers, in triplicate.

"Keep the pen," he tells me as he puts the papers into various folders and finally hands me back two folders. "One for you and one for Hank." Then he shakes my hand. "Congratulations. And good luck on your project."

By Friday afternoon a check has been issued from the loan company, and all the real-estate paperwork has been completed and signed by both Dad and me. Judy tells me that she's faxing the contract and as soon as the sellers sign off, the house is officially ours.

"I'd say it's official now," she says. "But I need to get this paperwork back from them first. Anyway your work here is done."

"Thanks. Does that mean I can have the key?"

She considers this. "I really should get their signatures first."

"Oh, that's okay," I tell her. "I'll have plenty to do this weekend anyway. There's so much to plan and figure out."

"Good for you. Consider yourself a homeowner, or house flipper. My guess is that I'll be handing you the key to the castle first thing Monday."

"That's great," I tell her. "I'll use this time to check out the local home-improvement stores. Even if I don't buy anything yet, I'll start making lists and budgeting and pricing things and getting information."

"Sounds like fun," she says.

And it does sound like fun. Much better than sitting around my crummy apartment, porking out on ice cream and watching HGTV. This is like having a real life!

On Saturday, after taking Riley for a long stroll on the beach, where I dusted off my camera and took some great shots of him, I'm hoping he's so worn out that he'll take a nice nap and refrain from chewing up anything too valuable. I tell him to be a good dog, and promising that things are going to change as soon as school is out, I stick a notebook in my bag and head for the local home-improvement stores. I considered inviting Dad to join me, and at some point I will, but for now I just want to process this on my own. I think I need to figure out some things for myself on the front end—like what kind of countertops, appliances, hardware, and all that fun design stuff that doesn't require contracting expertise to choose well.

By the end of the day, I have dozens of pamphlets and price lists and material descriptions. Not only that, but after talking to a helpful window salesman, I even applied for what they call a "project" card. It's six months of interest-free credit that earns points toward future purchases. I'm already thinking about the next house I'll be fixing up—the one I'll buy from the profits of my flip house—maybe as soon as August, before school starts back up.

"The first thing you need to do is start measuring everything," the window guy told me just as I was finishing up. "And then measure it all again just to be sure."

"Measure twice and cut once," I shot back at him with confidence.

This barely-out-of-high-school dude seemed duly impressed. "Sounds like you've done this before."

"Sort of. My dad's a retired contractor."

"Then you've got it made in the shade."

And as I sit in my apartment Saturday night, sorting out all the stuff I've collected, marking file folders and organizing everything into an oversized bag, I think maybe I do have it made—or at least I'm on my way. After going over the costs of the upgrades I know I'll need, I think maybe I can afford granite countertops and stainless appliances—real top-of-the-line items.

On Sunday after church Dad and I meet to look at the house again. We don't have the key yet, but he wants to check the exterior more thoroughly. I think maybe he's getting a little worried. He told me about a dream he'd had the night before in which the house we were working on collapsed.

"I'm thankful we have until tomorrow to cancel the loan," he says as I get out of my car.

"Why's that?" I ask, suddenly worried.

"Well, I was in a hurry when Betty and I stopped by here last week. And I suppose I was distracted, but I didn't notice a couple of things."

"A couple of things?"

He nods with a concerned frown. "That roof needs to be replaced."

"Really?" I peer up at the roof and just shake my head. "How can you tell?"

"See how those asphalt shingles are curling on the edges. They've definitely seen better days. I'm guessing that roof is about twenty years old."

"Oh...will that be expensive?"

"Yeah. I'm afraid it would take a good-sized bite out of your budget, sweetie."

"And you said 'a couple of things'?"

"Well, as you mentioned, the windows definitely need to be replaced. I'm surprised to see they still have the original aluminum ones. Most folks upgraded that kind of thing ages ago. But, besides that, some of that siding may need to be replaced as well."

I feel myself gulp. "And that'll be expensive too?"

"Depends on how much we can save."

"Do you have any idea how much these exterior things will cost?" I ask as I pull out my notebook and pen.

"Well, offhand, I'd guess about ten grand. But that's only if we do most of the work ourselves, Gretch. And that doesn't include the cost of windows, which could be another ten grand."

"Yikes."

He nods and adjusts his sunglasses. "I wish we had the key to go inside."

"Judy said we can probably have it tomorrow."

"Well, we should just be really thankful for that three-day cancellation law. We may need it, sweetie."

"Oh, I hope not..." But I feel my spirits seriously slumping as Dad puts an arm around my shoulders and gives me a squeeze.

"Don't worry," he says. "If this house isn't the right one, there's probably another one. Maybe we jumped the gun a little. I take partial blame... I'm sure I was too distracted with Betty."

I peer curiously at him now. "You really like her, don't you, Dad?"

He smiles. "She's a good lady."

I nod. "I think I like her too."

"I know she's very different from your mom, Gretchen. But I always knew that your mom was one of a kind...irreplaceable."

"I know..."

"And I never thought I'd actually consider settling down with a wife again."

"You want to marry her?" I feel a wave of shock, but I guess I should've seen this coming. Why wouldn't he want to marry her?

"Oh, I haven't said anything to her yet. But, yes, I do think I'd like to marry her, Gretchen. It's not easy being alone...when you're old."

I want to add that it's not easy being alone when you're my age either, but I think that might be a little self-centered.

"And Betty has a very nurturing spirit."

I nod. "Yeah. I like that she cares about your health, Dad."

He kind of laughs. "Well, I don't want to marry her to be my nurse."

"I know. But sometimes a woman has more sense when it comes to dietary needs. Betty seems to understand things like fat and cholesterol."

"Speaking of fat and cholesterol, I'm hungry. How about I take my favorite girl and new business partner out to lunch?"

"Sounds great."

At Outback Steakhouse, after I talk Dad into ordering a heart-healthy meal, we discuss the house. I tell him about all the things I found yesterday and how I even opened up a credit account.

"I'm not so sure I like the sound of that. You don't want to be going over your budget, Gretchen."

"No, I just thought it might be handy."

"The worst thing would be to end upside down with this house."

"Upside down?"

"Putting more money into it than it's worth."

"Oh..." I recall how some people have done that on *House Flippers.* "Well, Dad, if we decide to move forward, I'll be really careful. I promise." I smile and hope privately that everything works out and we don't have to cancel the loan.

"How about if I pick up the key from Judy tomorrow," he offers, "and I can do a thorough walk-through while you're at work? Then you can meet me there as soon as school gets out, and we can discuss this whole thing rationally. And we'll still have time to rescind the loan...if we need to."

"That's probably the wise thing to do," I agree. But to be honest, I don't agree. I know it's totally irrational, totally beyond reason, but I don't care what's wrong with it; I so want to flip that house. If a house ever needed to be flipped, the one on Lilac Lane is begging for it. We would be doing the whole neighborhood an enormous favor to turn that place around. But I don't admit to this. I feel fairly certain that Dad, a savvy businessman, would not get it. He'd think I was making a foolish decision based completely on emotion. And maybe he'd be right.

"You know that I'm not one to put much stock in dreams," he finally says to me in a very serious tone, "but maybe the one I had last night...well, maybe it was meant to be a warning. Maybe God was trying to tell us something."

I consider this. "Yeah, I suppose that could be." But the truth is, I don't really care about Dad's dream at the moment. The selfish truth is, I'm not willing to give up my own dream yet.

# 6

"It's pretty bad in there," Dad tells me as soon as I show up at the house on Monday afternoon. Nothing like an encouraging word to start off our time at the house. His red pickup, with "Hanover Construction" still painted on the sides, is parked in the driveway. The tailgate is open like a bench, and he is sitting on it when I arrive.

"You mean the smell?" I ask. Riley tugs at his leash to get to my dad, like he thinks Dad may be hiding one of those yummy ribs in his back pocket. Maybe it was a mistake to bring my dog here today, but I felt sorry for him being all cooped up.

Dad shakes his head. "No, I don't mean the smell. Although that's bad too."

"What do you mean then?" I ask. "Specifically."

He scratches his chin. "Boy, I hardly know where to begin. There's dry rot in one of the bathrooms and the laundry room. Looks like all the plumbing fixtures need replacing. What I could see of the hardwood floors wasn't promising. I can hardly think of anything that's good about it."

"Really?" I feel an unexpected lump in my throat. "It's that bad? Like completely hopeless?"

"I think it'd take more cash than you have to restore it. And even if you could, Gretch, this is a really tough house to take on for your first flipping experience. I wouldn't wish a place like this on my worst enemy."

"So that's it?" I say hopelessly. "We just give up."

"It's not like giving up. It's simply being sensible. There's got to be another house out there—something that's not in this kind of shape. The renters really messed it up." He sighs. "That's what comes from trying to manage property from out of the country. The seller may not realize what a mess this is."

"According to Judy, they knew it was bad. The wife was happy that someone was going to fix it up."

"Well, I hate to be the bearer of bad news, but that will have to be someone besides us." He glances at his watch now. "There's just enough time to make it to the finance place. You want to give them a call and tell them I'm on my way?"

I nod sadly. I feel totally defeated, but I trust my dad's judgment. "Yeah… Do I need to come?"

"No." He digs his keys out of his pocket. "It only takes one signature to cancel the loan. But I'll assure them that we'll be back. I'm sure we'll find another, more appropriate house in time. Meanwhile, you can head over to talk with Judy. I'm sure she'll understand. Tell her that we'd like her help in locating the next house but that it'll have to be in better shape than this one."

"Okay." I pull Riley's leash. "Let's go, boy."

"And really," Dad calls out as he gets into his pickup, "I know it's sad, but believe me, we should be thankful that we can get out of this nightmare."

"Yeah, right," I mutter as I force my unwilling dog back into the car. He's looking at me like *What's wrong?* Like he wanted to stay and run around in the yard. Not that the yard is ready for him yet. Now I guess it never will be. I try to think positively, like my dad, telling myself we probably did just dodge a bullet. Even so, it's hard to give up the dream of renovating that house.

"You're serious?" says Judy after I quickly explain the situation.

"I wish I wasn't."

"But it's a great deal, Gretch. Fixed up, that house could make you good money."

"My dad says there too many things wrong with it. He's stopping the loan right now."

She looks puzzled. "Well, I'm surprised he can stop the loan at this stage of the game. I sent the works, including the check, on Friday afternoon by FedEx overnight delivery to the sellers. They would certainly have it in their hands by now. I'm not sure we can get out of this gracefully, not to mention ethically."

"Well my dad seems to be pretty confident about the whole thing. But I really am sorry to put you through all this," I glance outside to make sure that Riley is still in my car since the top is down. He's never jumped out before, but just to be sure, I tied his leash to the door handle. "And Dad said to tell you that we'd appreciate your help in finding another, uh, more suitable house."

She nods. "I'm not sure what the sellers will think of this. But at least I won't have a problem selling that particular house again. I had three other buyers asking about it by the end of last week."

I reluctantly hand her the house key, then look outside just in time to see my big brown dog literally hanging himself from the passenger door of my car. "Oh no!" I cry out. "My dog's trying to commit dog-icide."

"What?"

I point out the window as I run for the door. Judy follows, and together we manage to untangle Riley's mess. By the time we finish, she's laughing. "What a crazy dog!"

Just then my cell phone rings. "Can you hold his leash a minute?" I ask as I do a juggling act just to get into my purse. It's my dad on the phone, and he sounds a little upset.

"What's wrong?" I ask.

"The loan has already gone through..."

"What about the three-day cancellation thing?"

"Apparently they count Saturday as a business day."

"What does this mean?"

"That the sellers cashed the check and we now own a wreck of a house."

"That's great!" I'm jumping up and down in the parking lot, smiling at Judy as she holds on to the end of Riley's leash.

"You think that's great?" My dad does not sound the least bit convinced or happy.

"I know it looks hopeless right now, Dad, but I am really excited about this, and it must have been for a reason. I know we can make it work."

"I don't know how you possibly know any of this, Gretchen. I just pray to God that you're not wrong."

"Want to meet back over there?" I ask happily. No amount of Dad's discouragement can bring me down right now. Plus, I really believe at this moment that God would have closed the door if he didn't want us to have the house. Instead, he closed the door to getting rid of it. "We can do a walk-through together. Maybe it's not as bad as you think."

"I really hope so."

"See you in about fifteen minutes, Dad." Then I hang up, and as I relieve Judy of my dog, I tell her the good news.

She seems pleased. "To be honest, I wasn't sure how your dad was going to put the brakes on this deal after the three-day rescission period had passed, but I didn't want to be the one to rain on your parade until I spoke to the sellers."

"Hey, I couldn't be happier," I tell her. "I know Dad's a little worried, but I really think we can do this. Somehow we will make it work. I really believe it's going to be a great house by the time we're done." I'm imagining granite countertops, cherry cabinets, sleek stainless appliances, and gleaming wood floors.

She hands the key back to me now. "Well, here you go, Gretchen. Congratulations. And let me know if you want my help when it comes time to list it."

"For sure," I say as I open the passenger door. Then, using both hands, I shove a reluctant Riley back into my little car.

Okay, I feel a small stab of concern as I drive back to the house. Am I completely selfish? I'm fully aware that my dad's condo is on the line here, and if this house flip goes flop, I will be extremely upset for him as well as for myself. Consequently, I know I should be taking this all very seriously. But I think it's because I truly believe we can do this that I'm not that worried. I guess I'm feeling more confident than usual that God really cares about me and about this project. And with his help, I think we can pull off the impossible.

Dad gets back to the house right after I pull up, and I don't need to see his expression to know that he is not pleased. He slowly walks over to where I'm letting Riley out of the car—no more hanging-dog tricks.

"It's going to be okay," I say to Dad. Then I hug him. "I have a really good feeling about this. I think it's going to turn out to be a miracle."

He frowns. "It's going to take a miracle, Gretchen."

"I know. Anyway, I'll tie Riley out here," I say as I wrap the leash around a post that supports a handrail near the driveway.

"Yeah, I wouldn't let a dog I liked in there."

"Not yet anyway."

"And not in that backyard either," warns Dad. "Don't let Riley go back there until we get a cleanup crew in. It's not safe." Dad offers a small laugh, and I'm glad.

"Right." I smile. I unlock the front door, bracing myself for the smell as I push it open. "Maybe we should open up the other windows and doors before a walk-through," I say. "Let it air out a little."

"Sounds like a plan," he says.

So I go around to unlock and open the back door. I can hear Dad stomping around inside, jerking open a window and using words that come as close to swearing as I've ever heard from him. I can tell he is very unhappy with this house. Hopefully, he'll change his tune after we get a few things done. Then, thinking I can't deal with the smell any longer, I pull out the scarf that I tucked in my purse and tie it around my nose like a bandit. Hopefully, Dad will think this is funny...not depressing.

But Dad ignores my little costume, simply taking me from room to room and pointing out flaw after flaw. "This whole bathroom will need to be torn out," he says as he bounces on the floor so hard that I'm afraid he might go straight through it. "And probably part of the other bathroom too, at least around the sink area anyway."

Finally I can't take the smell anymore. "I need some air," I gasp. Then I hear a loud crash, and the next thing I know Riley is trying to get in through the front door, dragging the whole post and handrail behind him. Fortunately the pieces of wood keep him from getting inside.

"Bad dog," I scold him as I go out and work on disconnecting him from the rotten wood.

"I don't know about that." Dad joins me outside, cracking a small smile. "I think Riley has got it right. He's a *demo* dog. He knows that the best answer would be to demolish the whole house and start over."

"Dad!"

He tosses a piece of broken handrail into the weed patch of a front yard, then scratches his head. "You're really excited about taking on a stinking pile of crud like this?"

"It's hard to explain," I admit. "I know it probably seems crazy, but I really do want to do this. And I don't want you to feel like it's your responsibility," I add quickly. "Like I said before, I want you as a consultant only, Dad. I don't expect you to lift a finger."

He makes a grunting noise like he's not convinced.

"I'm serious," I say sternly.

"Well, for starters I plan to get a cleanup crew in here ASAP." He frowns at me. "It's a good thing one of us speaks Spanish. The best crew I've ever worked with is a group of guys who speak very little English."

"You'll never let me off the hook for taking German instead, will you?"

He shakes his head. "We practically live in Mexico, Gretchen, and yet you picked German for your foreign language."

"Well, it all started with this certain cute guy in high school," I admit to him for the first time. Taking German has always been a bone of contention between my dad and me. I figure, on a day like today, maybe it's a good time to clear the air.

"Huh?" He looks surprised.

I nod sheepishly. "Yep, he was a senior, and I was a sophomore. He had this great curly blond hair and big blue eyes. His name was Todd Vincent, and he was an academic assistant in the first-year German class. I had the worst crush on him. So I transferred from first-year Spanish and took German instead."

"I always knew there was more to that." He actually laughs now. "So what happened to this Todd fellow?"

"He went to Germany as an exchange student at Christmastime. I never saw him again."

"But you kept taking German anyway?"

I shrug. "Yeah, well, I didn't want to have to start over with Spanish by then."

"Well, anyway, I'll order a couple of Dumpsters and get a work crew in here to clean this place out. Hopefully ripping out that carpet will take care of some of that smell."

"It'd be great to be able to go through the house more slowly," I admit. "It's awfully hard to focus on the renovations when I feel like I'm about to hurl."

"I'll have the guys clean up the yard some too. Just remove the trash and do some sanitizing so that Riley can roam around without any threat to his health. Is he current on all his shots?"

"He is."

Dad pats Riley on the head. "Okay, Demo Dog, we'll get this place cleaned up and safe for you. Then we'll set you loose on it, and you can tear out anything you like. We can use the help." Dad tells me about a few other things he'd like to take care of soon. And the more he talks, the more I think that maybe he's getting into this just a little.

We lock up the house and go our separate ways. I try not to feel discouraged, and I especially hope that Dad isn't preparing for financial demise. He obviously knows more about houses and construction than I ever will, but more than anything, I would love to prove him wrong on this one.

# 7

There's trouble in Paradise," Dad informs me over the phone Friday as I leave school for the day. It's been four days and four Dumpsters since my dad's cleanup crew started emptying the house of all the trash and debris. And yesterday I started to feel really hopeful. Not only was that nasty carpeting and all the linoleum totally removed, but the smell had decreased significantly as well. I had commended the crew for doing such a great job, and in my best Spanish, which is admittedly lame, I presented them with a case of cold Sierra Mist and a box of cleaning supplies and asked them to scrub down the surprisingly sturdy kitchen cabinets. There appeared to be at least a decade's worth of grease and grime coating the wood, which Dad says is probably alder. After doing a patch test, I could see that the wood has a rather nice grain. With some refinishing and new nickel hardware, along with sleek granite countertops, I think the cabinets will look great. Plus reusing the cabinets will save us enough money to nearly cover the expense of a new roof.

"What do you mean?" I ask Dad as I walk to my car.

"Come on over, and we'll discuss it when you get here," he says stiffly.

"Let me pick up Riley first, and I'll be right over." I want to tell Dad that I don't expect him to be at the house every single day and that he better not be doing any of the actual labor, but I've said it so many times that I'm starting to get sick of hearing it myself. As I drive home, I wonder what's gone wrong now. Hopefully it's nothing too big. I've already noticed how Dad can overblow things when it comes to this house. Like it's a personal vendetta—him against the house. Or maybe it's simply his way to remind me that he was opposed to this project from the start...and that he expects it to turn out badly.

I hurry up to my apartment, change into my "renovation" outfit: a T-shirt, overalls, and Havaianas rubber flip-flops. Then after I leash up Riley and allow him a quick pit stop in the park, we're on our way to the house.

Dad meets me in the driveway with an impossible-to-read expression. When I ask him what's up, he simply says, "Come and see for yourself."

"No hug or anything," I tease him. "Must be pretty bad..."

"You can be the judge of that." Then he offers me a halfhearted side hug, nudging me up the driveway.

I glance up at the house now. It looks much like it did yesterday. Nothing appears fallen or crumbled...no huge catastrophe that I can see.

We go inside, and I let Riley off his leash to explore. Then Dad leads me to the kitchen, and I notice the room looks strangely spacious. Like something has changed.

"The cabinets!" I suddenly exclaim. "Where are the cabinets?"

"The cleanup crew demoed them."

"Demoed? As in totally destroyed?"

He nods with a somber expression.

"But why?"

"They said you gave instructions to remove them."

"I gave them cleaning stuff and told them to clean them."

"In English?"

"No, I've been trying to use what little Spanish I know." I dig in my bag, pulling out the little English to Spanish dictionary that I've been relying on.

"Tell me exactly what you told them," says Dad.

So I repeat, as best I can, what I think I said, and he just nods.

"What did I say?" I ask.

"To remove the cabinets."

"Oh…"

"That was an expensive mistake, Gretchen."

"Oh my goodness. What do we do now?"

"We order new cabinets. Fortunately one of the guys on the crew has a brother-in-law who's a cabinetmaker. They won't be top-of-the-line, but they should be okay."

"I'm sorry, Dad." I'm on the verge of tears. I can't believe I blew it so badly. From now on I will keep my mouth shut or make sure my dad translates for me.

He forces a smile now. "Maybe it's for the best, sweetie. They say kitchens are the most important selling feature in homes these days."

"And bathrooms," I add.

He frowns now. "Well, don't get me started on that. Those bathrooms are a disaster."

"A disaster that you don't need to worry about," I remind him for the thousandth time.

"Then who are you going to get to replace those floor joists?"

I consider this. "Well, I don't know right now…but it won't be you." I put my face close to his and look into his eyes. "Okay?"

He grumbles something I can't hear, then asks if he can borrow my phone. I hand it to him and start walking around to inspect my house. Most of the hardwood floors seem to be fairly solid but, as Dad pointed out, are in need of serious refinishing. At least I didn't ask the work crew to "clean" them too.

"I asked Noah Campbell to stop by today," Dad tells me as he hands me my phone.

"Why?"

"Because we need some help, Gretchen."

"But why Noah?" I persist. It's not that I don't like Noah Campbell, but last Christmas my dad tried to fix us up at his annual Christmas party, and I guess I just wasn't ready for it. Then Dad seemed offended when I gave Noah the cold shoulder. Later he asked me what was wrong with the guy. Well, obviously, there was nothing wrong with Noah. I mean, not only is he a perfectly nice guy, but he's also gorgeous. In fact, that might've been part of the problem. Gorgeous guys tend to scare me. So as Dad continued to pester me about Noah, the only thing I could come up with was to say it bothered me that he is divorced.

And, okay, I know lots of divorced people. And, really, it's nothing personal, but the truth is that I have absolutely no desire to get involved with a guy who's been divorced. Call me stubborn or judgmental or narrow minded, but I've always imagined myself marrying someone who's never been married. It's just an expectation I've carried with me since childhood. And to make matters more complicated, Noah has a child that he and his ex share custody for. Because

I teach kindergarten, I've seen what that does to kids and parents and exes and everyone. And, I'm sorry, but that is just too much baggage for me. Especially considering I have my own baggage to deal with. As much as I like to think that time heals all wounds, I know I still have some scars. And that's basically what I told Dad. Without going into all the details, I told him I was not interested. Fortunately, it shut him up and got him off my case about Noah. Until now.

"Noah is an excellent carpenter…and he's not busy."

"If he's such an excellent carpenter, why isn't he busy?"

Dad shrugs. "I'm not sure. But I was chatting with him a couple of weeks ago, and he mentioned that he was trying to slow things down."

"Why is he slowing things down?" I ask, knowing that it's none of my business and that I'm acting like a very wet blanket. "He seems a little young to retire, don't you think?"

"I don't know, Gretchen." Dad's voice sounds irritated now. "Just be thankful he's available."

"But shouldn't I have some say in who we hire to help us?"

"Sure. Who did you have in mind?"

I shrug now. "No one. But maybe I'd like to take a shot at doing some of these things myself, Dad."

Now he actually laughs. "I have to admire your courage, Gretchen Girl, but you need to know exactly what you're doing when you replace something as structural as floor joists." He scratches his head now. "I didn't think we needed a building permit when we started this project. We weren't going to change the footprint or anything structural…just basic renovations. Now I'm not so sure."

"Meaning?"

"Meaning I'll look into it."

I point to the wall that separates the living room from the dining and kitchen area. "Like what if I want this wall removed?"

"You want that wall removed?"

I'm sure I've mentioned this several times to Dad, but he keeps acting like it's a big surprise. "I want to open up the place," I say. "One big great room. Remember?"

"Well, this happens to be a load-bearing wall."

"And?"

"The roof might collapse if you remove it."

"Really?"

"We'd have to set up some posts and a beam to support the ceiling."

"That's fine."

"And there's electrical here too," he points out. "We'll have to hire an electrician."

"So..."

"Well, I agree that it would be an improvement for this house. And it would probably help the salability of the place if we open it up a bit. But that means I'll have to go file for a building permit." He glances at his watch now. "I can just make it before they close."

"What about Noah?" I ask.

"You're calling the shots," he says. "You deal with it."

"But I don't know what to—"

"Just let him in the door, Gretchen. I already gave him a quick lowdown on our situation. He'll probably want to walk around and check things out. Hopefully, he won't turn around and walk straight out once he sees it."

"Where did the cleanup crew go?" I ask as I put on a pair of yellow rubber gloves and reach for a bottle of cleaner.

"I paid them and told them we'd be in touch." He looks slightly sheepish now. "I also took them to task for ripping out the kitchen cabinets. Now I'll have to apologize."

"I should probably be the one to apologize."

He nods. "Yep, you should. Now I better head over to the city office for that permit."

After Dad leaves, I go straight into scrubbing down a kitchen wall. Then I hear someone call out "hello" from the front door. I get there just in time to see Riley jump up and place both dirty paws on Noah Campbell's clean white T-shirt.

"Riley!" I scold, grabbing him by the collar. "Down!"

Noah attempts to brush the brown marks off his shirt and then smiles. "It's okay."

"Sorry about that." Once again I am struck with how incredibly good-looking this guy is. And, once again, it just bugs me. Almost every gorgeous guy I've met has turned out to be (1) slightly shallow, (2) somewhat full of himself, and (3) looking for an equally gorgeous woman so he can be part of a matched set. Sorry if I sound bitter, but that's been my experience.

As I attempt to peel off a rubber glove, Noah bends down to scratch Riley behind the ears. "You're a friendly one, aren't you?"

"His name is Riley, and I guess I need to work with him on his social skills."

"Chocolate Lab?"

"And part something else—probably some wild and crazy breed."

Noah stands and looks at me now, and I'm aware that I must

look like a wreck. "It's been a while. How have you been, Gretchen?"

I'm surprised that he actually remembers my name. "Okay, I guess...although my dad thinks I've bitten off more than I can chew with this house flip. Did he tell you much about it?"

"Just that it's in need of help."

"Yeah. And I don't want Dad doing the physical labor himself. You know he's had some serious health problems."

He nods. "Yeah, I heard."

"Of course, he thinks he's much better now that he's been on medication for a while. But I still don't want him doing too much."

"That's understandable." His dark brown eyes glance about, quickly taking it all in, and he doesn't appear terribly impressed.

"And anyway this is really *my* house flip, not Dad's. He's only supposed to be my consultant. In fact, I wasn't sure I needed outside help just yet. Dad didn't even ask me before he called you. And when school gets out, just a week from now...well, I'd sort of hoped to tackle this myself."

"Really?" I see the same skeptical look in his eyes that I saw in my dad's earlier. But at least he's not laughing at me.

"I know a little about carpentry. I mean, I grew up watching my dad."

"I'm sure you know a lot." I think I sense some sarcasm, but I ignore it.

"And when I'm not distracted with my teaching responsibilities, I can give this remodel my full attention."

"Right..."

"So it might've been premature for Dad to call you."

"Oh..."

"I mean, feel free to walk around and have a look, if you want. There's not that much to see. We've been mostly trying to clean it out this week, getting it ready for paint and things. It had been a rental, and the renters were pretty bad. They must've had a lot of pets. I guess you can still sort of smell it."

"It definitely looks like it's seen better days."

"But it does have potential," I say in a slightly defensive tone. "And it'll be great once I start doing the real improvements." He's followed me to the kitchen now. "I had hoped to reuse the existing cabinets; they weren't too bad really. But we had a little communication problem with the cleanup crew."

"They tore them out?"

"Yeah." I sigh. "Things got a little out of control. I think that's why I want to slow it down just now. Dad is all like 'get 'er done,' and I want to take more time and plan it a little better. I have lots of ideas… I know how I want it done. I'd like to take my time, you know?"

"I can understand that." He nods politely, though he still doesn't look convinced.

"And so I'm not sure I really want to hire anyone just yet."

He glances around the gutted kitchen with a slight frown. "And I don't want to force my services on anyone. I only came as a favor to your dad. He's a good guy."

"Of course. I just don't want him to take over this house flip." I press my lips together, thinking I'm saying way too much. Really, this is none of Noah Campbell's business.

"Well, I can see you're busy," he says stiffly. "I won't take up any more of your time."

"Thanks for stopping by, though. I'll tell Dad you were here."

"Good luck on your house flip." He heads for the front door now with Riley at his heels as if he's planning on going with him.

"Riley," I call out, "stay!"

Naturally, Riley ignores my command, making it awkward for Noah to slip out the door gracefully. He uses one foot to gently push Riley backward, then makes a quick escape. Standing in the shadows of the living room, I watch out the big front window, past the cracked glass and fly-specked grime, as Noah walks down the driveway toward a nicely restored turquoise pickup, complete with wooden side rails. I'm guessing it's from the sixties—and probably a classic.

But it's Noah I'm watching. Observing the way his long legs amble along in faded jeans and sturdy work boots, the fit of his white T-shirt over his broad shoulders, the casual cut of his sandy brown hair. And I'm thinking, okay this guy may be divorced and carrying some baggage, but he is one hot guy.

Then it's like I want to slap myself. What am I thinking? So to purge these crazy thoughts from my mind, I plunge back into cleaning with a vengeance. Nothing like a filthy wall to take your mind off a man.

I'm just finishing up in the kitchen when I hear Riley barking happily at the back door and my dad greeting him and asking, "How's Demo Dog doing?"

"Thankfully, not too much damage. Did you get the permit?" I ask as I drop a sponge back into the bucket.

"It should be ready by next week."

"Great."

He glances around the room. "No sign of Noah yet?"

"He was here."

"What'd he think?"

I shrug. No way will I tell him how I shooed Noah away. "I don't know."

"Didn't he say anything?"

"Not much."

"Gretchen?" Dad looks perplexed now. "Did he look around?"

"A little. I sort of told him that it was premature to hire him."

"Premature?" Dad looks upset. "Have you even seen this place, Gretchen?"

"I told him that I have one more week until school's out and that I plan to really jump into it then."

Dad almost smiles now. "That's fine, and I'd like you to jump into it. But there are certain things you can't—"

"You don't know what I can or can't do yet, Dad. You haven't even given me a chance." I realize I'm being stubborn, but I'm a little tired of being condescended to. "Like I told you in the first place, I've been watching these home-improvement shows. And for years I've watched you. I really do think I can do this. I want to do this."

"But you might need some help."

"Why don't you let me figure that out, Dad?"

He lets out an exasperated sigh and just shakes his head.

"And if and when I need help, I'll ask."

"What if Noah has taken on another project by then?"

"Noah's not the only carpenter in the world."

"Maybe not, but he's affordable and one of the best. And he's a good man, Gretchen."

I point my finger at Dad now. "So *that's* it."

"What?" He gives me his best innocent look.

"You're trying to set me up with him again, aren't you?"

"No, I'm not." He waves his hand at me in dismissal.

"*Sure* you're not..."

"So what if I am, Gretchen? You could certainly do a lot worse than Noah Campbell."

"What's that supposed to mean?"

"You know what it means."

"Collin?"

Dad shrugs. "I never really trusted that guy, Gretchen. I think you were lucky to get out of that relationship when you did."

"Lucky?"

He nods firmly. "More than lucky. I think God was watching out for you. I think there's someone far better for you."

"Someone like Noah?"

"Maybe."

"Okay, Dad, I've already told you that I don't like that Noah's divorced. I will never marry a guy who's been divorced. And he has a kid." And he's way too good looking, I'm thinking, but I don't say this.

"Betty's divorced," Dad points out. "Do you think it's wrong for me to marry her?"

"I can't say what's right or wrong for you, Dad. I can only speak for myself. I just cannot imagine marrying a guy who is divorced—a guy who didn't take his wedding vows seriously." Okay, I realize that I don't know Noah's whole story, but besides the fact that I do feel strongly against divorce, this is my best shot at getting Dad to leave me alone. "After the whole Collin fiasco," I remind him, "I know what it's like to be on the receiving end of a broken promise."

Dad looks like he's about to spout steam through his nostrils. "Well, I'm sure glad that you aren't God, Gretchen."

"What's that supposed to mean?"

"It means that I'm glad God is much more gracious and forgiving than you."

I blink. I'm not used to Dad talking to me like this. Maybe it's because of this house—maybe he's just frustrated.

"And if you'll excuse me, I'm tired and hungry, and I'm going home." Then without saying another word, Dad leaves through the back door, and I'm still standing in the kitchen, wondering how I offended him like that. Maybe it has to do with Betty. Or maybe it's something more. I guess we'll just have to sort it out later.

# 8

The weekend passes quietly. I continue cleaning the house, but Dad does not come by. On one hand, I'm relieved. It's sort of nice to have the place to myself. I bring Riley, a CD player, and a small cube refrigerator that I stock with sodas, and I just plug along with the cleaning. But by Sunday night I'm feeling a little irritated. Is this Dad's way of punishing me? Is he trying to teach me a lesson? So before I go home, I give him a call and ask him what's up.

"I played eighteen holes with Gary Gordon on Saturday," he tells me in an offhanded way. "And after church this morning, I came home and read the newspaper, and then I watched an NBA play-off game, and after that I took a nap."

"Oh…"

"Have you been working on your house?" he asks.

"Yeah."

"How's it coming?"

"Okay…but kind of slow."

"I thought you wanted to slow things down."

I consider this. "Yeah. It was actually kind of nice. I got a lot of cleaning done, and it smells a lot better now."

"Good for you."

So I make a little more small talk, then admit I'm tired and about to head home.

"Take care, sweetie," he says in a kind voice.

"You too."

"And I think you're right to slow things down some," he adds. "Maybe you should wait until school's out to get going on the actual renovations."

"I think you might be right," I admit. "The last week of school is usually pretty wild anyway. I should probably make sure I give the kids my best. Maybe we should both just take the week off. Then come back at it fresh and new as soon as school ends."

"That sounds wise."

"Thanks, Dad."

I feel like things are pretty much okay between Dad and me as I drive home. I know from watching HGTV that remodels can stress even the best of relationships, and I sure don't want to see my house flip undoing my relationship with Dad. In the future I'll have to be on guard against that.

~ ~ ~

Packed with all those end-of-the-year activities, the week passes relatively quickly, and finally it's the last day of school, which is also the day of the kindergarten picnic. With the help of my room mothers and teacher's aide, Claire, I merge both classes for a day of fun and games at a nearby park. Fortunately, I remembered to bring my camera and am getting lots of good shots.

“Miss Hanover?” calls a voice from behind me, and I turn to see Marion, the school secretary, hurrying toward me and waving her hand.

“What’s up?” I ask.

“We tried your cell phone,” she says breathlessly.

“It’s turned off. Why? What’s wrong?”

“It’s your dad.”

“Dad?” I feel my throat tighten.

“He’s at Saint Joseph’s.”

“The hospital?”

“Someone just called from ER and said you need to come right away.”

“Go ahead, Gretchen,” says Claire. “We can take care of things here.”

“And explain to the kids?”

“Yes,” says a room mother as she gives me a gentle push. “Just get yourself over to the hospital and hurry!”

“I know you rode over on the bus with the kids,” says Marion. “But I’ve got my car, and I can take you straight to Saint Joseph’s if you like, Gretchen.”

“Thanks,” I tell her as I grab my bag and start jogging toward the street. As Marion drives, I try calling the hospital to check on Dad but end up on hold.

“Here you go,” she says as she pulls up in front of ER. “You call and let us know how he’s doing, okay?”

“Yes. Thank you!”

I run inside and go directly to the desk, asking where my dad is and if I can see him. After what seems like an hour but is probably only minutes, a middle-aged doctor introduces himself as Dr. Fontaine and tells me that he's been treating my dad.

"Your father was brought into ER a little before noon with acute MI," he explains.

"What does that mean?" I demand.

"MI stands for myocardial infraction, more commonly called a heart attack."

I want to ask why he didn't just say that in the first place but decide I'll make more progress by being polite. "How is he now?"

"He's stabilized enough that we can run a few tests, and then he'll be moved to ICU, maybe within the hour."

"Can I see him?"

"Not until we get him settled into ICU."

"Is he going to be okay?" My voice is shaking now.

"The first few hours are the most critical."

"Meaning?"

"Meaning he's getting the best care possible." He puts a hand on my shoulder. "He's lucky he got here when he did. Things could've gone much differently." Then he excuses himself. By "differently" I assume he means that my dad could be dead.

I go to the waiting room and sit down. I am thrown off and scared, so I pray. I ask God to watch over Dad, to make sure he gets the best treatment, and to help him get well. I take out my phone and consider calling someone. But who? Betty is off on a ship, cruising through the Mediterranean, and I doubt she's using her cell phone. And what would I say at this stage anyway? Wouldn't it be better to have more information before I get her all worried? Dad has an older sister in Detroit, but other than an occasional greeting card, they don't really keep in touch. I'd call Holly just for moral support, but she's still at work, and her boss hates it when she gets personal calls.

That's when it hits me—and it hits me hard. When it comes to family, Dad and I are almost all we have. And that's when I start to cry. I don't want to lose him. I need my dad.

~ ~ ~

It's after three by the time I'm allowed into ICU. But even then, I'm not ready for what I see. Dad is pale, and he looks much older than he did last week. And even when I quietly say, "Hi, Dad," he doesn't open his eyes. Doesn't flinch or move a muscle. He's hooked up to several things. One tube, that I assume is for oxygen, goes into his nose. And then there's an IV, which is connected to his arm. And finally there's a heart monitor with irregular beeping noises that make me uneasy.

"Visits in here are limited to five minutes," a nurse informs me as she checks on the heart monitor.

"Bye, Dad." I gently squeeze his hand, which seems abnormally cool. "I love you." I wait for some response, but there is none. "See you later," I say quietly.

I find Dr. Fontaine looking at a laptop computer by the nurses' station, and I ask if he can fill me in a bit regarding my dad.

"From what I can see, your father is going to need bypass surgery, or a CABG, otherwise known as coronary artery bypass surgery. I thought we might attempt an angioplasty at first, but after going over his medical records more carefully and looking at the test results, I no longer think that's the best treatment."

"What exactly happens with bypass surgery?" I ask. "I mean, what does it entail?"

"It's major surgery. To put it simply, we open his chest and replace the diseased artery to the heart with a healthy blood vessel from somewhere else."

"Is it dangerous?" I ask, knowing this is probably a stupid question. "I mean, what if his heart stopped while you were doing this?"

"Actually, his heart will stop. We use a heart-lung machine to take over the blood circulation during the surgery."

"Oh…" The image of Dad on an operating table with his heart stopped makes me feel weak.

"Coronary bypasses are becoming a fairly common procedure," he continues, and I can tell he's trying to reassure me.

"So it's not really that risky?"

"All surgeries involve some risks."

"Right…so when do you plan to do it?"

"We're prepared to do an emergency bypass today, but we're hoping that your father will respond favorably to the medication and that we can delay the surgery."

"Why do you want to delay it?"

"For the optimum outcome, we want him to be in the best possible shape. I'd really like to keep him here a few days before we do the surgery."

"When will he wake up?" I ask weakly.

"When he's ready. The pain meds are probably helping him rest. But don't let it worry you. He needs a good rest right now."

"He felt so cold," I say. "Is that normal?"

"It's a new treatment for heart patients who are unconscious. We use cold packs to lower the body temperature a few degrees."

"Is that safe?"

"Absolutely. The cooling allows the body's metabolism to slow down, to preserve and protect cells that might otherwise be damaged. And, of course, all this is carefully monitored. But the outcome with this cooling treatment is nothing short of amazing."

Then he tells me that the nurse is preparing a release form for me to sign, and I thank him for his time. He excuses himself, and I just stand there like a dummy next to the nurses' station, wondering what I should do next. I'm so used to asking my dad this kind of question. Whenever I have a problem or a crisis, I turn to him. He's the one who always has the answers. Of course, this reminds me about my house flip, which suddenly seems like the lamest thing I've ever attempted, and I wonder if there's any chance I can sell the ranch house as is. Would I even be able to find a buyer who'd want a run-down old house with a gutted kitchen, a bad roof, and bathrooms with dry rot? What have I gotten myself into?

It's after five, and I've been in to see Dad several times, each time for only five minutes, but he's still unconscious so no response. And he still feels cold when I touch him—and I suppose that worries me even though the doctor said it shouldn't. Finally I know it's time to call Holly. I catch her in a parking garage on the way to her car, and choking back sobs, I explain to her what's happened today, and she promises to come straight to the hospital.

"Th-thank you!" I blurt out with tears now streaming down both cheeks.

People in the waiting area look up when Holly enters the room. She's dressed for work, but she's so stylish she looks like she could be heading to fashion week in New York. Oblivious to the attention she's getting, probably because she's used to it, she comes straight for me and wraps her arms around me, holding me as the dam breaks and I let it all out. After a couple of minutes I feel bad for getting the shoulder of her pale pink button-down soggy. And finally, feeling self conscious, I step back. "Sorry for falling apart…"

She shakes her head. "Don't be sorry. This is what best friends are for, honey. Now tell me everything…like how is he, when did this happen, and what's next?"

So I go into all that I know, and after I've exhausted my information and most of my brain cells, I pause to take a deep, choppy breath.

"Where did it happen?" she asks.

"The heart attack?"

"Yes. Was he home? Did he call an ambulance?"

"I don't really know."

She nods. "I guess I just wonder…what would you do if you were alone and felt chest pains? Would you call 911 or just wait to see? Or what if you were driving in traffic? Would you get out and ask for help?"

These sound like Holly questions. Which is probably one reason she makes a good legal assistant—and why she might make an even better attorney if she ever gets the confidence to go back and finish her law degree.

"Dad doesn't even use his cell phone anymore," I tell her. "So maybe he was home and simply called for an ambulance from there. However he did it, the doctor said he made it here just in the nick of time."

"Good for him." Holly's big brown eyes get misty now. "I know he's going to be okay. He has to."

"I just wish I could talk to him," I say.

"Does the doctor have any idea when he'll regain consciousness?"

"When he's ready. The doctor said he needs this rest...to help prepare him for surgery."

Holly takes both my hands and squeezes them now. "It's going to be okay, Gretch."

"How can you know that for sure?"

"I just feel it." She nods firmly. "I prayed for him all the way over here. I know he's going to be fine."

I want to question this, because I'm not so sure about God today. After all, he took my mom when I was thirteen, and there was Collin and the wedding that never happened. It seems my life is full of losses. Where was God then? But I don't have the energy to argue just now.

"What about your house?"

"What about it?" I ask flatly.

"With your dad, well, kind of incapacitated, won't it be a challenge to get the renovations done in time?"

"I'm thinking about just putting it on the market as is."

"As is?" Holly frowns. She's already seen the house. And even though it was somewhat cleaned up by then, she was still pretty shocked by how bad it was. "What if you lose money on it?"

I consider this, then shrug. "It doesn't seem to matter now..."

"I'm sorry. I shouldn't have brought it up. I'm sure it'll work out."

"It seems pretty minor in light of Dad's health." Well, other than the fact that the security of his home is hinged to the loan for that house. But I don't want to think about that now. I notice Holly looking at her sleek Gucci watch, the one Justin got her for their one-month anniversary. I can't imagine what he'll get her for one year.

"I hate to leave," she begins with a worried brow. "And I don't expect you to make it now, but tonight is Tina's—"

"Tina's bridal shower!" I slap my forehead as I remember that Holly's younger sister is getting married in a couple of weeks. Naturally, Holly is Tina's matron of honor and hosting a shower for her tonight. "I totally forgot, but I do have a gift for her. It's all wrapped and everything. It's at my—"

"Forget about it. I'll tell Tina what happened. She'll understand."

"I'm sorry, Holly. I was supposed to help you too."

"Don't give it another thought. I just wish I didn't have to go. Tina will have a fit if I don't pull this off."

I nod. Tina, who used to be a fairly sweet girl, has turned into a real Bridezilla. I even suggested to Holly that she should call that TV show and see if they want to feature Tina the Terror for their next June episode. I'm just thankful that Tina has never really liked me that much. So far, other than being invited to the wedding and a couple of showers, I've gotten off fairly lightly.

"Good luck with the shower tonight," I say to Holly.

"I'll need it." She sighs. "The truth is, I would rather be here with you, Gretch."

Holly gives me a sad smile and a little finger wave as the elevator door closes.

But as I walk back over to ICU to check on my dad, I know that I would gladly endure the worst of Tina and endless showers if only Dad were healthy. I peek through the window to see that he's still resting quietly. Then I check with the nurse before I slip back into the room. It's amazing how in just one day everything's beginning to feel so familiar. The slightly raised mechanical bed so the medical staff can easily help him and observe him from the nurses' station, the various machines, the sound of the ECG, the soft lighting, the tubes, the smell, which is kind of stuffy—a strange mixture of cleaning supplies and something more organic and human.

"I love you, Dad," I whisper again, gently holding his hand, which is quite cool and completely lifeless. I can see by the slight up and down movement of his chest that he's breathing, but if not for that, it would be hard to tell he's alive. "Holly told me that she knows you're going to be fine. She's praying for you. I'm praying too. I need you, Daddy. Please hang in there and get better." Then I just stand there with tears streaming down my cheeks. What if he doesn't get better? What if he doesn't make it through the night? Should I have insisted on the emergency bypass surgery? Does the doctor really know what's best?

I feel a gentle nudge on my shoulder, and the nurse nods toward the clock. "I hate to disturb you," she says, "but time's up."

"Sorry." I look back down at Dad, smoothing his fuzzy eyebrows with a forefinger. "I love you, Daddy… I'll be back in a little while."

It's after six when I return to the waiting area, and I suddenly realize that Riley has been home alone all day. I tell myself that he's probably okay. As always, I left him with a big bowl of dry kibble and water and his toys. And he has his doggy pad to relieve himself on if need be, which he has probably used by now, although he prefers to go outside. I feel sorry for him, but it's Dad who concerns me most. Riley will be okay.

"Gretchen?" I hear someone calling my name. Thinking it might be the doctor and fearing that something has changed with Dad, I turn to see. But it's not the doctor. It's Noah Campbell. What is he doing here?

"How's your dad?" he asks with what looks like real concern in his eyes.

"Not so good," I admit.

"What happened?"

I quickly explain about the heart attack and the need for bypass surgery. "How did you hear about him?" I ask curiously.

"I happened to be driving by your house in Paradise—"

"Happened to be?"

"Well, I was driving out there not too far from the subdivision, and I wondered how it was going."

"And?"

"I saw your dad's pickup there, and—"

"Dad was at the *house*?" I demand.

"No, he wasn't there. But the front door was open, and the radio was on, so I assumed he was inside. I went in and called for him and looked around, but I didn't see him."

"Dad was at the house?" I repeat my question, trying to wrap my mind around this surprising fact. Why was Dad at the house? Hadn't we agreed to take a week off? What was he doing there anyway?

Noah gives me a curious look but simply nods. "Hank had definitely been there. Looked like he'd been working in one of the bathrooms. His tools were still there, and my guess is that he'd been fixing some of those rotten floor joists."

"He wasn't supposed to be there."

"Why not?"

"We'd agreed to take a break this week—until school ended for me."

"A break?" Noah looks somewhat confused. "When there's so much that needs to be done?"

"But I didn't want Dad doing it."

"Right..." Noah almost seems to be biting his tongue now.

"So Dad had been at the house," I repeat, trying to act like that was just fine. "But he was gone?"

"Yes. I went outside to look around, and a neighbor lady came over and told me what had happened."

"What happened?"

"She said she was getting her mail when she noticed your dad by his pickup. He was clutching his chest, and she went over to see if he needed help. Then she realized it was a heart attack, so she ran back to the house and called for help."

"So an ambulance picked him up?"

"Yes. The woman—I think her name was Marsha or Martha—said she stayed with Hank until help arrived, but she was sorry that she didn't know CPR or anything. She said he was in a lot of pain. She asked me to let her know how he was doing."

"Thank God for that neighbor calling for help. That's just one reason I wish Dad kept his cell phone with him." But even as I say this, using a slight scolding tone, all I can think is, *Dad was working on my stupid house when he had his heart attack. If it hadn't been for me and my impossible plan to flip a house, Dad might be perfectly fine right now.* And once again I feel tears coming. I choke back a sob, quickly excuse myself, and dash for the rest room, where I turn on the faucet and just cry and cry. This is all my fault. If Dad dies, I can only blame myself.

# 9

Are you okay?" asks Noah when I finally emerge from the rest room with a swollen red nose and puffy eyes. I had assumed he'd be gone by now.

"Not really," I say in a somewhat uptight voice, possibly a hint that I don't need his help with this, that I wish he'd leave me alone.

"Want to get a bite to eat?"

"Not really," I say again, sounding I'm sure like a recording.

"Come on," he urges. "I'll bet you haven't had dinner yet."

"No, but I—"

"No arguments," he says firmly, actually taking me by the arm and guiding me toward the elevator. "I know your dad would agree with me on this."

Well, I can't argue with that, so I let him take charge, and before long we're sitting in the cafeteria, and there's a bowl of chicken-noodle soup sitting in front of me. I don't even remember if I ordered it or not, but I take a hesitant bite, and it's not bad.

"For what ails you," he says with a nod, "my grandma was always a firm believer in chicken-noodle soup."

"Thanks."

Then to my utter surprise, he actually takes my hand, bows his head, and prays. Not just a blessing for the food either. He prays for the doctors to have skill and wisdom and for my dad to have a quick and complete recovery. I murmur a quiet but heartfelt "amen" and actually feel a tiny bit better.

We both eat quietly, and although the soup revives me a little, I also am beginning to feel self-conscious. I look down at my lap and notice the grass-stained knees on my khaki Capri pants from playing with the kids and taking photos at the picnic. Was that today? It seems like a week or more ago. "This has been a long day," I say finally as if to explain something, although I'm not sure what.

"Was it the last day of school?"

I nod. "We were just finishing up the kindergarten picnic when I heard about Dad... Fortunately I had helpers there. They told me to go, and Marion gave me a ride,...and I didn't even get to tell my students good-bye."

"That's too bad, but I don't blame you. Obviously, you needed to be here." His eyes get cloudy now, as if he's remembering something. "If the worst had happened, and you weren't here, well... I never got to tell my dad good-bye."

"I'm sorry."

"I was in college—about to graduate and obsessed with my own life. I hadn't seen him in months."

"That's too bad."

"Yeah. Anyway, it's really good that you're here."

A wave of fear washes over me again. "Do you think he's going to die?"

"No no, that's not what I mean," he assures me.

"How did your dad die?" I ask cautiously.

He glances away uncomfortably, like he doesn't want to say.

"Was it a heart thing too?"

"It's the number one cause of death for men in that age group."

"Really?"

"That's what I've been told." His face brightens. "But medical science is improving every day."

"I talked to Dr. Fontaine, and he told me that Dad's chances for recovery are good...with bypass surgery." I lean my elbow on the table and hold my head, which feels heavy. "But I'm worried... What if they wait too long? I mean, he said they could do the surgery today if needed, but he wants to wait. How does he know that Dad will be okay in a day or two? What if he needs that surgery right now?"

"Hank is being carefully monitored. This is a good hospital. I think you can trust that they will do whatever is best for him."

"Where was your dad when he died?"

"In Central Washington...a small hospital. Nothing as good as this one."

"I'm sorry," I say again.

"Hank reminds me a lot of my dad."

"How's that?"

"My dad was a building contractor too. He never took on big projects like Hank has done. Mostly it was single-family homes. But he was really good at it. He believed in quality and was respected by the community."

"In Washington?"

"Yes, that's where I grew up."

"What brought you down here?"

He sighs. "It's a long story."

"Oh…"

"And I'd be happy to tell you the whole thing, but I need to go take care of something."

"Of course," I say quickly. "Don't let me keep you."

"I'd stay if I could."

I wave my hand. "No no, that's okay. There's really nothing that can be done."

"Do you need a ride or anything?"

"No…I can't go home."

"Right… But what about your dog?"

"Riley…" I forgot again. "He's probably destroyed my apartment by now."

"Why don't I go and get him for you?"

"Oh, I can't ask you—"

"It's no problem."

"But you said you have something you have to—"

"Yes. I just need to pick up my daughter…at her mother's. But she and I could go by and take care of Riley." He smiles. "We could even take him home with us…if that's okay."

"Seriously?" I look up at his eyes, which are acutely caring. "Riley is a sweetheart, but he can be, uh, well, a little destructive. My dad nicknamed him Demo Dog."

"My place is on the beach. We could probably wear Riley out so much that he won't want to destroy a thing." He grins. "And, trust me, there are few things at my place that I'm worried about."

"No designer shoes?"

He looks puzzled.

"Riley has a thing for devouring expensive shoes—but never the whole pair. He always leaves one shoe for me to remember them by, and he seems to prefer the flavor of the left shoe. But he never bothers with cheap knockoffs. He's too sophisticated for that."

Noah laughs. "You girls and your fancy shoes. I just don't get that."

I'm starting to think I don't either. Really, what's the point? "You're sure you want him?" I ask as I reach in my bag for my apartment key.

"I promise to take excellent care of him, Gretchen. I know he's your baby."

I take the key off the ring and hand it to him, telling him where the building is and my apartment number, which he jots down on the napkin.

"Oh yeah," he says. "I had to leave the house in Paradise unlocked since the lock on the doorknob was broken and there was no key for the deadbolt. But I locked your dad's toolbox inside his truck since it was still open. Hopefully the tools will be safer there."

"He won't need those tools anytime soon..." And I'm thinking he may never need them again. "Although it would be a shame for them to be stolen. And I suppose I could use them."

"If you'll give me your deadbolt key, I'll go by and lock up the place," he offers, "in case you're worried about vandals or anything."

"I doubt there's much they could hurt." But I pull out the key and hand it to him. "Still, I appreciate it."

"Anything else?" he offers. "How about your dad's cats?"

I slap my forehead as I remember Mowzer, Wowzer, and Bowzer. "I totally forgot about the cats."

"Want me to go—"

"No, I think they're okay. Dad has those continuous feeders and a self-cleaning kitty-litter box. I'm sure the cats will be fine for a day or two anyway."

"If you're sure."

"Yeah. Dad leaves them home alone for up to three days without being checked. I'm sure they're just fine." Then I look at the clock to see that it's been forty-five minutes since I've been with Dad. "I think I should check on him now," I say, standing.

"Give him my best." Then he hands me a business card. "Here…in case you need to see how Riley's doing, or if you want me to check on the cats. Also, I'd appreciate hearing about Hank's condition."

"Thanks…" I slip the card into my already overloaded bag, which is bulging with my camera and other things I'd brought along for today's picnic. I stand straighter as I adjust the strap on my shoulder, smoothing down the front of my rumpled cotton shirt. "Thanks for everything."

Noah heads for the front exit, and I trudge back to the elevators again, preparing for what I know will be a long night. But it's a vigil I must make. Dad seems to be the same—cool and pale—but I suppose that should be encouraging. At least he's not worse.

"I'll be in the waiting room all night," I explain to the nurse in ICU when visiting hours are officially over. I write down my cell phone number and ask her to call if anything changes.

"I wish I could offer you a place to sleep," she says, "but we're full up right now."

"It's okay," I tell her. "I noticed a couch that I can curl up on. Hopefully I can sleep."

"You're sure you don't want to go home?" she asks now. "We would call you if anything—"

"No," I say firmly, remembering how things had been strained between Dad and me last week. How we'd disagreed over the stupid house. "I want to be here if he wakes up or anything."

"I understand." She nods. "And there's a chapel on the third floor...in case you need a quiet place to meditate."

Visiting the chapel sounds like a good idea, so I go to the third floor and into the little room. But I don't meditate. Instead, I pray. I beg God to make Dad well again. I even bargain with him, which I know is ridiculous, but I can't help myself. I just don't want to lose my dad. Not like this.

I sleep off and on during the night. Every time I wake up and look at the clock, it seems that only thirty minutes or so have passed. At 3:47 a.m. I check my cell phone for missed calls, and when there are none, I decide to just walk into the ICU. I stand by the window and look into Dad's room, making sure he's still here, still okay.

Finally it's morning, and after a quick cleanup in the rest room, I go to check on Dad. Nothing has changed; he is still sleeping, but the nurse tells me that his ECG is looking better today.

"Does that mean he can have surgery sooner?" I ask hopefully.

"That's for the doctor to say, but it's definitely a good sign."

So, feeling slightly hopeful, I go down in search of coffee, but what I find is disappointing. The coffee has definitely been sitting in the pot all night. Even after adding cream and sugar, which I normally don't do, it's barely palatable. Still, I think I need the caffeine today. I'm taking a sip when Holly calls on my cell phone.

"How is he?" she asks anxiously.

"About the same...maybe a little better."

"Oh, good."

"How was the shower?"

"Don't ask. I'm actually on my way back from Tina's final fitting for the wedding dress, and she was in a serious snit because she's gained a whole pound."

"Poor thing," I say with sarcasm. Tina, like Holly, is long and lean and wouldn't look bad carrying an extra pound or twenty.

"Anyway, I'm not far from your place, and I still have your apartment key and thought I could check on Riley and—"

"Actually, Riley's being taken care of."

"That's cool. One of your neighbors?"

"No...just a friend. Riley's not even home right now."

"Oh, that's probably good. But I could still pop in and get you some things, Gretchen, like some fresh clothes or whatever."

I look down at my sad outfit, which is not only grass-stained but hopelessly wrinkled and frumpy, and I've just dripped coffee down the front of my white shirt. "That would be awesome, Holly."

"Any specific requests?"

"You'd probably know better than me right now," I admit. "I'm pretty groggy from a bad night's sleep."

"How about some Starbucks too?"

"Oh, you're an angel!"

"See you in about an hour."

I've just checked on my dad again when Holly gets here. In typical Holly style she's brought me a choice of clothes and more cosmetics than I normally use. We go to the rest room where Holly decides what I will wear and then lectures me about not using face moisturizer. Instead of resisting like I might normally do, I give in, and by the time Holly's done with me, I actually look much more refreshed than I feel. And I even look somewhat stylish.

"Thanks," I tell her. "You should dress me every morning."

"That's the truth."

"Where did you find this shirt anyway?" I ask as I check out my image more carefully in the mirror. The soft aqua blouse brings out the color of my eyes. Or maybe it's just that I've been crying so much.

"In the back of your closet, which is a total mess by the way. And what's the deal with those chewed up shoes? Your dog has expensive taste."

"Tell me about it," I say before taking a sip of my hot and delicious mocha grande.

"And your apartment, Gretch. It's such a mess."

"I know..." Then I feel a small shock wave going through me as I realize that Noah was in my apartment too. "Oh no..."

"What?" Holly's eyes widen.

I wave my hand. "Nothing."

"What?" she demands again.

"The guy who picked up Riley for me at the apartment," I explain. "It's just kind of embarrassing to know that he was in there."

She nods. "I'll say. If I were you, I wouldn't let anyone in that place."

"Considering the circumstances, I didn't have much choice."

Holly grabs the oversized bag she brought, and we go out to the waiting area again. "Hey, who picked up Riley anyway? Someone from your school?"

"Do you remember the guy that my dad tried to set me up with?"

"At the Christmas party?"

"Yeah. Noah Campbell."

"I remember that he was seriously beautiful." Her face brightens. "He has Riley?"

"Yeah."

"So what's up with *this*?" She pokes me in the arm with a sly look. "Something you haven't told me?"

"No, not at all." I quickly explain how Dad had wanted him to help, how I had declined the offer, and how he just happened to stop by the house.

She frowns. "So your dad had his heart attack at the house?"

I nod, swallowing back a lump in my throat. "I feel really bad about it, Holly. Like it's sort of—no, not just sort of—almost entirely my fault."

"You can't blame yourself for—"

"If I hadn't wanted to do a house flip, and if I hadn't been set on that particular house, Dad would probably be out playing golf right now."

"And maybe having a heart attack on the ninth hole."

"Maybe...but at least it wouldn't be my fault. I know it's selfish of me to think that way, but I guess knowing it's my fault makes me feel guilty on top of scared. And scared is hard enough."

Holly nods sympathetically, then kindly changes the subject, telling me about last night's shower and how everything seemed to go wrong. From the sheet cake Justin picked up from the bakery that said "Happy Bar Mitzvah, Sammy" to the shower-game booklet her mother brought, which turned out to be for baby showers.

"I think that was just wishful thinking on Mom's part." Holly shakes her head, laughing. "She's dying to have a grandbaby—not that I plan to help anytime soon."

"How did Tina take all that?" I ask as I imagine Tina's face turning purple with rage.

"Not too well. And I'm sure she thought I was trying to ruin everything on purpose. Even the punch was terrible. I tried a new recipe and forgot to add the simple syrup until someone finally complained." Holly's laughing so hard now that she's almost crying. "But I honestly wasn't."

We talk awhile longer, and although she's a good distraction and I'm laughing with her, which feels nice, I know it's time to check on Dad.

"I understand completely," she says as she pats me on the knee. "And I should probably go home and clean up the condo. It's still a mess from the shower."

"Thanks for everything," I say as we stand.

"No problem. And keep me informed. Let me know if there's anything I can do."

Then I remember my car, still parked at the school parking lot. I barely mention this, and she promises me that she and Justin will take care of it. I hand her my car keys and hug her. "Thanks!"

I go to see Dad, hoping against hope that maybe he'll be awake by now. But when I get to ICU and stand in front of the window by the nurses' station, he is still motionless with his eyes closed. So quiet and still he could be mistaken for dead.

# 10

I'm Dr. Swenson." A woman not much older than me sticks out her hand to shake mine. "I'll be keeping an eye on your father over the weekend. Dr. Fontaine told me that we're looking to do a CABG on Monday, if not sooner."

"So it's scheduled for Monday?" I ask hopefully.

"As far as I know."

"But if he needs it sooner, you'll be ready?"

"Of course."

"This is just so hard," I admit. "Not knowing…and not having him conscious to talk things through. I mean, I signed the surgery release for him, but this is all so new to me. I don't want to make any mistakes…"

She nods with a look of understanding. "It's hard, I know. But we really do have your dad's best interests in the forefront. And Saint Joseph's may not be the biggest hospital, but our cardio unit is one of the best. Did Dr. Fontaine explain the cooling treatment to you?"

"Yes. Do you think it'll help?"

"It should definitely improve his prognosis.

"That's reassuring."

"If you have any other questions, please feel free to ask."

"Do you have any idea when he'll wake up?"

"That's hard to say…"

"But it's good for him to rest?"

"Well, that depends. But, don't worry, he's being closely monitored. He's in good hands here."

And that's what I tell myself after my next five-minute visit with him. Because the truth is, I am beginning to doubt. His unconscious state concerns me. A lot. And I wonder what Dr. Swenson meant when she said "that depends." Still, I don't see her around right now, and the nurses look busy. Finally I wander back to the waiting room, which is beginning to feel like my home away from home. Only less cluttered.

"Miss Hanover?"

I turn to see a young blond girl peering curiously at me. At first I think it may be one of my students, but she's not familiar. "Yes?" I say to her. "Are you looking for me?"

"Are you Miss Hanover?"

"I am."

"Hank Hanover's daughter?"

"Yes, I'm Hank Hanover's daughter. Who are you?"

"Kirsten."

I smile at her. "And you know my dad?"

She nods now, carefully looking at me…as if taking inventory. "You're supposed to come with me," she finally says, turning to head back to the elevator.

"Come where?" I ask.

"Downstairs."

"Why?"

"Because my daddy sent me up here to get you is why."

"Who is your daddy?"

"Noah Campbell."

"Oh." I nod as I piece this together. "He sent you up here by yourself?"

"I'm seven years old," she proudly tells me as she punches the Down button. "I can do lots of things myself."

"I see." I smile as we go inside and she punches the 1 button.

We are both silent as the elevator goes down. But I'm taking her inventory. For seven, she seems small. Not much bigger than my kindergarten kids. But she's also very pretty in a delicate, blue-eyed blonde sort of way, and as far as I can see, she doesn't look much like her dad. Wearing a pastel blue T-shirt and pale yellow shorts, she reminds me of cotton candy. And I get the impression that for a little girl, she is more capable than the average.

"This way," she tells me, leading me out of the elevator.

"Where are we going?" I ask as I follow her, watching as her short, slender legs almost march toward the front entrance.

"Out there," she points to the double-glass doors, and I can see a turquoise blue pickup.

"Why didn't your dad come in too?" I ask as I push open the door. But as we step outside, I can see why he didn't come in. He appears to be containing Riley in the back of his pickup. Riley is perched with his front paws on the wooden rails, his tongue hanging out one side of his mouth in a goofy-looking grin. He barks when he sees me and begins to run back and forth in the pickup bed.

"Riley," I say as I go around to the tailgate, where Noah is standing.

"I think he misses you," says Noah as he puts down the tailgate.

Then, before I can say a thing, Riley lunges out of the pickup, coming straight at me. He plants both front paws onto my midsection, and I topple backward, tripping over the curb and landing not so gracefully in the bark-o-mulch.

"Riley!" scolds Noah, pulling my dog off me. "You weren't supposed to kill her." Then Noah extends his other hand to me, helping me to my feet. "You okay, Gretchen?"

"Sure," I say as I brush bark off my back section and then lean over to pet my dog. "Silly thing."

"I didn't know he was going to take you out," says Noah. "Sorry about that."

"It's not your fault," I tell him as I squat down to give Riley the attention he's demanding. "I just haven't trained him very well."

"I like him," says Kirsten quietly.

"And I'll bet he likes you too," I say, still down at Riley's level, which is also her level.

"We played on the beach. He's good at fetching."

"He is good, isn't he?" I say. "I think it's his favorite game."

"Can we keep him longer?" she asks with hopeful eyes that are stunningly blue.

"Wow, you have pretty eyes," I tell her.

She just shrugs it off. "Can Riley stay with Daddy and me for the weekend?"

I stand up now, looking curiously at Noah, and he looks slightly apologetic. "I didn't promise anything… I just told her all we could do was ask, I mean, offer."

"You don't mind having him?"

"Not at all." He digs in his pocket now. "And here are your keys.

I locked up the house, and everything looked pretty much like before."

"Like a mess, you mean?"

He smiles. "It's definitely in need of some TLC."

"That's for sure." I don't ask him for his impressions. I don't think I want to know. I can't imagine what he must think of me. I don't even know why I should care.

Now Kirsten wraps her arms around Riley's neck, giving him a hug that he doesn't even try to shake off. I wish I had my camera turned on and ready to go, because this is a real Kodak moment.

"Can we take him home again, Miss Hanover?" begs Kirsten.

"Only if you promise me something," I say seriously to her.

"What is it?" She gives me a very somber look now.

"Please don't call me Miss Hanover," I tell her. "You see, all year long I'm a teacher at Lincoln Elementary, and all the kids call me Miss Hanover. But school's out now, and when I hear you say it, I think I'm back in school all over again."

"Oh…"

"Just call me Gretchen, okay?"

"Okay."

"And I'd love for Riley to spend the weekend with you. It would actually take a load off my mind."

"How's your dad?" asks Noah.

"About the same."

"Still unconscious?"

I nod, feeling close to tears again.

"Well, we didn't want to keep you from him, but Riley needed to see you."

"I appreciate it," I say as I give Riley another good ear rubdown.

"And I had to send in Kirsten because I wasn't sure that Riley would stay in the pickup."

"That was wise." I tell him about Riley nearly hanging himself from my car.

"Yep, I had a feeling."

I turn my attention back to my dog. "Now, you'd better be a good boy for Noah and Kirsten," I tell him. "Mind your manners, and don't eat any shoes." I glance at Kirsten. "You don't have any expensive shoes, do you?"

She gives me a funny look, then shakes her head no.

"Good. You should be fine."

"We'll let you get back to your dad then," says Noah.

"Thanks."

"I'll try to come by and see him sometime soon," he says. "Keep me posted, okay?"

"Sure."

"Tell Mr. Hanover hello for me," says Kirsten politely. "I hope he's feeling better."

I want to ask Noah how Kirsten knows my dad but can't think of a polite way to put it. Besides, I know that Noah is friends with Dad. Why wouldn't his daughter be friends as well? It's not like I spend all my free time with my dad. Especially these past eighteen months when I've been hiding from pretty much everyone.

"Thanks again," I tell both of them. "Riley's probably having such a great time with you guys that he'll never want to come back home to me."

"I doubt that," says Noah.

I wave and go back inside the hospital, which seems stuffier than ever after I just spent a moment outside in the morning sunshine.

~ ~ ~

The day passes slowly. About every half hour I go in and spend five minutes with Dad. But I begin to wonder if my being here really makes any difference. My hope is that, one of these visits, he will wake up, open his eyes, and give me one of those great sunny smiles. But all I get in return is a blank, cool silence—like I'm standing at the edge of a frozen lake or very near death.

It's late in the afternoon when I go to the chapel again. This time I don't have any agenda. I don't even have any words to pray. But I get on my knees and close my eyes, and for no explainable reason I feel certain that God can hear my heart—maybe even better than I can hear it. I no longer want to bargain with him. And I don't want to give him my answers. I am too tired, too scared for my dad's future—and my own—and I just want to surrender. I feel like letting go. "Do what you will," I say out loud for no one but God to hear. "All I can do is trust you..." I don't know how long I've been in the chapel, but my knees are stiff and sore by the time I stand up. But I feel strangely renewed. And even at peace.

I go back to ICU and into Dad's room. I just stand there looking at him and thinking how lucky—how blessed—I have been to have such a great dad. Does that mean I'm ready to lose him now? No, not at all. But I know this is out of my control. I take his cool hand in both of mine and gently squeeze it, closing my eyes. "No matter what happens, Dad," I say quietly, "I will always love you. You are the best." Then I just stand there for a moment, knowing that my five minutes are nearly up and that visiting time will soon be over too.

"I'm hungry," I hear a gravelly voice say.

I look down to see Dad's open eyes. "Dad?" I cry with excitement. "You woke up!"

"Where am I?"

"Saint Joseph's Hospital," I say, reaching for the nurse's buzzer and pushing it hard.

"It's freezing in here." He reaches for the oxygen tube that's going into his nose and pulls it off.

"I think you're supposed to leave that—"

"What's going on here?" asks the nurse as she pushes in front of me.

"He's awake," I tell her.

"Welcome back, Mr. Hanover," she says as she reinserts the tube in his nose. "You need to keep this oxygen going."

"I'm hungry," he says again. "And thirsty."

She chuckles. "We'll see what we can do about that, sir."

"And I'm cold."

"I'll bet you are," she says as she checks his monitor.

"You're in good hands," I say, peeking at Dad from behind the nurse and smiling. "They've been doing everything possible to help you."

He frowns at me now. "Did I have a heart attack?"

I nod. "You did. The neighbor lady called an ambulance for you."

"I want you to stay quiet, Mr. Hanover," warns the nurse. "I'll let Dr. Swenson know that you're conscious now. But take it easy, okay?"

"No dancing the Watusi?"

She laughs. "You know how to do the Watusi?"

"Sure. Want to see?"

"Not yet. You take it easy."

"Is it okay if I stay?" I ask, knowing that my five minutes have expired.

"Yes. Please do. And he can have a couple of sips of water. Just to wet his throat."

So while the nurse pages Dr. Swenson, I give my dad a little water. "I'm so glad to see you again," I say as he sips. "I missed you, Dad."

"I'm right here, sweetie."

# 11

After several minutes Dr. Swenson and the nurse come back into Dad's room, and the small space is too crowded for all of us, so I step out and wait by the nurses' station as they examine him and check the machines and whatnot. I want to call Holly and tell her the good news, but cell phone use is not allowed in the ICU. Apparently it can interfere with the monitors. Finally, after about forty minutes, they're finished with Dad.

"He's pretty worn out," says Dr. Swenson, "but you can go in for a quick visit if you want. Then he'll need a good night's rest."

"How does he seem?"

"Pretty good. We removed the cooling pads. But he'll still be on oxygen and the monitor…probably until he goes for surgery. But we may do that as soon as tomorrow morning."

"Why so soon?"

"Based on your dad's condition, sooner is better. And he's probably as stabilized as he's going to be. But we'd like to have his consent."

"Did you ask him?"

"I mentioned it, but he didn't seem ready to discuss it just yet. Maybe you can bring it up with him too. I'm sure he's still somewhat in shock."

I nod. "Yeah, it's a lot to take in."

"Well, don't visit with him too long. He may think he feels strong, but his heart isn't."

"Thanks," I tell her as I turn to go back in. Dad's eyes are closed now, and for a moment I think that maybe he's unconscious again. But then he opens them and barely smiles.

"Dr. Swenson said I could visit with you briefly." I stand by his bed and take his hand. To my relief it's almost a normal temperature now.

"How're you doing, sweetie?"

"Mostly I've been worried about you, Dad. You've really been out of it."

"What day is it?"

"Saturday."

"Oh..."

"You know that the doctors are recommending coronary bypass surgery, don't you, Dad?"

He seems to consider this but doesn't answer.

"It sounds like it's a fairly standard procedure now... They say that you'll be almost as good as new if you have it."

Still, he doesn't respond.

"I signed the release form...because you were unconscious. I didn't know what else to do, Dad. It seemed to make sense. I wanted to talk to someone about it, and I thought about calling Betty for some—"

His eyes flash. "You didn't, did you?"

"No."

He looks relieved now. "Good. No sense spoiling her vacation."

"You don't plan to call her at all?"

"Nope."

"Oh..."

"The doctor told me about the surgery."

"Did she explain how it works?"

He nods, just barely.

"And that it'll really take care of that blockage? It'll be like having a brand-new set of pipes going to your heart."

"My doctor talked about angioplasty...before this."

"I know," I tell him. "I remembered your mentioning that before, but both Dr. Fontaine and Dr. Swenson agree that bypass is the best treatment." I glance at the clock, knowing that the nurse could come in here at any moment. "Why don't you just sleep on it tonight, Dad."

"Yeah, that's what I am going to do. We can make a decision tomorrow," he says, obviously weary and a little overwhelmed.

"By the way, Noah and Kirsten send their regards."

His eyes seem to brighten at this. "They were here?"

"They're keeping Riley for me."

"You haven't been home?"

"No...I couldn't leave you, Dad."

"Thanks. But go home tonight."

"I'll think about it... Oh, and Holly sends her love too." I lean down to kiss his cheek. "We've all been praying for you."

"I can tell."

"I love you, Dad."

"Love you too, Gretchen Girl."

I smile. "Rest well."

"You too." Then he closes his eyes and instantly falls asleep. I squeeze his hand once more, then quietly slip out. I'm not sure I'm going home tonight. I do realize that I'm hungry, but the idea of eating in the hospital cafeteria is not appetizing. I go to the waiting area and call Holly to tell her the good news about Dad and that they may even do the surgery tomorrow.

"Oh, I'm so thankful," she says. "Justin and I almost brought your car over there this afternoon, but I didn't know if you'd want it stuck in the parking lot all night. So we parked it at the apartment. I can come over and give you a ride home if you want."

"I'm not sure I want to leave him yet."

"But you must be exhausted, Gretchen. And if you're dad's having surgery tomorrow, maybe you need a good night's rest."

"Maybe. Right now I'm starving."

"I haven't had dinner yet either. Justin is having guys' night out. Why don't I come and take you to dinner."

"Sounds great."

"I'll pick you up at the main entrance in about ten minutes, okay?"

"I'll be there."

After a quiet but rejuvenating dinner at a bistro downtown, Holly drives me to Dad's condo, where I refill the cats' food and water containers. They don't seem any worse for wear, and I promise them that their papa will be home in about a week. Then she drops me off at my apartment. "Sorry. I'm not very good company," I say as I reach for the door handle. "But I do appreciate your help tonight."

"I was glad to be here for you. And please give yourself a break, Gretchen. You've been through a lot these past couple of days. Hopefully, you'll get a good rest tonight."

"Yes...and back to the hospital first thing in the morning."

"Keep me posted."

I nod and get out of the car, realizing that I haven't told Noah about Dad yet. I promised to keep him posted too. As I trudge up the stairs, I dig his card out of my bag and slowly punch in his number. While the phone rings, I stand in front of my door, fish out the apartment key, and let myself in. No matter how messy and tiny my apartment is, it feels really nice to be home. Finally, as I drop my purse and lean against the wall, Noah answers his phone, and I tell him about Dad waking up.

"That's great!"

"And they might even do the surgery tomorrow."

"On a Sunday?"

"I guess Sunday is just another day in the hospital."

"Well, it does seem like the sooner they can fix him up, the better."

"I know I'll be relieved... I'm home now but plan to go back first thing in the morning."

"Well don't worry about Riley. I think he and Kirsten have fallen in love."

"I'll try not to get too jealous."

"Oh, don't worry. I can tell that Riley's heart belongs to you. Kirsten is just a fleeting fancy."

"Fickle dog."

He chuckles. "Well anyway, take care of yourself tonight," he says. "And give Hank my best, okay? Tell him that Kirsten and I will be praying for him to come through with flying colors."

"Yeah...sure." I don't know why this catches me off guard, but for some reason it does. It's still hard to grasp that Noah is the praying type. "Thanks again for keeping Riley."

Now that I'm off the phone, I can think of nothing better than sleep, so I make a beeline for my bed.

~ ~ ~

I wake up early the next morning, and all I can think about is Dad as I hurry to shower and dress and head back to the hospital. I pray for him on the way, but as I park my car and go inside, I'm still plagued with questions. Is he okay? Did he have a good night? Will they be able to do the surgery today?

As I reach the ICU unit and his room, I am shocked and scared when I see that he is not there. I turn and look for a nurse, then run down the hall until I find one just coming out of another room. "My dad?" I say breathlessly. "What happened? Where is he?"

"Hank Hanover?" she asks, although I know she must remember me since she's shooed me out of his room enough times.

"Yes! Is he okay?"

"They're prepping him for surgery."

"It's not even eight o'clock yet," I point out.

She gives me a blank look.

"And no one even called me."

"Since Hank regained consciousness and signed the release, there was no need to call you."

I hold back my irritation now. "So...when will he go to surgery?" I ask in a tightly controlled tone.

"The surgeon should be here around nine."

"Who is the surgeon?" I demand.

"Dr. Swenson."

Okay, at least that makes me happy. I have a good feeling about that woman. She seems intelligent and caring. Still, does that make her a good surgeon? I consider asking the nurse but assume she'd feed me a line.

"Will you be in the waiting room?" she asks, or perhaps it's a hint.

"Yes, of course."

"I'll let Dr. Swenson know."

"Thank you." I force a smile now, realizing that this woman will probably still be caring for Dad after his surgery. No need to make any enemies here. Then I go back to that detestable waiting room and prepare to wait. I pick up a recent issue of *Renovation Style* magazine and open it. Then, for one long hour, I attempt to lose myself among the glossy pages. I try to distract myself by focusing on all the wonderful things I might do to the house on Lilac Lane—and how proud Dad will be when it's done.

"Miss Hanover?"

I look up to see Dr. Swenson. She's wearing scrubs and a serious expression. I quickly stand, and the magazine falls into a puddle of pages at my feet. "What's wrong?" I ask fearfully.

"Nothing's wrong. Nurse Kelly said you wanted to see me."

"Oh well, I was just taken by surprise that Dad's surgery was scheduled so early. I mean, no one called me. Is everything okay? I mean, is my dad— Has his condition worsened?"

She smiles now. "No, he seems to be fairly stable. I just happen to be a morning person, so I like doing surgeries like this as early as I can."

"Oh..." Relief washes over me now.

"It's still something of an emergency procedure," she points out. "I think it will be a double bypass, but we may decide to do more once we're in there and are able to look around."

I cringe at the idea of Dr. Swenson with her hands in my dad's open chest cavity, poking around his heart and making assessments. It's a good thing I didn't go into the medical field.

"Any other questions?"

"How long will it take?"

"That depends, but I expect to be finished around noon."

"Oh..."

"I'll let you know how it went as soon as I'm done. Okay?"

"Yes." I nod eagerly. "I'd appreciate that. My dad, well, he's all I really have. I mean, I do have a dog. But my dad...well..." I feel my face flushing, and I know I probably sound like the village idiot.

She puts a hand on my shoulder. "I understand. Trust me; I will do my very best."

"Thanks."

And I actually do trust her. But I'm still scared. I replace the magazine on the table, then head for the chapel to do some serious pleading with God.

# 12

It's close to one by the time Dr. Swenson makes another appearance in the waiting room. I can tell by her expression that things went well.

"How is he?" I ask before she has a chance to say anything.

"He's in recovery, and everything looks good."

"So it went okay?"

"Yes." She nods. "Although I was surprised that we ended up having to do a quadruple bypass."

"Four?"

"Yes. But better four now than having him back here six months from now to do it again."

"That makes sense...I guess."

"He'll be in recovery for a few hours, then it's back to ICU for careful observation for at least twelve hours and probably more like twenty-four."

"When can I see him?"

"In a couple of hours. But then only briefly."

"And after twenty-four hours?"

"If there are no complications, he'll be moved to a regular patient room, and he'll remain there until he's strong enough to go home."

"When will that be?"

"I'd count on at least five days...maybe a week."

"Will he need help when he does go home?"

"Probably. We can talk about all that later."

"Yes." Then I reach out and shake her hand. "Thank you, Dr. Swenson. Thank you so much!"

She smiles. "You are very welcome. Your father seems like a really nice guy. He was even making jokes before they put him under anesthesia. And the nurses in ICU seem to like him."

I chuckle. "Yeah, sounds like my dad."

I call Holly and then Noah, telling them that the surgery went well. Holly offers to come over and keep me company, but I assure her I'm fine. And Noah asks when I want my dog back.

"I do miss him," I admit. "But I'll probably be here all day again. Of course, you may want to get rid of him by now."

"No, he's fine. Although I'm afraid Kirsten might go through withdrawal when it's time for him to go home."

"Doesn't she go back to her mother's?"

He sighs. "Maybe..."

"Maybe?"

"We're having a little disagreement about custody just now."

"Oh, I'm sorry."

"No, it's okay. It's just that I thought Kirsten was going to stay with me this summer, and now Camille is changing the rules."

"That's too bad... I hope you work it out." There's that baggage thing.

"I'm sure we will. Why don't you give me a call later and let me know what you want to do about Riley."

"Thanks. I want to be here when Dad wakes up, but that might be a couple of hours still." Noah says that's fine and not to worry. Then I hang up and head out for a quick bite to eat at a nearby deli. After which I come straight back to the hospital, where I get to wait some more. I keep checking, but it's close to four by the time I'm allowed to see my dad. At least he's awake, although he seems really groggy, and my attempts at conversation are mostly one-sided. His brain is surely scrambled, and I'm not even sure that he's cognizant of what just happened—either his heart attack or the bypass surgery. But I make fluffy chitchat, and when he eventually drifts off to sleep, I quietly exit.

"My dad seems a little mixed up," I say to the nurse at the desk. "He hasn't suffered any brain damage or anything, has he?"

"No no, I really don't think so. It's normal for someone to be confused after surgery. It's simply the aftereffects of anesthesia combined with the pain meds."

"Okay. When do you think he'll be more normal?"

"Probably not until tomorrow. They usually sleep a lot during the first twelve hours." She smiles at me. "If I were you, I'd just go home. I doubt that he will even miss you. Then you can come back tomorrow and spend as much time as you like with him."

So I take her advice, and after one more "visit" with Dad, where I do all the talking and he's pretty much out of it, I finally tell him I love him and that I'll see him tomorrow, and then I go home. I get here at around six but realize I need to turn right back around and get Riley, so I call Noah to arrange a time for me to come by.

"Why don't I bring him to you," he offers. "I have to drop Kirsten at her mom's anyway. And it might make the trip a little easier if I have Riley with me."

I make a joke about him turning my dog into a codependent,

but then I thank him for bringing Riley home. I look around, and without any hesitation I go to work straightening my messy apartment. Okay, there's not a lot I can do about boxes and stuff, but I do get rid of the dirty dishes, hiding them in the oven since I don't have a dishwasher and there's just no time to wash them. I take out the garbage and open up the place so that it smells a little fresher. I toss shoes and clothing and junk into my room and shut the door. I quickly run the vacuum cleaner and even put on a jazz CD, then fluff the pillows and light several scented candles.

Wait. What do I think is going to happen here? Feeling foolish, I quickly blow out the candles, waving my hand through the air to disperse the smoky smell of hot wicks. But I leave the music on, turned down low.

Now I start pacing nervously around my small space. Good grief, what is wrong with me? Why should I even care if Noah Campbell is coming to my apartment? I have absolutely no interest in him. Do I? No, I don't. I can't anyway, not after experiencing the tremendous pain of a broken relationship. He may or may not be the primary guilty party in his divorce, but I'm sure he's not completely innocent, and I can't take any risks. Plus, not only is he divorced, but he has a child, and from what I can see, he has custody challenges—baggage times twenty. I've seen enough of my students caught in this trap, and I agree with the experts who say the kids suffer most. No way do I want to be involved in something like that. Not that Noah's giving me the option or anything, but I just need to set some boundaries in my own mind. I turn off my CD player and even consider undoing what little cleaning I did but then realize that's pretty ridiculous. Instead, I turn on HGTV and check my e-mail.

I'm beginning to get totally engrossed in *Buy My House* when I hear a knock at the door and an anxious, familiar bark. I jump up to let Riley in before the neighbors complain. Despite the huge pet deposit I paid, having a big dog in a small apartment is still an issue.

"Hello," I say as I jerk open the door, allowing Riley to leap through and nearly knock me over again. "Down!" I command, trying to remind him who's boss but also feeling relieved that he's glad to see me. I think I'd started to develop a complex over his attachment to Kirsten. After Riley and I exchange greetings, he bounds past me as if he needs to investigate the apartment and see if everything is still in its proper place. Maybe he thinks another dog popped over to play with his doggy toys.

"Thank you again for keeping Riley," I say to Noah. "You have no idea what a relief it was not to worry about him."

"Like I said, it was our pleasure. Kirsten even suggested that I could set up play dates for the future."

"Play dates?" I puzzle over this terminology. Is he asking me out?

He laughs. "That's what mommies do when they need a babysitter; they take turns letting their kids visit each other's houses and call them play dates."

"Oh, right." I nod as I recall what it means. How dumb can I be? Or maybe I'm just sleep deprived and stressed.

He's still standing in the doorway, and I realize the polite thing is to ask him in, although I don't want to look overly eager. "Uh, do you want to come in?"

"Oh, you're probably busy." He peers over my shoulder now, noticing the TV still running. "Is that *Buy My House*?"

I glance back and nod. "Yeah. Do you like HGTV?"

He grins sheepishly. "Not that I'd want my guy friends to know."

"You're welcome to come in and watch it if you want."

"Sure. I had my cable turned off after I caught Kirsten watching something inappropriate. I haven't seen HGTV in months."

"Make yourself comfortable," I tell him, "if you can. I know it's pretty crowded in here."

He grins. "Yeah, I noticed that when I picked up Riley. You getting ready to move or something?"

"Long story…"

He nods as if he understands, then flops down onto the sofa. "Hey, this is comfortable."

"Do you want something to drink?" I offer, hoping I can follow this through if he says yes. I open my fridge and peer cautiously inside. "I have sodas and iced tea."

"Iced tea sounds good."

"Raspberry?" I ask tentatively.

"Great."

So I pour us both a tall glass, hand his to him, and then sit down in the armchair that's wedged between the sofa and the dining table. The commercials are on now, and without thinking, I mute the TV like I usually do during commercials. But suddenly the room feels too quiet. Riley is happily chewing a rawhide bone on his bed, and I feel the need to say something to fill the void.

"This isn't really my decorating style," I say, waving my hand over the clutter. "But I didn't expect to still be living in this apartment by now."

"Yeah, I guess life doesn't always meet our expectations," he says like he knows what's behind my comment.

I nod. "That's often been true for me."

"Is that why you're flipping the house? To make enough money for someplace else?"

"Exactly...although I'm not so sure anymore. I may just have to sell the house as is and hope I can break even."

"Why's that?"

"My dad... Obviously, he can't help me at all now."

"I thought you wanted to do it on your own anyway."

I laugh. "Yeah, I guess I said that, didn't I?" I let out a long sigh. "Sometimes I say things without thinking."

"Well, I'm still available...if you need some help."

I consider this. On one hand, it makes perfect sense. I need help if I'm going to move forward with the flip. But on another hand, I wonder if I'm just setting myself up for something. Something I don't want...something that could end up hurting worse than a flopped flip. "I'll think about it," I finally say. "Right now I feel like life is up in the air. I need to figure out how Dad's doing and what he'll need for recovery. His girlfriend is off on a big European trip, and I might need to be his nurse and housekeeper."

"Betty already took off?"

"You know Betty?"

"Sure. And now that you mention it, I do recall that she was going to be gone for a long time."

"Yeah, so, anyway..." The show's back on now, and I'm thankful to turn the sound back on. "It might be up to me to care for Dad."

He nods, and the show goes into full gear. As we watch, we make random comments on some of the couple's renovations and choices of materials. When the show ends, he stands up, thanks me for the tea and TV, politely sets his glass in the sink, and lets himself out the front door.

"Thanks again," I call out. "For helping with Riley."

He waves. "No problem."

Then I just shake my head. "Gretchen, you are hopeless," I say out loud, and Riley's tail goes *thump, thump, thump* against the floor as if to say he totally agrees with me.

~ ~ ~

When I arrive at the hospital, a nurse tells me that Dad's already been moved to a regular patient room. I take the elevator to the fifth floor, where I find him happily situated in his sunny new digs.

"I ate breakfast," he excitedly tells me. "I don't know if it was any good or not, but I finished off every last bite." He gingerly pats his midsection. "And I'm still hungry."

"Well, you probably shouldn't overdo it at first," I point out as I pull up a chair and sit down.

"Don't worry. They have me on soft foods now anyway. I won't get to sink my teeth into anything good for another day or two."

"So, you're feeling better then?"

"Yeah, all things considered."

"I was surprised they did a quadruple bypass," I admit.

"You and me both. But like the doc said, better now than later." He chuckles. "Pretty nice-looking doc, don't you think?"

"Dr. Swenson?"

"I never had a lady doc before," he says. "I told Dr. Swenson that I wouldn't mind seeing her on a regular basis."

"What about Betty?" I ask indignantly.

"I meant professionally...as my physician."

"Right..."

"So how are you holding up? How's Demo Dog doing?"

I explain how Riley spent the weekend at the Campbells' and added that Noah and Kirsten sent their best wishes. "Noah said they'd been praying for you."

He nods. "It helped; I think the good Lord intervened."

"Really?"

"Yep. There was a time when I thought I was a goner. Man oh man, Gretchen, I never felt so much pain in my life. It felt like someone had dropped a thousand pounds of bricks on my chest." He rubs his arm as if reenacting it. "And my right arm hurt so bad, I'd have let someone cut it right off."

"Glad you didn't."

"Yeah me too. And I'm on the mend now. I told the doc that I want to be out of here as soon as possible."

"You'll probably need help at home."

"Oh, I don't know about—"

"You'll definitely need help, Dad. At least for a while. And I'm pretty much done with school now. I have a couple of days to clean things up, but about the time you get out of here, I'll be free to come help."

"What about your house flip?"

I let out a long sigh. "I don't know, Dad... Maybe it was a mistake."

He gets a worried look now. "A mistake? Don't forget that my home is riding on this little venture."

"Believe me, Dad, I haven't forgotten. In fact, I think it might be best to just cut my losses, sell the place as is, and pay back that loan."

"No, Gretchen." He scowls. "I don't want you to give up. You've already put too much into this to just let it go."

"I don't know. And anyway, if by chance I do finish it, there's no way you can be involved in the renovations now." I don't mention my guilty frustration over the fact that he suffered his heart attack while trying to help at the house, even after I asked him not to. No need to add insult to injury.

"Not even as a consultant?"

I consider this. "Maybe not, Dad."

"That's no fun."

"I just don't want to add any more stress to your life."

"Being a consultant doesn't have to be stressful."

"I don't know..." I frown at him. "I'm not sure you can do anything halfway, Dad. You might just be one of those all-or-nothing kind of guys."

He grins now. "The Good Book says it's better to be hot or cold than to be lukewarm."

"In the case of my house, you'd better remain cold."

"Then how about you reconsider letting Noah help out? He's a master carpenter, Gretchen. You really couldn't ask for better."

"I'm thinking about it," I say, mostly to console him.

He smiles. "Well, then, maybe all this hospital business and surgery was worth it after all."

"Dad!" I shake my finger at him. "Don't act like you did this on purpose just to force me to hire Noah Campbell. That is perfectly outrageous."

He chuckles. "Hey, that just happens to be something else the Good Book says, Gretch: all things work together for good for those who love the Lord and are called according to his purposes."

"Well, I can't disagree with that, Dad. But like I said, I haven't decided about the house yet."

He nods with a somber expression, putting his hand to his chest as if he's in pain. "Don't feel bad for me, sweetheart. Never mind that I've had my heart set on—"

"Dad," I laugh, seeing right through his little act. "Don't be a drama king."

He smiles. "It was worth a shot."

"Speaking of shots," says a stout, middle-aged nurse as she enters the room. "Time for your meds, Mr. Hanover."

"Hopefully you're talking about the kind of meds that don't involve needles."

She chuckles. "Oh how I miss the old days of injecting a cantankerous patient."

"Is my dad cantankerous?" I ask.

"No," she tells me, "he's actually quite a charmer."

"Well, charmer," I tell him, "I'm feeling coffee deprived. If you don't mind, I'm going to run and get a Starbucks. Can I bring you anything?"

"You go get your fancy coffee," he says. "Even open-heart surgery isn't going to change my opinion about that nonsense. Give me Folgers any day."

I giggle to myself as I leave. Yep, same old Dad.

# 13

As I'm returning to Dad's hospital room, I see him speaking, it seems, to the wall. "How's the boat, Noah?" he says. I almost drop my coffee, stopping to figure out if my dad is losing it again.

"It's coming along," says a voice from the bathroom. Then Noah Campbell emerges with a pitcher of water and sets it on Dad's bed table.

I laugh out loud as I come fully into the room. "Well, that's a relief."

"What?" Dad looks up at me curiously.

"I assumed you were by yourself when I heard you asking Noah about a boat, and I thought you were imagining that Noah from the Bible was in here with you. I figured next you'd be asking about the animals and whether they were all lined up yet."

Noah chuckles. "Well, so far I haven't considered putting animals on the boat. But if Kirsten had her way, I'm sure she'd ask to borrow Riley when we finally take it out."

"So you have a boat?" I ask Noah as I pull up a chair on the other side of Dad's bed and sit down.

"Noah's been building a thirty-six-foot sailboat for a couple of years now," says Dad. "And she's a beauty. The woodwork alone is nothing short of amazing."

"Really?" I glance at Noah, imagining him on a boat. "So are you a sailor?"

"Well, kind of."

"But you're building a boat?"

"Well, I've sailed some. My ex-father-in-law had a forty-five-foot boat that we'd take out on Puget Sound occasionally. And then I used to borrow a friend's smaller boat, just to learn the ropes, so to speak. But I'm not what you'd call a seasoned sailor."

"When do you expect to finish it?" asks my dad. "When's the big launch?"

"It's getting close," says Noah. "Maybe by the end of the month."

"That's great," I tell him. I can imagine that a boat would be an ideal way to release anxiety built by custody battles.

"Do you sail?" Noah asks me.

I shake my head. "Never. But it looks like fun."

He nods. Then, as if I'm not in the room at all, Noah and Dad start talking about woodworking and types of woods and tools, and I feel like odd girl out.

"You know," I say, standing and feeling awkward. "If you guys don't mind, I think I'll head out for a bit. I really need to check in at school, let them know how things went, and start packing up my classroom."

Dad waves his hand. "You go ahead. I appreciate how much time you've already spent in this crusty old hospital."

"See you later then." I glance at the clock. "Probably around three."

"That'll be fine," he assures me. "Take as much time as you need."

I lean down and kiss him on the cheek, which is now smoothly shaved. "It's so good to see you back to your old self, Dad."

"See you, Gretchen," says Noah as I head for the door.

"Take care," I tell him. Then, relieved to be out of there, I hurry toward the elevators. I can't quite put my finger on it, but something about the easy way those two guys were talking just made me feel at odds. Sort of left out. And after I've spent so much time concerned about Dad these past few days and have been pretty much the only one here for him, it hurts to be pushed aside now. Okay, I know that's not exactly what happened, but that's how I feel. And not for the first time, I feel resentment toward Noah Campbell. And I remember how he compared my dad to his dad…and I almost want to go back there and set him straight, remind him that Hank Hanover is *my* dad and that I don't care to share him just now, thank you very much.

Of course, I know that's not only embarrassingly juvenile but incredibly selfish. I should be thankful that Noah came to visit Dad today. Also for watching my crazy dog this past weekend. Really, he's been helpful…and he's doing me a big favor by freeing me up to go to school and tie up loose ends. But the childish side of me just can't see it that way. Oh, get over yourself, Gretchen!

Everyone at school is concerned and understanding about my dad. My principal assures me that she doesn't expect me to have my room all packed up this week. "Take as much time as you need, Gretchen," she says when she stops by my room. I'm just taking down the front bulletin board, tucking butterflies and flowers into a big manila folder. "The cleaners and painters won't be in until the end of the month anyway."

Thinking of cleaners and painters only reminds me of my house flip, and getting my room packed up seems even more urgent. "That's okay," I tell her. "I'd like to wrap it up as soon as I can anyway. My dad's doing so well that I'm guessing he might be released from the hospital before long. I need to be ready to help him when he goes home."

She gives me a compassionate pat on the back. "You're a good daughter."

I shrug, remembering with a stab of guilt how it was possibly my stupid house project that induced Dad's heart attack in the first place. "Oh, I don't know..."

I work like a whirlwind for the next several hours, and it's after three by the time I quit. But at least the whole room is packed up, and I won't need to come back again until the end of August. I turn off the light with a sigh of relief. But then I remember Dad and that I promised to be back by now and that Riley is still at home and probably chewing up something he shouldn't. I feel like that old song "Torn Between Two Lovers," only I'm torn between my dog and my dad. Deciding that Riley will have to wait, I head straight to the hospital.

But when I get to Dad's room, Noah is still there, and suddenly I feel perturbed, although I tell myself not to show it. Just chill, Gretchen. No big deal.

"You're still here?" I say lightly as I go directly to Dad and plant a kiss on his cheek.

"Of course, I'm still here," says Dad in a slightly grumpy tone.

"Not you, silly. I mean Noah."

"Actually, I just got here," he says. "Your dad asked me to stop by again."

"Oh..." I turn my attention back to Dad. "How are you doing?"

"I'm tired of this place," he says impatiently. "I want to go home."

"Well, that's not going to happen, Mr. Hot or Cold...at least not for a few days. Dr. Swenson said five days was the minimum."

He scowls. "I know. Anyway, I asked Noah to stop by to talk to you, Gretch."

Noah looks slightly apologetic. "Hank asked me if I'd be willing to talk to you again about helping out with the house. Seems he knows his daughter can be, umm, independent, and I can't argue with a guy wrapped in tubes."

I glower at Dad. "Interesting..."

"I want him to go with you to the house," commands Dad. "I want him to do a thorough walk-through...to get his opinion."

"Didn't we already do that?" I ask.

Dad just shakes his head. "It's just too big a project for you to tackle on your own, Gretchen. You need help."

Okay, I feel like I've just been put in my place, and it's kind of embarrassing. But Noah's right: it's hard to argue with Dad while he's stuck in a hospital bed, just a couple of days past what could've been death's door, and his chest is bandaged from his quadruple-bypass surgery. So I just nod and say, "Okay."

"I'm tired," says Dad. "So you two might as well head on over there now since you're together anyway. Noah can ride with you, Gretchen."

"Why?" I ask.

"Because I want him to pick up my truck for me. He's got the keys."

"Oh..."

"And he can take it back to my condo, and you can pick him up there. And while you're there, you can get my mail and go inside and take care of the cats—"

"The cats are fine," I assure him. "I saw them yesterday."

"Still, I want you to go in and water the plants since I usually water them on Saturdays. And you can bring me a few things from home. I made a little list there on the table for you."

"Wow, you've got this all worked out, haven't you?"

"Not much else to do...stuck in this doggone bed all day."

After making sure Dad's nurse knows we're leaving, Noah and I head out and say nothing as we ride down in the elevator. Just before we reach my car, he finally speaks. "I know you don't want me involved in your house renovation, Gretchen, but—"

"It's nothing personal," I say quickly. "It's just that I want to do it myself. I've watched *House Flippers* so many times that I think I should be able to do this."

"But that show makes it seem easier than it is," he points out, "and if you've noticed, some of the house flippers are unsuccessful."

"I know..."

"I'm not going to force my help on you," he says in a firm voice. "I'm only going over there this afternoon as a favor to Hank. I'll give him my assessment and then walk away if you want me to." It almost feels like a challenge.

I don't know how to respond, so I say nothing as I dig my keys out of my purse. I just unlock my car, and we both get in. As I back out of the parking spot, I think of my dog. "Do you mind if I pick up Riley first?"

"Not at all. I'd like to see him."

So I stop by my apartment, and Riley, eager for some action, quickly does his business in the park, then happily hops in the back of the car and hangs his head over my shoulder as I drive to Paradise. Other than a few dog comments, Noah and I are both quiet during the trip across town. I feel guilty now because I think I've hurt his feelings…or at a minimum insulted him. Yet I don't know how to undo it either.

Once we're at the house, Noah and I go our separate ways. I take Riley to the backyard but realize it still needs some more cleaning before it'll be a safe place for him to play. Plus portions of the fence don't seem secure. I decide to put this on my priority list. If I'm really going to flip this house, it will make life much easier if I can bring Riley with me. And he'd be much happier here than in my stuffy little apartment.

With Riley still on his leash, I let myself into the house through the back door and look around with dismay to see there really is a ton of work to be done. Where the washing machine should be, there is a hole in the laundry room floor, and part of the Sheetrock is torn out. My dad's handiwork, I'm certain. Leave it to him to go looking for trouble. Okay, I know that it's wrong, but part of me would've preferred to simply cover the dry rot with new flooring and paint the wall. Hide it and move on. Of course, then I have to ask myself, would I want to live in a house like that?

I go into the kitchen next, looking at where the cabinets had been. I wonder how much it's going to cost to replace them…and who Dad knew who could give me a good deal. I pull out a notepad and write down some questions. I don't have my fancy house-flipping bag with me, but I figure I might as well try to get on top of things. And suddenly as I'm walking around this dilapidated house, it hits me: I still want to do this. I really do want to do this. And for no explainable or intelligent reason, I still think I can.

I write down more notes, making a fairly long to-do list that starts with fixing the fence in the backyard.

"I think I've seen enough," says Noah as he rejoins me in the living room.

"Meaning that it looks hopeless?"

"No, not at all. I actually think you can turn this place around… with some help."

"Meaning you?"

He shakes his head. "Nope. Like I said, I don't force my help on anyone."

"I know." I sigh loudly. "I also know that I'm acting like a spoiled brat, Noah. And I know I'm not being very gracious or appreciative."

"But you still don't want help," he fills in.

"No," I agree, "I don't *want* help, but the truth is, I need it."

"You do if you plan to finish this in six weeks."

"It's five weeks now," I point out.

He just shakes his head. "Have you ordered anything yet? Windows or cabinets or anything?"

"No…"

"Those things alone can take up to six weeks, Gretchen."

"Really?"

He nods soberly, then kneels to scratch Riley's ears, almost as if he's giving me a moment to think this through.

"Okay, I admit it," I say with reluctance. "I do need your help, Noah. But I wouldn't blame you if you told me to take a hike."

He stands and smiles now. "Why would I do that?"

"Because I've been such a brat."

"You're just being honest, Gretchen. And territorial."

"Yeah, I guess I do feel territorial. Maybe you wouldn't understand, but I have this need to prove I can do something big like this—maybe more for myself than anyone else."

"I do understand."

"Oh..."

"And I'll tell you what. If you want me to help you with this, we will set our boundaries right now. You are the general contractor, and I am the sub."

"Really?"

"Absolutely. You call the shots. You tell me to jump, and I'll ask how high."

"Seriously?"

He nods.

"Jump," I tease.

"How high?"

I use my thumb and forefinger to show about two inches, and he jumps about two inches, which gets Riley all excited so that he's jumping too. I laugh as I stick out my hand. "Okay, it's a deal."

He takes my hand and gives it a firm shake. "Deal. And for the record, I won't send my bill until the house is sold."

Of course, I realize this means I'll need to keep a tab of his hours so I can budget for this. Still, what other choice do I have?

Then I lock up the house, get in my car, and follow him as he drives my dad's pickup to my dad's condo. We both go inside, and while I clean some perishables out of Dad's fridge, Noah waters the plants. When we're done, he rides with me to my apartment to drop off Riley before we return to the hospital so he can pick up his truck.

"How's the custody thing going with Kirsten?" I ask as I drive through town. I'm mostly just trying to make conversation, although I am curious. I just hope I'm not stepping over the line. "Will she get to spend the summer with you?"

"It's not looking good."

"I'm sorry."

"Me too."

"How does Kirsten feel about it?"

"She's disappointed. She's also pretty miffed that she has to be in day care now."

"Day care? Isn't she a little old?"

"Her thinking exactly. Unfortunately the day-care center has a summer program for school-aged kids up to seven. But it also still has a lot of little kids…or *babies* as Kirsten calls them."

"So instead of being with you, she's in day care?"

"Yep."

"Of course, you wouldn't be able to watch her while you were working," I point out.

"I was going to take the summer off. Just finish my boat and hang with Kirsten."

"What are you—independently wealthy?" Of course, I regret my nosiness as soon as I say this.

But he just laughs. "I wouldn't say that. But I have rearranged some of my priorities when it comes to work and money and living. I think life's too short to spend all your time trying to get more and more. I'd rather just be happy with what I have and enjoy what's going on around me more."

I consider this. Maybe that works for him, but I'm not ready to settle for being cooped up in a tiny apartment. I wonder if he thinks I'm wrong to want something more. Maybe he thinks I'm one of those people who just want more and more. Maybe I am. Okay, that's a little unsettling, but I decide not to think about it too hard as I drop him off by his old turquoise blue truck.

"I like your pickup," I admit.

"Thanks. So do I."

"Did you do the restoration yourself?"

"I did."

"Looks good."

"I still have a few things I need to address, but for the most part, it runs pretty well, and I'm happy with it."

I look curiously at him now. "You're just a pretty happy guy, huh?"

He laughs. "I try to be. The truth is, I spent too many years being unhappy. I guess I'm trying to make up for it now."

"Oh..."

"Tell Hank I'll pop in tomorrow morning to tell him my assessment of your house, if he still wants it. But I'll only do that if you're there too...since you're the boss, Gretchen."

"Do you want to come up now?" I ask.

He glances at his watch. "I would, but I've got a dinner date that I'm already running a little late for. I better get going."

"Sorry to keep you," I say quickly.

"No problem."

I watch as he gets into his truck, wondering who his dinner date could be. Then I realize that, of course, a guy like Noah has to have a girlfriend. Duh. For all I know he might have several. Most women wouldn't think twice about his divorced status or baggage, not with a good guy like Noah. And nowadays most single women in their thirties realize that you can't be so picky if you want a good guy.

Most women except for me, that is. Maybe I need to have my brain examined!

# 14

I told Noah he can help me," I announce to my dad as I sit down by his bed. It looks like he's just finished his dinner and maybe getting a little groggy. But he does seem relieved at my news.

"I don't think you have much choice," he says in a tired voice, "that is if you still want to turn the house around and make some money."

"I really do want to flip it, Dad. I wasn't sure earlier. This whole thing with your surgery and all…well, it was a setback. And I'm willing to admit that I do need help. And Noah still seems interested in helping." I almost add, *I don't know why,* but keep it to myself.

"Good girl. I was hoping you'd come around."

"And Noah has agreed—actually it was his recommendation—that I will act as the general contractor, and he will be the sub." I study Dad's reaction, which is minimal, but then again, he looks tired. "Does that work for you, Dad?"

"Not much I can do about it one way or the other."

I pat his hand. "I know you're worn out."

He lets out a big yawn. "I have to agree with you there."

"So I'll let you get your beauty rest…unless there's anything I can do for you before I go."

"Just hearing your willingness to work with Noah is more than enough, sweetie. It puts my tired old heart at ease."

I go to the window and adjust the blinds so the setting sun won't be too bright in here. "Glad to be of help."

"How's Demo Dog?"

"He's fine. I wish I could sneak him up here to visit you."

Dad smiles faintly. "I don't think you could sneak that dog in anywhere."

"I know it. By the way, I sorted the mail. There's nothing that can't wait."

"No postcards…from Betty?"

"No. But you know how slow overseas mail can be."

"And she's probably got better things to do than write to an old coot like me."

"You're not an old coot," I tell him. "Oh, also, I have your keys. But I might as well hang on to them until you go home."

"Safer with you than here, I expect."

"That gives me an idea, Dad. Do you think I could use your pickup while you're recuperating, to pick up building supplies and things?"

"That's a smart idea."

"Great. I started making a list at the house. First thing tomorrow I'll fix the fence and clean the yard for Riley, and then I'll measure everything. And, of course, I'll measure it again, and then I'll order windows, and…" But I notice his eyelids drooping, and I realize that he's too tired to hear any more. Poor guy. He was so eager to get out of this place this morning, and now he's beat. I quietly remove his food tray from the bed. Then I partially fill his water cup, and after carefully pulling the blanket up over his chest, I lean over and kiss his wrinkled forehead. Without opening his eyes, he smiles.

"Night, Daddy," I whisper, then tiptoe out.

I feel strangely energized as I drive back to my apartment, so I pick up Riley and head back to Dad's, where I exchange my car for his pickup. Riley is thrilled to jump into the back of my dad's truck, and I start to feel like a real carpenter as I drive through town. I consider stopping at Home Depot to pick up a few things but realize that Riley can't be trusted to stay in the back of the pickup. And I don't trust him not to chew up something in the cab if left unattended. But then I think, *It's time this dog got some discipline.* So I take my chances and head to Home Depot. I get out of the truck, tell Riley in no uncertain terms to "stay," and then pretend to go into the store. I actually hide behind a nearby minivan, keeping an eye on my dog as he trots back and forth in the pickup bed, sort of whining and acting nervous. Then he settles down, and I think maybe he's getting this. But the next thing I know he leaps over the tailgate.

"Riley!" I shout, popping out from behind the minivan and startling a customer who's wheeling out a cart loaded with lumber. "Bad boy!" I shout, deciding I don't care who hears me. My dog needs to learn. Then I make a big deal of scolding him, force him back into the pickup bed, and once again tell him to "stay!" We go through this entire procedure about seven more times, and I am getting seriously exhausted, not to mention fairly certain that my dog is academically challenged in the area of obedience.

Then suddenly he seems to get it. I'm crouched behind another pickup now, no longer caring what curious bystanders think of me, and it hits me that Riley is staying in the truck. I sit down on the curb of the parking divider now, deciding to wait a good long time to make sure that he's really with the program, but after twenty minutes, I think he gets it. I also think Riley deserves a little praise.

I pretend like I'm just casually walking from the store now, like I've actually been shopping instead of sitting on a curb. I approach Dad's truck and calmly encourage Riley, "Good boy. You stayed." His tail wags happily, and I continue to praise him, stroking his head and promising him a special treat when we get home. And to my utter surprise, he seems to understand this. I think we have turned a corner. Maybe I won't be enrolling Riley in doggy reform school after all.

~ ~ ~

The next day I awake to my cell phone ringing. I scramble to find my purse, then dig out my phone and groggily say hello, hoping that nothing's wrong with Dad. Fortunately, it's not the hospital. It's Noah.

"Sorry to call so early," he says, "but I forgot to mention that your dad wanted me to go over things with him regarding the house."

"So are you going to the hospital?"

"Yeah, but I wanted to check with you first. After all, you're the contractor."

I consider this and smile, curious. Has he forgotten his promise to wait until I'm present too? "I think it would be great for you to go talk to Dad this morning. And why don't you tell him that I'll pop over there around noon. I want to get some fence stuff and see what I can do to clean up the backyard and make it safe for Riley."

"Sounds like a plan. And if it's any help, I noticed a pile of free fencing in front of a remodel over on Parker Avenue...about Ninth Street, I think it was."

"Really? When was that?"

"Just yesterday evening."

"Cool. I'll drive by and take a look. Even if I only use it temporarily to keep Riley in, it might be worthwhile."

As it turns out, Noah is right. There is a pile of used fencing at the end of a driveway with a piece of cardboard with "Free" spray-painted on it. I park the pickup, then get out and cautiously open the tailgate. I brace myself to be tackled as I command Riley to stay. And to my amazement, he stays. Today, I remembered to bring a box of Milk Bones to use as rewards. And after I load all the lumber, which actually looks to be in fairly good shape and similar to the fencing that's already at the house, I give Riley a treat and tell him he's a good boy. He happily wags his tail, and I'm thinking perhaps dog training isn't as tough as I'd imagined.

Of course, I've picked up some splinters along with the fencing. It occurs to me that my dad often wears heavy gloves when working with wood, so I decide I'll have to get a couple of pairs. Next I go to Lowe's, and once again I give Riley his command, but I stick around for a minute or two, hiding behind a car, as I make sure he's still on board. Then, pulling my list from my bag, I go inside and allow myself twenty minutes to get what I need for this morning. I can't find everything, but at least I'm off to a good start, and to my relief Riley is too.

"You're a good boy," I say as I pet his smooth head and hand him another half of a Milk Bone. "Next stop and you can stretch your legs."

By the time I make it to the house, Noah is already there, and the front door is wide open. I'm curious how he got in, but then I realize that Dad probably gave him the key when he asked Noah to pick up his truck. I try not to feel irked. After all, Noah is working for me. I should be pleased that he's already at it.

"Hello," I call as I set a bag of things by the door. "Anybody home?"

"Back here," he calls, and Riley dashes off to find him in the bathroom. Actually he's several feet down in the bathroom.

"Did you fall through the floor?" I joke.

"Not yet. I'm removing some of these rotten joists and decided to have a good look around down here, make sure the moisture problem doesn't go farther than we expected."

I grimace. "Does it?"

"A little. But fortunately it doesn't seem to be past the perimeter of the bathroom. I think we can leave this wall intact." He taps the wall near the door.

"Oh."

"Anyway, I'm trying to figure out what you'll need in the way of lumber."

"Don't let me bother you," I say quickly, feeling like I'm the one intruding here. "By the way, that fencing was still there, and it looked pretty good. Thanks for the tip."

"No problem, boss."

I roll my eyes as I walk away. Right, like I really know what I'm doing. Still, I don't have to reveal just how much I don't know. I leave Riley in the house while I take a shovel and a five-gallon bucket that I've lined with a trash bag, and I go thoroughly through the backyard, scooping up doggy doo-doo. It's a stinky job, but somebody's got to do it. And once this is cleaned up, I'll only be picking up after my dog, and I'm used to that.

As I walk around the yard, I imagine how nice it could be back here with some rollout grass and landscaping and maybe some flowering shrubs against the fence. But with the mature trees and shady privacy, it's really not half bad. It just needs some serious TLC. Finally I think I've pretty well sanitized the dried-up brown grass, and I want to tackle that fence. I decide to start by removing the broken pieces. After I get the hang of it, it's actually sort of fun to muscle them out with Dad's oversized hammer and a crowbar. And these gloves are great. No more splinters for this girl. When I'm done, the fence looks sort of ridiculous with all its gaping holes. Like an old prizefighter with a bunch of missing teeth. But before long, I'm replacing those missing teeth, and to my relief the salvaged wood actually blends in pretty well with the original fence.

"Hey, good job," calls Noah from the back deck.

"Thanks," I tell him.

"That old cedar is a good match."

I nod, shielding my eyes from the sun. "And a lot cheaper than replacing the whole thing with new stuff."

"And I think it actually looks better too," he says.

I consider this and think maybe he's right. A brand-new fence might look out of place in this yard.

"I'm heading to the lumber yard to pick up some wood. Anything you need?"

I glance at my watch to see that it's getting close to eleven now. "No. I'll probably be gone to see Dad by the time you get back. Do you mind if I leave Riley behind?"

"Not at all. He's actually being a good dog in the house."

"That's probably because there are no designer shoes in there." I laugh and try not to remember the Stuart Weitzman shorty boot that I found chewed up in my apartment yesterday when I got home from the hospital. I really thought I'd put all the good shoes up high, but he must've found the box under my bed and then gone at it all afternoon, because that little brown boot looked like a twisted raw-hide chew stick by the time I saw it. Maybe it tasted like one too. But to be fair, I wasn't terribly sad since they were boots I'd splurged on for my honeymoon. The honeymoon that wasn't. Perhaps Riley has been doing me a favor by destroying the evidence. The only thing that really makes me sad is how much money I wasted buying designer shoes in the first place. Sure I got deals on them, thanks to Bluefly.com. But just the same, I was living an illusion, both financially and romantically. Really, what was I thinking?

"It's almost done," I say to Riley as I snap out of my depressing brain fade, "but not quite ready for you yet. Maybe I'll finish it up when I get back." Then I tell him to be good until Noah returns. He's not eager to be left alone and lets out a few barks of protest, but I leave anyway. The dog has got to learn that he's not the one calling the shots.

Knowing that Dad loves ice cream even more than I do, I decide to stop by Ben & Jerry's and buy him a treat. But as I study the menu, I realize that he may be seriously restricted from fats from now on, and I finally have the girl make him a nonfat, orange-cream sorbet shake. I'm tempted to get something less healthy for myself but then realize that Dad might get a bad case of ice-cream envy, so I have her make one for me as well.

"Treats," I say as I go into Dad's room.

"Ice cream?" he says hopefully, eying the B&J bag.

"Sort of," I say as I hand him the shake and stick a straw into it. "Only healthier. I'm having one too."

He frowns but takes a cautious sip anyway. "Not bad."

"And not bad for you."

He doesn't argue as he continues to sip.

"I didn't ask if it was okay," I admit, glancing over my shoulder. "I hope I don't get you in trouble."

"I'll blame it on you," he says.

Then I tell him about the free wood and how I'll soon have the fence fixed and the yard ready for Riley.

"Good! You'd be smart to scavenge all you can for that house. Funds are going to be tight."

"I know… Already I can tell I'm going to have to cut back on some things. Speaking of that, can I get the name of the cabinet guy?"

"What cabinet guy?"

"I thought you mentioned someone."

His forehead creases. "Oh, it was a brother of one of the cleanup crew guys. But I don't have a name or phone number."

"Then how do we find him?"

He brightens now. "I'll do some calling around today. That's one thing I can do from this confounded bed."

"Do they tell you to stay in bed all the time?"

"No. I have a therapist who comes in several times a day and makes me do my exercises and breathe into that contraption there. She said that starting tomorrow I can be up and walking around more." He winks. "But I think I might sneak out and walk around today. Glad you brought my robe. I don't like the idea of traipsing down the hallway with my hind end hanging out of this gown."

I laugh. "Yeah, I've always wondered what was up with hospital gowns. It's like they're designed to humiliate patients."

"Probably to put us in our places…make sure the medical staff keeps the upper hand."

We chat awhile longer, and then I start getting itchy to go back to the house. "I should probably get back to work," I finally tell him. "I left Riley in the house, and I'd like to secure that yard for him."

Dad nods. "Yep. You run right along. I'll be fine."

I throw our empty cups away, then kiss him on the cheek. "Be a good patient, Dad."

He gives me a sly grin. "Be a good contractor, Gretchen." He chuckles but then turns serious. "Would you mind checking my mail today, Gretchen? I'm sort of hoping that Betty will send a card or something."

"No problem."

"And while you're there, want to pick up my vitamins for me? Betty would be miffed if she knew I hadn't been taking them."

"Good idea," I tell him. "I'll bring them by this evening, okay?"

"Thanks, Gretchen." He's smiling, but his eyes are sad.

"You okay?" I ask.

He shrugs. "Just missing her…I guess."

"Betty?"

He nods.

As I leave, I feel a mixture of envy and admiration. It must be nice to have someone special to miss.

# 15

Noah is still hard at work when I get back to the house. I don't interrupt him but go straight to work finishing the fence in back. In less than an hour, it's secure enough to let Riley come out and join me. I fill an unused cleaning bucket with fresh water for him and then throw a stick for him to chase for a while. He acts like he's in doggy heaven, and I suspect he wouldn't mind living here. And, who knows, maybe when the house is a little more functional, I could bring over a few things, and he and I could camp here. That would subtract the commute and give me more time to work.

"Okay, you're going to have to entertain yourself," I tell him. "I've got to measure those windows."

I've just finished measuring windows when I hear Noah calling my name. I go to find him still at work on the bathroom floor, and to be honest, it doesn't look much different than it did this morning. I'm tempted to point this out but decide to hold my tongue.

"I don't know if you're going out for any building supplies," he tells me, "but there are a couple of things you could pick up for me for this bathroom, if you don't mind."

"Not at all. I was actually about to head out to order the windows."

"Did you measure them?" he asks as he stands up and uses the back of his hand to wipe perspiration from his brow, making a brown dirty streak across his forehead. I'm tempted to wipe it off for him, but I don't.

"Yes," I say a little indignantly. "I measured twice on every window just to be sure."

He wears a slight frown now. "Do you want me to check the measurements for you?"

"No," I say even more indignantly. "I know how to read a measuring tape."

"I'm sure you do, but have you ever ordered windows before?"

"No, of course not."

"There are a couple of tricks to it. Did anyone explain it to you?"

"Well, no...but..."

"Wouldn't you rather have me check them than order the wrong windows, Gretchen?" He suddenly sounds bossy, but I've spent enough time around contractors, including my own father, to know this is how they talk. "Do you realize how expensive it would be to have to purchase two sets of windows?" he continues. "And then you'd have to wait for the second set to arrive, and your schedule would be shot to pieces, and—"

"Okay, okay!" I hold up my hands as in "I surrender," not sure whether to laugh or sulk. I hand him my list of window sizes and the tape measure and say, "Go ahead and check it. I mean, what would a kindergarten teacher know about measuring?"

I follow him into the living room, where he begins to measure, then stops. "Which measurement is the width here, Gretchen?"

"Huh?" I look at the paper, then point to the right spot.

"For starters, you should always list the width first when ordering windows."

"Why?"

He sort of smiles as he remeasures the width of the front window. "Because that's how it's done."

"Oh well, that's easy. I can change that."

"Okay, come here and look at this," he tells me. "This window's width is seventy-eight inches, but look what you wrote down."

I look at my list again and see that I've written down seventy-four inches. Then I look at where he's holding the tape. "But that's the outside of the window," I point out. "I measured the glass."

"But that's not how you order windows," he explains with a hint of that contractor tone again. "They come already put together with the frame on them. It's easiest if you replace them in the same size. Then you don't have to mess with the headers or siding. You just slip them into place."

"Oh..." I nod, taking this in. "That makes sense."

"So, you see, if you'd gone in and ordered the windows like this... well, you would've been sorry when they got here, because they'd have been too small, and you probably would have had to re-side the whole house and redo the headers, and then there would have been the Sheetrock to be filled in, and you'd—"

"Okay, already. You made your point. I'm stupid."

He shakes his head. "Not stupid, just a little inexperienced. Trust me, when we're done with this house, you'll be a real pro."

I force a smile. "I hope so."

"How about I help you remeasure these windows. One of us can measure, and one can write; it'll go much faster that way."

"Thanks," I tell him as I wad up my faulty window list and toss it into the garbage can. "I'd appreciate that."

And it does go quicker. Noah measures, and I write, and before long we have a proper list.

"Have you decided what kind of windows you want?" he asks.

"Glass?"

He laughs. "Yes, that's a good place to start. But I mean like which brand, and do you want wood or clad, double hung or casement, or—"

"Here we go again…" I try not to show my frustration or inexperience. "I want the windows to be nice but not too spendy."

He nods. "But you don't want them to be too cheap either. Cheap windows on a nice house is like a pretty woman with a bad hairdo."

Without thinking, I absently reach up and touch my hair, which is pulled back in my usual grunge-day ponytail.

"Your hair is fine." He smiles.

"Right."

"Anyway, my point is don't go too cheap on the windows. And if you do clad, which I'd recommend, you might want to consider what color you plan to paint the house later on. Pick out an exterior color that will go nicely."

"I was thinking a sage sort of green."

"Why don't you stop by the paint section and get some samples along the lines of what you think you're going to paint. And what about those patio doors in back?" he asks. "Are you going to replace them too?"

"Definitely. But I thought I could deal with it later."

"Why put it off? They'll take about the same amount of time as the windows, and if they come sooner, we'll be that much ahead of the game."

"I thought french doors would be nice," I tell him.

"I agree."

"Want to help me measure the doors?" I ask meekly. "I mean, I know you want to keep working in the bathroom, but it—"

"I think getting the doors measured and ordered is a priority," he says. So we go back to measuring.

"Okay," I say when we finish. "I think I have my work cut out for me now."

"Good luck."

"And Riley should be fine in the backyard," I tell him. "But this might take awhile. Do you need those pieces really soon?"

"No, I'm fine. Maybe I'll start tearing into the other bathroom; I think the dry rot in there is only under the sink. We'll be able to leave the toilet and tub in for a while."

I tell him his plan sounds good, then head out the door. And I feel more hopeful than I have in a long time as I drive Dad's pickup through town. Our first official day working together, and we seem to be getting along. To be fair, I think it has more to do with Noah than me. I can't believe how patient he was about my ignorance. My dad, as much as I love him, isn't always that kind. Sure, he means well, but it just seems like he expects everyone to know as much about building as he does, and when you don't, well, watch out. Noah's got a softer way of dealing with overconfident, inexperienced me.

It takes a couple of hours to order the windows and doors, but when I'm done, I feel good about my choices. Well, other than the expense, which is a considerable portion of my budget. But it's also unavoidable if I want the house to look good and also function well. And while I didn't pick the costliest windows and doors, the quality is a major upgrade from the house's current ones. I think Noah will approve. I kept the designs simple—or classic, as the woman helping me described it. And I followed Noah's advice to get some paint samples, and the exterior clad I chose, in a nice, neutral taupe, looked great with all the greens I selected. Best of all was the wooden front door, which is more of a craftsman style but simple enough that it works for modern/contemporary too. Plus I think it will really set the tone for the house. And I already know what kind of porch lights will be perfect with it.

Since I'm halfway to Dad's place, I decide to go by to check his mail, get his vitamins, and say hi to the cats. I'm hoping Betty has sent a postcard by now since I know that will lift his spirits, but when I unlock the box, I only find a couple of bills and junk mail. I put these with the rest of his mail on the dining room table, then go to look for his vitamins. As I'm about to leave, the phone rings, and I decide to answer it.

"Gretchen?" says a woman's voice.

"Yes."

"Oh, I'm so glad I reached you. It's Betty. We're in port in Valencia, Spain, and my cell phone is finally working. Is Hank there?"

"Actually, he's not."

"Is everything okay?"

I try to think of the right answer. "Yes, everything is fine…now."

"I tried to call him a couple of times last weekend. It should've been nighttime there, but he wasn't home. I began to worry."

"Well, Dad hasn't been home," I say, wondering how much to tell her. I know Dad doesn't want to spoil her trip, but now that he's out of the woods, or seems to be, maybe she should know.

"Where did he go?"

"He had a heart attack last Friday and—"

"Oh no," she gasps, "is he okay? Should I come home?"

"No no, don't come home. He's okay now. And he would feel terrible if you came home. He didn't even want me to tell you, Betty."

"But how is he?"

So I explain about the surgery. "And he's doing really great now. He will probably be home by the end of the week."

"But he'll need someone to help him, Gretchen. A quadruple bypass takes weeks to recover from."

"Yes...six to twelve weeks."

"I think I will come home."

"No," I practically yell. "Please don't. Dad would hate to ruin your trip. I'm here. I'll take care of everything. Please don't worry."

"But what about your house, Gretchen? How will you ever manage to do it now?"

Then I explain about Noah.

"Oh, Noah is a dear!" she exclaims.

"You know him?" Okay, I already know this, but for some reason it catches me off guard, like I've been missing out on something.

"Oh yes, his mother and I are neighbors and good friends. In fact, it was Noah who introduced Margaret and me to Hank in the first place. Lucky for me, Margaret decided that Hank was not her type."

It suddenly feels like all these people—my dad, Noah, Betty,

Kirsten, and now Noah's mother—were enjoying this secret social life I wasn't part of.

I offer a laugh. "So you can see that everything is totally under control here, Betty. Please, do not even think of ending your vacation sooner than you planned."

"I just wish I had been there for him, Gretchen." Her voice breaks now. "I really care about him. A lot."

"And he cares about you too," I assure her. "In fact the main reason I'm here is that he was hoping you'd sent him a postcard."

"I've sent him at least seven. Haven't they arrived yet?"

"Not yet."

"Ugh. International mail is so slow."

"But he'll be pleased to know that I spoke with you."

"Is it all right for me to call him at the hospital?"

"Of course." Then I give her his room number. "He'd love to talk to you—except that he didn't want you to know. I hope he's not mad at me for telling you."

"Well of course you should have told me. I can explain that I wormed it out of you."

"And assure him that you're not going to let it spoil your trip. He needs to know that. Otherwise, he will feel guilty."

"Yes. I totally understand. Don't worry. I'll smooth it all over."

"Thanks."

"And thank you for telling me, Gretchen. I'm so glad that you're there for your dad. I know he acts like he's so self-sufficient, but he needs us."

"I know the feeling."

"Well, good luck on that house of yours. I can't wait to see it. You are taking photos, aren't you?"

I slap my forehead. "You know, I was, but then this whole thing with Dad kind of threw me off. I will make sure to take my camera over tomorrow."

"Well, I better say 'adios' before I wake up my sister."

"What time is it there?"

"After midnight."

"Oh, it's just a little past four here."

"Well, give your dad a great big hug for me, okay?"

"I'll do that."

I feel slightly guilty as I hang up. I know that Dad didn't want Betty to know about his heart attack. But how could I not tell her? Hopefully, she'll help him understand that. And I know he'll be happy to hear from her. It was nice to hear her say how much she cares about him too. Maybe their affection for each other really is mutual. Who knows, there might be a wedding in our family after all. I wonder if Betty would like to use any of the things I still have from my wedding that wasn't. I tried to pass some things off on Holly, as well as her sister, but they were worried that the things might be jinxed.

By the time I get back to the house, Noah has made good progress by tearing out the sink and cabinet from the other bathroom. But the expression on his face is not encouraging.

"This is worse than I thought," he says, poking a screwdriver into a piece of Sheetrock that's already crumbling. "This whole sink wall will have to be replaced."

"Oh..." I feel my spirits crumbling just like the wall.

"How'd the door and window shopping go?" he asks more cheerfully.

I quickly give him the lowdown, and he nods with approval. "Sounds perfect. And don't worry about this dry rot, Gretchen. It's all fixable."

"Why do they call it dry rot anyway?" I ask. "I mean, isn't it caused by water? Why don't they just call it wet rot?"

He smiles. "That's a good point. But don't worry, whether we call it dry rot or wet rot, we'll get it whipped."

"Yeah, but it'll just take longer now." I throw my arms to my sides. I feel like a whiny child, but this is so frustrating. "What if everything just keeps taking longer...gets more expensive...is harder to finish? What then?"

"You know, I've learned from certain experiences...over these past few years..." He stops now, as if he's unsure he wants to continue. But that only makes me curious. I hate when people start to tell me something, then change their minds. It's one of my pet peeves. And he looks now like he's about to change the subject.

"What?" I persist.

He smiles. "Oh, it's a long story."

I frown at him. "You shouldn't start to tell someone something and then stop like that, Noah. It's not nice."

"How about if I tell you about it later?"

"Yeah, right." I give him a skeptical look.

"It's just that I want to finish ripping this dry rot out before I quit for the day."

I nod. "Actually, that's a good thing. I'll forgive you for leading me on like that."

"And if you're really interested in hearing my story, you'll have to treat me to a cheeseburger for dinner."

"A cheeseburger?"

"Yep." He turns his attention back to tearing out Sheetrock. "I've been craving one for the past hour. Have you been to Henry's yet?"

"You mean that new diner downtown?"

"Yeah. Want to try it out with me tonight?"

"And if I treat, you'll talk?"

"That's the deal."

"Then it's a deal." Okay, I'm telling myself this isn't a date, but I still want to run home and get cleaned up. "I'll just need to go check on Dad first. Oh yeah, and Betty called." So I fill him in on that as he works. "And I need to take Riley home. You want to meet at Henry's?"

"Sounds good. I'm thinking around six thirty. Does that work for you?"

"I'll see you there."

Then I unload the rest of the things from the pickup, do a little more cleaning, and finally decide it's time to take Riley back to my apartment, get in a shower, and check on Dad.

# 16

"Is it a date?" Holly asks as I towel dry my hair. She stopped by on her way home to pick up the present I was unable to take to Tina's shower last week.

"No, it's not a date." I tighten the belt of my bathrobe. Okay, I honestly don't think it's a date, but I suppose there's a little part of me that wishes it were. And that bugs me.

"But you're going to spruce up a little, aren't you?" she asks hopefully.

"*Spruce* up?" I laugh. "Who says that anymore?"

"My mom. And me." She reaches over and gives my hair a fluff. "Anyway, aren't you going to fix yourself up a little, Gretch?"

I narrow my eyes at her. "Why?"

"Because, in case I haven't mentioned it before..." She laughs. "You kind of let yourself go this past year and a half."

"Thanks, Holly. With friends like you who needs—"

"I'm sorry," she says, "but if your best friend can't be honest with you, who can?"

I roll my eyes at her. "Look, I need to hurry, Holly. As it is, I'll only have about half an hour with Dad. I can't waste time fix—"

"Then get moving!" She grabs me by the arm and drags me into the bathroom, positioning me in front of the mirror. She quickly digs through my weird assortment of cosmetics—mostly things that she's talked me into buying since I'm not naturally talented when it comes to this sort of thing—and she starts having her way with my face. And I must give her credit, not only is she quick, but she's good. Unfortunately, I'm not paying very close attention to her techniques. "You know, Holly," I say as she finishes up with some powder blush over what I can only assume are my cheekbones, "someday you should teach me how to do this for myself."

She laughs. "I've tried. You never listen."

"Maybe if you wrote it down."

But she pulls me into my bedroom and rips open my closet to forage for…for what? "You really need to go clothes shopping, Gretchen. Or else lose some weight."

"Just keep the compliments coming, Holly," I say sarcastically. "I needed that little ego boost."

She turns and looks at me, then her expression changes. "Actually, now that I'm looking at you, I think you have lost weight," she says.

"Okay, now you're just messing with my mind—"

"No, seriously, you look thinner." She pulls the scale out from where it's tucked next to the cabinet, then forces me onto it.

I'm about to give her a piece of my mind, but I notice the number. "Hey, you're right. I have."

"See, don't you feel better now?"

I stand up straighter. "Actually, I do."

"It's probably from giving up ice cream and working on your house project."

"That and Dad's heart attack. I haven't had much appetite since he was rushed to the hospital."

"So..." Holly pulls out a broomstick skirt that's various shades of earthy greens and golds and holds it up. "This is pretty, and it should be no problem since the waist is elastic."

"A skirt?" I frown at her.

"Yes, sometimes women wear skirts, Gretch." She points to the bottom half of her light blue business suit, a knee-length, fitted skirt I could never wear.

"And it looks fantastic on you, Holly, but I am not—"

"Shut up. You're wasting time," she tells me. "Put on that skirt while I find a top."

So, without arguing, I put on the skirt and submit to several tops until Holly decides on the moss green camisole topped with a pale yellow, sleeveless silk blouse and then adds a woven belt and jewelry.

"Voilà!" Holly proudly shoves me in front of the full-length mirror on my closet door.

"This is too much," I tell her as I remove the beaded necklace. "Noah will think I'm trying too hard."

"Spoilsport." She puts on a pouty face now.

"It's my life, Holly."

"Well, you have to leave the rest, Gretchen, or I will give up on you completely."

"Unfortunately, I don't have time to change it," I tell her.

"What about shoes?" She rushes back to my room.

"That could be a problem," I admit.

"How about those Michael Kors sandals that you got—"

"Riley ate one of them."

"That bad dog. You need to break him of that." She pulls out a pair of gold-beaded ballerina flats that I got at Target a couple of summers ago, back when Collin was still in the picture. "These will be perfect with that skirt."

"And they're comfortable," I admit as I slip them on. "And now I gotta go."

"And you're welcome." Holly picks up Tina's package, then checks me out and gives me one last nod of approval.

"Yeah, thanks," I say as I reach for my bag. "Tell Tina she can take that back to Pottery Barn if it doesn't work for her." I chuckle as we go out and I lock my door. "Don't tell her that I didn't even check her wedding registry. The glassware set is actually something I got awhile back but have never used."

"She'll probably hate it," admits Holly.

"Probably."

"Have fun on your date with Noah," she calls as we part ways in the parking lot.

"Very funny!" I yell at her.

Dad whistles as I walk into his hospital room. "Well, look at you, Gretchen Girl. Let me guess… Big date tonight?"

I frown at him. "No, Dad, no date. And the only reason I look like this is because Holly insisted on dressing me."

"My kudos to Holly. You should make dressing nice a habit."

I sit down in the chair next to his bed and let out a discouraged sigh. "So, do I really look that bad…I mean, usually?"

"Well, honey, you can't deny that you've let yourself go a little. Back before that nasty business with Collin, you were looking real pretty. Then after the breakup, well, you know how it's gone."

I nod. "I know. And that's changing. I mean, I can say for the first time in a long time that I am over him. And doing this house... well, it's like the world is opening up to me now."

He smiles. "I hope so." He reaches out and takes my hand now. "Call me old-fashioned, but I like my girls looking pretty."

"Speaking of your girls, did you, uh, well, did Betty call?"

"She did."

"Are you mad at me?"

"Mad at you? Why?"

"Because I told her what happened...and you had told me not to."

"Oh well, now that I'm on the mend there's no reason for her not to know. And I made her promise not to cut her trip short."

"I did too."

"Although she admitted that she's already wishing she was home. She's afraid that six weeks is going to be too much."

"Oh..." I try to imagine this. "Six weeks in Europe sounds pretty fantastic to me."

"Not me." He shakes his head. "Right now all I want is to be at home sweet home. I never knew how much I loved my little condo until getting stuck here."

"It won't be long, Dad."

"So, you haven't told me, Gretchen. What are you all dressed up for tonight? Or did you doll up just for your old man?"

"Oh, my outfit is just the result of Holly having fun. And

tonight I'm grabbing a cheeseburger at Henry's with Noah after a long workday. He had some thoughts on homebuilding he wanted to share with me." It was only a half truth, but I thought it was my best effort at sounding casual and keeping his matchmaking at bay.

"Hmm… I'll leave that one alone for now," he says mischievously. "I've wanted to try out that diner myself. I asked Betty to go a couple of times, but she didn't think it was a very healthy choice. But maybe while she's gone, I'll see if they deliver."

"Dad," I say in a warning tone, "just because you got some new pipes to your heart doesn't mean you no longer have to watch what you eat."

"We'll see about that…"

I glance at my watch now and realize that it's time for me to leave. "Sorry I can't stay longer, but I told Noah I'd meet him at six thirty."

"And so you shall."

I lean down and give Dad a big hug now. "That's from Betty. She told me to give you a big hug for her." Then I kiss his cheek. "And that's from me."

"Thanks."

"And you know what, Dad?"

"What?"

"I really like Betty."

His eyes light up. "So do I."

"And if she ever becomes a more permanent part of our family, I want you to know that it's perfectly fine with me."

He winks. "Thanks for your blessing, honey."

I laugh. "Like you needed it."

Now he looks serious. "I couldn't be happy with someone you didn't like, Gretchen. You must know that. You and I have been a pair for quite a long time now."

I nod. "Yeah, like twenty years."

"Well, you better run along. Don't make Noah wait."

"Yeah, he sounded pretty ravenous."

"And I hope you have a nice evening. Noah is a good man." He winks.

"Thanks, Dad." I leave it at that.

He just grins as I walk out the door.

*Oh well,* I think as I head for the elevators. *If my poor, old, sick dad wants to be delusional, why should I spoil it for him?*

It feels odd to be dressed up like this and driving Dad's big four-wheel-drive, diesel, club-cab truck. But if anything, it makes this seem less like a date. And that's a relief because, despite Dad's wishful thinking, I do not intend to develop anything with Noah besides a good working relationship. I just can't see it being anything but messy—considering all my objections—and I've been through enough mess already. Plus, I think it could cause problems with my house-restoration project. I've seen enough HGTV shows to know the strain that renovating can put on people who have been happily married for years. I can't even imagine how it might complicate things if the couple was just starting to date. With all the ups and downs of romance, a relationship with Noah could be the undoing of my house flip.

Not that he'd even be interested. Good grief, who am I fooling here anyway? I'm sure Noah must have a flock of women—probably beautiful women—waiting in line for him. Maybe he's already in a serious relationship. And why am I even thinking about this in the first place? I guess I can blame Holly and my dad. They were trying to plant the wrong things in my head.

Why did I allow Holly to fix me up like this? It's like a setup for a disaster. Noah will probably get the wrong impression, and I'll end up totally embarrassed. And what's new with that? If it wasn't 6:29 right now, I'd zip back home and put on jeans and a T-shirt.

Then, as I park the pickup, I start to feel indignant. There's no reason I can't look nice if I want to. Dad's absolutely right; I have let myself go for too long. And, like Holly always says, I could run into Mr. Right anywhere along the way. Wouldn't it be better if I looked halfway decent when it happened? I think about the interesting guys I could meet while shopping for building materials. Maybe I need to "spruce up" for those times too.

As I walk across the street to the fifties-style diner, I wonder about the good-looking guy that Holly said owns Henry's. I wonder if his name is actually Henry as I push open the door and go inside and look around. The place is fairly full, but I don't see Noah anywhere. In a way that's a relief because it will give me time to regroup and get my wits about me.

"Table for one?" asks a dark-haired guy wearing a red and white bowling shirt.

"Actually, I'm meeting someone," I tell him. Then, remembering Holly's encouragement, I smile directly at him. You just never know.

He returns my smile. "Have you been here before?"

"No, it's my first time. But I've heard that it's good."

He nods modestly. "Well, I hope you'll like it. We've only been open a month, so I really look forward to customer comments."

"Are you the owner?" I ask as he leads me to a table toward the back.

"I am." He pauses, waiting for me to slide into the shiny red booth.

"So does that make you Henry?"

"That's right. Henry Barrett. May I ask your name?"

"Of course. I'm Gretchen. Gretchen Hanover."

He sets the menus on the table and shakes my hand. "It's a pleasure to meet you, Gretchen. And welcome to Henry's. I hope you'll become a regular."

"So do I."

"Caroline will be your waitress, but can I get you anything to drink?"

I order iced tea, and just as Henry leaves the table, I notice Noah coming in the door. I'm relieved to see that he's cleaned up too. He's wearing neat khaki shorts and a light blue polo shirt. I wave, and he sees me and quickly comes to join me. Rubbing his hands together, he grins happily. "I'm starving."

"Have whatever you like," I tell him. "Remember, it's on me."

"I've been fantasizing about cheeseburgers for the past couple of hours."

"Maybe you should order two."

"Or maybe I'll just go for the half pounder."

"That sounds like a lot of red meat."

He nods eagerly. "It does, doesn't it?"

As it turns out, he orders the half pounder with fries and a large chocolate shake. I follow suit, only I order the regular cheeseburger and a regular chocolate shake. "I probably shouldn't have the shake," I admit after Caroline leaves with our order. "I gave up ice cream a few weeks ago. But I just don't think I could sit here and watch you drink one without having serious chocolate envy."

"You gave up ice cream?" he asks with a worried look.

"Well, it was kind of an addiction," I admit. "Not a very healthy one either."

"There are worse things than ice cream," he points out.

"Maybe for other people, but for me it was a pretty dangerous obsession with some form of very rich Ben & Jerry's chocolate ice cream and HGTV."

He laughs. "I think that sounds like a pretty good combination."

"It served me well for a while," I admit. "But then I switched ice cream for low-fat, sugar-free frozen yogurt, and HGTV for my very own house project. And you know what, I'm not even sorry." Now I look evenly across the table at Noah. "But you've got me talking about me, and the deal was I would buy dinner if you would tell me a story, remember?"

He nods as Caroline sets the shakes in front of us. "Yup, but not until I get a nice long sip of this baby."

# 17

My name is Noah Campbell, and I am a recovering workaholic," he confesses somberly. Then he pauses to take a second long drag on his straw, decreasing the height of his milkshake by another full inch. I hope he doesn't get brain freeze. But I keep my concerns to myself and simply nod as I wait for him to continue what's starting out as an interesting story. I never would've guessed this laid-back guy was a workaholic.

He goes on to tell me that he started working with his dad's construction company in his teens, earning enough money to buy a car…and then a motorcycle. "But construction was hard work," he admits. "So when I got to college, I decided there were easier ways to make a buck. So a buddy and I started up this little software company." He shrugs apologetically. "I guess it was just the thing to do back then, back in the early nineties. But for some unexplainable reason, our company actually took off."

"That must've been cool."

"Yeah, it actually was pretty cool…at first. It seemed our future was launched even before we graduated from college. Of course, my dad was disappointed because he'd been hoping I'd come home and go into construction with him full-time, handling the business end of things…and then, like I told you, he died."

"That must've been hard."

"Yeah, I blamed myself for a while. It seemed like the good son would've taken over the family business for the sake of his parents, you know? But the software company was just coming into its own right then, and I knew I couldn't do both. Not successfully."

"So you continued with the software?"

He nods and takes another long sip of his shake. "I made the selfish choice."

"You chose what seemed right to you. I'm sure your dad would've understood."

"Maybe... Anyway, Daniel—my partner—and I set up an office in Seattle. Pretty predictable, huh? Just like everyone else was doing at the time. But we worked hard and smart, and things just kept getting better, and the business grew. Of course, to keep that ball rolling, or maybe we were just chasing after it, we both put in really long hours. We worked weekends, and lots of times, if something big was going on, we'd work 24/7. It got to the point that we often spent nights at the office. There were a couple of leather couches and a little kitchen and bathroom. So work was pretty much my entire life back then."

I shake my head. "It's hard to imagine that. I can't quite picture you in the three-piece suit and the executive office and—"

"It wasn't so much like that. We were fairly casual...unless we did a presentation, say to an Asian company. That's when the Armani would come out, and we'd shine our shoes."

As our cheeseburger baskets arrive, he continues about how the software business took on a life of its own and ultimately controlled him. Finally, I encourage him to take a break and enjoy some of this food, which is fantastic. He does and then gradually returns to his story; it's as if something is compelling him to get the whole thing out.

"Anyway, just as things were taking off for us, while we were the toast of the town, I started dating Camille. It seemed to go with the territory."

"How's that?"

"She was this gorgeous fashion model with expensive taste, and I was the computer-geek whiz kid on his way to making his first million."

"Really?" I want to point out that he's not exactly a "geek" but don't.

"Well, that was the plan." He laughs as he shakes the bottle of ketchup onto his fries. "Before long, we were just one more predictable component of the Seattle scene."

"And then you got married?" Okay, as soon as I ask this, I wish I hadn't. Why not just let him tell the story? But he doesn't seem to mind.

"Yep. That was almost ten years ago now. I had just turned thirty, and we'd been going out for a couple of years, and Camille had started pushing for an engagement ring. Her friends were starting to get married, and she got caught up in the whole wedding thing. Eventually, it seemed like the easiest thing was to agree. And to be honest, I was so caught up in the business that I liked the idea of having someone at home, making the place nice, cooking good meals." He chuckles. "All those bachelor illusions of what married life might be."

He pauses to take another big bite of his burger, and I wait for him to chew, swallow, and continue. I'd ask another question, but it would probably sound stupid, and it seems like he's already telling me way more than I imagined he would. And I must admit, I'm finding it rather intriguing. It's like a whole different Noah Campbell.

"And, man, was that some wedding," he continues. "Camille's parents were pretty wealthy, but they had good friends who were megamillionaires with this incredible estate on Fox Island and no kids of their own. Anyway, they offered to host the ceremony, and Camille went all out. People were talking about that wedding for..." He laughs now. "Well, at least a couple of weeks." Then his expression gets serious. "The talk probably died down about the same time the honeymoon ended."

"You guys honeymooned for two weeks?"

"Actually, we didn't even take a honeymoon. But that was mostly my fault. I was too consumed with the business, and we were landing a big account just then. And, of course, Camille wanted us to be rich. Very rich. So she agreed to postpone the honeymoon and—" He stops abruptly. "I can't believe I'm telling you all this, Gretchen. Am I boring you to tears yet?"

"Not yet." I smile.

"Honestly, I don't usually go into all this detail about my past, but I think maybe I'm feeling slightly intoxicated just now."

Feeling uncomfortable, I suddenly wonder if he means me. Can he possibly find me intoxicating?

"I suppose that sounded weird," he admits. "I mean, this food. Aren't these cheeseburgers incredible?"

I nod with what I decide is relief. "They're fantastic."

"So, anyway, about a year into the marriage, I realized we were in serious trouble. Camille wanted me to make more money, but she also wanted more of my time. I didn't know how to give her both. I was still working those long hours and still sleeping at the office a lot. Probably even more than was necessary. Because when I did make it home, it never seemed to be the sweet marital bliss that I'd imagined." He waves his hand as if to erase that. "I won't go into all the details, and I do take the blame for how our relationship deteriorated. I can't really blame Camille for having a packed social life since I sure wasn't giving her the time and attention she needed. But we just kept growing further apart. We hadn't even been married two years when I realized our marriage was doomed. But then Camille got pregnant."

"Kirsten."

"Yes. But at the time Camille didn't want to have a baby, didn't want to ruin her figure or her social life. She even talked about an abortion. But I told her I would leave her if she did. It was a real standoff for a while. But finally she seemed to change. I thought maybe it was those maternal hormones kicking in, and I began to feel hopeful. She got caught up in planning for the baby and started ordering things for a nursery. In the usual Camille style, it was way over the top, but I didn't care. I thought this might be our chance for happiness. I promised to start taking more time off from work. And for a while, I did. But then Kirsten came along, and things got hectic, and I returned to my workaholic ways. The business obsessed me. Even when I wasn't at work, my mind was at work. It was very unhealthy."

"And hard on your relationship." Okay, I'm trying to understand this guy, but it's not exactly easy. Also, I wonder why he wants to tell me all this. Even more than that, I wonder why I'm so eager to hear it.

"Yes, that's why I really do blame myself for how things went." He dips a fry in ketchup and sadly shakes his head. "At Kirsten's third birthday party, which was quite an event with pony rides and a clown and magician—the works—Camille told me that she was leaving me and taking Kirsten with her."

"That night, after I tucked Kirsten in bed, imagining how empty my life would be without my little princess, I begged Camille to rethink her decision. I promised that I would change, that we would change. I even suggested we get counseling. To be fair, I wasn't fighting as much for Camille as I was for Kirsten. I couldn't bear the thought of losing my daughter. And Camille had already told me that she wanted to relocate to San Diego. She said that she was tired of the Seattle rain, that it depressed her."

"I've heard it can be pretty dreary," I admit.

"It takes its toll on some."

"So is that why you moved down here?"

"Sort of. But first I sold my share of the software business to Daniel. He got a great deal, but the timing wasn't the best for me, because I still was so invested in the business development. Even so, I didn't care. I knew I couldn't put off that decision for another day. I finally grasped that having a family, being with my daughter, was worth more than anything. It's like I woke up and suddenly realized that life wasn't just about making money. If I had to be home 24/7 to make my marriage work, to be a better dad, I would do it."

"But it still didn't work?"

He laughs, but it's a sad laugh. "Camille wasn't pleased at all. She thought selling my share of the business was a huge mistake. And as it turned out, she was already involved with someone else."

"Wow." I'm not sure how to respond, but I feel a genuine pang of sympathy for him now. Even so, why he did he marry a woman like that? Gorgeous or not, she sounds like a real witch. "What did you do?"

"Well, I finally had time on my hands. At first I got depressed, questioning everything about myself, about life, about God. Then I did some deep soul searching. And I borrowed a friend's boat and did some sailing. I also spent a lot of time with Kirsten. I felt like I was really getting to know her. Before she had seemed like a baby, but suddenly she was this little person, with her own thoughts and opinions and an interest in everything."

"That is a fun age."

"And eventually I returned to the faith I'd been raised with. I realized I couldn't make it on my own, and I really pursued a relationship with God. For the first time in years, I started to experience real peace. That's when I started to rearrange my priorities. I decided that I want to live the rest of my life totally differently."

"Was that when you started doing carpentry?"

"I realized it was something I had loved doing. I think because carpentry was so logical, sort of mathematical and predictable. I liked that. I'd rebelled against it in college, but the truth was, I liked making things with my hands. I liked the feel of wood, taking something rough and transforming it into something beautiful and useful. So I got a few tools and started messing around with it again. My dad had taught me a lot, and much of it came back to me."

"So did you get a job then? Or start your own construction company?"

"I didn't have that level of confidence yet. Also, I wasn't ready for my own business again. So I took a couple of classes at the community college, but I quickly realized that I knew as much as, maybe even more than, some of my instructors. After that I bought some good tools and just started building things."

"And what happened with Camille?"

"Shortly after the divorce was final, she married Peter, the stockbroker she'd been involved with. And they made plans to move down to San Diego."

"And that's why you came down here?"

"I could've stopped Camille. According to the custody agreement, she wasn't supposed to remove Kirsten from the state. But by then I'd had time to rethink a lot of things—my own selfishness and being a poor excuse for a husband and a workaholic to boot. Finally I gave in. I told Camille that she could move down here but that I would move too, and we would continue to share custody of Kirsten, and hopefully our daughter's life wouldn't suffer too much due to her parents' immaturity."

"Kirsten seems like a very well-grounded seven-year-old."

He smiles now. "She is wonderful, isn't she?"

"Very mature for her age."

"Unfortunately, I think divorce does that to kids—forces them to grow up too soon."

I consider this, thinking that the death of a parent isn't so different when you're still a kid, but I don't mention it. This is his story, not mine.

"Shortly after we got settled down here, my mom missed Kirsten and me so much that I encouraged her to move down as well."

"Ah, yes. And I hear that she's friends with Betty."

"Yes, they're neighbors in the same condo unit." He chuckles. "When I started working for your dad, I thought maybe he and Mom might hit it off. He sort of reminded me of my own dad, but while your dad and my mom are good friends, there's no spark."

"No spark..." I smile. "Well, fortunately there seems to be some spark with Betty. Dad was so happy to hear from her today. Her call was good medicine."

We both seem to be finished eating. All his food has vanished, and although I still have fries and some shake left, I'm stuffed.

"I guess I told you all that because I wanted to encourage you. My story proves that it's true what they say: God really does work in mysterious ways, and I know that's going to wind up true with your house flip too. I could tell you were starting to feel overwhelmed back at the house, and I wanted to say that things will work out, in whatever way is best from God's perspective. It was only after going through all that hard stuff—my job, my marriage, the possibility of losing my daughter—that I learned how to let go of things...and just trust God. Does that make any sense?"

"Of course." I feel slightly defensive now. "I mean, I'm a Christian too. And I try to trust God with things. But I guess this house flip—what with Dad being indisposed and the pressure of the loan—well, it's been freaking me out. I suppose I seem kind of stressed to you." I suddenly wonder if his whole talk wasn't meant to be some sort of a lesson to me. Not that it was a sermon exactly, but he did seem to be making a point.

"But what if you chose to hand this house flip over to God?"

"I know," I say quickly. "I've thought of that."

"It's natural to be worried about the details. But if you give your worries to God...well, it's just a lot better." He looks slightly uncomfortable now. "Sorry, I seem to be preaching at you. I've been told that it's a weakness of mine."

"I know what you're saying is true. And I'd like to be, you know, more like that..." I look down at the table, suddenly feeling self-conscious and ill at ease, like I just used the wrong fork or said something idiotic or made some serious fashion faux pas like walking out of the bathroom with the hem of my skirt caught in my panties. These are the sorts of things that usually cause me embarrassment. But this is different. I am feeling uncomfortable about not being a more faithful Christian. More like him. This is a surprising development.

I try to absorb all of what he's said, so I sit there quietly for a moment, and he lets me. "So are you saying that if my house flip totally flops or my dad loses his condo, after losing his health, that I should be happy?"

"I'm just saying that we need to trust God with all parts of our lives. Otherwise, we'll never be really happy. I know this personally."

Now Henry is approaching our table, looking at me with a concerned expression. "Was everything okay, Gretchen?"

I realize my face must look like I just ate a dill pickle, so I force a big smile. "Hey, it was better than okay, Henry. It was fantastic."

He points to my unfinished food. "But you didn't clean your plate."

"Trust me, I'm stuffed." Then I introduce Henry to Noah.

"And I'm going to be a regular here too," Noah promises. "It's great having a place in town that caters to something besides all that health-crazed California cuisine."

Henry laughs. "My thoughts exactly. Although, just so you know, I do have some heart-healthy choices on the menu as well. Including a buffalo burger with really low cholesterol."

"Seriously?" I say. "My dad just had bypass heart surgery, and he loves an occasional burger. He'll be stoked."

"Why don't you take him a menu?" suggests Henry. "I have some to-go ones by the door."

"I'll do that. Dad was envious that I was coming here tonight," I admit. "He wondered if you do takeout or delivery."

"We do takeout, and I'm considering delivery."

"Great. And I'll take the check whenever it's ready," I tell him. He looks mildly surprised, but I tell him it was a prearranged agreement.

"Yeah, we had a deal," says Noah, winking at me.

"Unless you want dessert," I offer. "I'm not trying to rush you."

"Yes, we do have a tempting dessert menu," says Henry.

Noah leans back and pats his stomach. "Not this time."

After I pay the bill, Noah walks me across the street to Dad's pickup and thanks me for dinner.

"And thank you for sharing your story," I say. "I'm sorry if I acted like I didn't appreciate it at the end."

"And my apologies if I came on too strong. Some of my friends have accused me of wanting to become a preacher, which I honestly have no interest in."

I teasingly shake my finger at him. "Never say no to God."

"You too."

"Right...and I'll admit that the idea of trusting God with all this house business sounds good. I'm just not quite there yet."

He grins. "Well, God has amazing ways of getting us places."

I roll my eyes as I imagine God taking me through a variety of trials similar to what Noah experienced. "Okay, that's a scary concept."

Noah laughs, then looks at me more seriously. "By the way, I was going to say something earlier. But before I forget, you look really pretty tonight, Gretchen."

I give him what probably looks like an embarrassed smile, and my cheeks grow warmer. "Oh, that was Holly's doing. She came by my apartment to pick something up, and, well, she's kind of a fashion freak. Anyway, before I knew what hit me, Holly gave me a mini-makeover."

He just nods. "Well, you look great, but don't get me wrong. I happen to think you look great in your working overalls too."

I feel my whole face getting hot now. This is more than I want to hear. And yet I'm loving it! Really, what is up with me? But I simply tell him that I better get home. "In fact, I'll bet Holly left my closet door open. For all I know Riley might be polishing off one of my favorite shoes right this minute."

As I drive home, I try not to think too hard about this evening. Certainly it was sweet of Noah to share his story with me. But hearing all about his personal life, his relationship with Camille—well, it was almost an informational, or maybe an emotional, overload. I don't think I was ready for it.

I decide to just shove it all aside for the time being. Like Riley with a bone, I'll just bury it somewhere. Then I turn on Dad's radio and am not surprised to find that it's tuned to his favorite country-western station, the kind that plays tunes going clear back to the fifties. Even so, I leave it on and listen as some old cowboy croons out one of those you-done-me-wrong kind of songs. And even though I'm not normally a country music fan, this one has some rather interesting lyrics. I think it sums up Noah's experiences with Camille just about perfectly. And then I feel irritated to realize that, despite my resolve, I am thinking about Noah again.

# 18

Hello there," calls a petite brunette who is, I'm guessing, about my age. I'm beginning to unload the pickup when she and a little boy approach me from across the street with a plate of something. "I'm so glad you bought this house," she says. "And I just want to welcome you to the neighborhood. I'm Jenna Stein, and this is Cory."

"Thank you," I say, staring at what appear to be homemade oatmeal cookies. It's nearly two, and because I was crazily running errands the past couple of hours, I forgot to take a lunch break. And right now my mouth is watering so much that I'm afraid I'm about to imitate one of Riley's long drools. "I'm Gretchen Hanover."

"Nice to meet you." She shakes her head with disgust. "I'm sure the house was as nasty inside as out. I mean, the other neighbors were total pigs."

"Yeah, it was pretty bad," I say as we continue up to the front door together. I'm hoping she doesn't want to come inside for a tour—not that there's much to see, but there is much to do. Already it's Thursday of the third week, and I'm seriously behind schedule.

"Is that your husband's construction company?" she asks, nodding to Dad's pickup. "Hanover Construction? Because we're looking for someone to do some remodeling in our—"

"No," I say quickly. "That's actually my dad's truck. He's a retired contractor. And he had a heart attack recently. I'm just borrowing the truck while he's recuperating."

"Oh yes, I heard that an ambulance was here. I was at Cory's school that day. I'm sorry about your father. Is he doing okay?"

I pause by the front door, quickly explaining his surgery and that he gets released from the hospital tomorrow. I'm trying not to show my impatience; she seems really nice, and I don't want to be rude.

"Oh, that's good. And I'm sure it must be handy having two pickups during your remodel." She smiles and hands the plate of cookies to me. "I made these this morning while it was still cool. Anyway, we're just so thrilled to finally have some good neighbors. Did you know that a lot of people on this street sold their homes just to get away from the family who lived here?"

"That's too bad." I open the door behind me, as in "Hint, hint, got work to do."

"And their kids were really mean," says Cory in a serious tone. "Jason pushed me off my bike one time." I look at him sympathetically.

"Well, I'm hoping this will turn things around for our neighborhood now." Jenna smiles happily. "Already I'm planning to do some landscaping in front, and maybe I'll paint the exterior. Then, later on, if we can find a trustworthy contractor, I'd like to do some upgrades in the kitchen." She peeks over my shoulder now. "Wow, you guys really are tearing into this place. I can't wait to see how it looks when it's done."

"We'll be having an open house," I tell her. "You're welcome to come."

"Fantastic! Let me know what I can bring."

Suddenly it occurs to me that she assumes I bought this house to live in. I'm about to set her straight, but she takes Cory by the hand and announces that she doesn't want to be a pest and then waves and dashes back across the street to the yellow house that actually does need a paint job. Oh well. I'll have to clarify later.

"Who was that?" asks Noah as he emerges from where he's been putting down the subflooring in the bathroom.

"A neighbor named Jenna," I tell him, holding out the plate of cookies. "Help yourself."

"Nice neighbor." He grins and takes a cookie.

"Yeah. But I think I gave her the wrong impression."

"Huh?" He asks with a mouthful of cookie.

"Well, it seems she thinks I bought this house to live here. She's really excited to have 'good' neighbors."

"Oh well," he says, reaching for a second cookie. "Eventually they will have good neighbors, don't you think?" He smacks his lips now. "Sure could use a cold glass of milk with these."

"I don't think milk would be too cold in that cooler," I point out. "In fact, I was wondering about ordering the refrigerator so we could use it while we're working here."

"It might get pretty dusty with all the construction still to come."

"I'm sure it would clean up just fine."

He nods. "Yeah, that's a good point. Does that mean you haven't ordered the appliances yet?"

"No, should I have?"

His brow creases. "Depending on what you want, yeah. It'd be a drag to get everything done and not have appliances in time for the open house."

"That reminds me," I say. "Dad got hold of the cabinet guy. He's coming to measure tomorrow. Is there anything I should know?"

"It wouldn't hurt for you to draw up a rough draft of what you'd like as far as the layout goes. Also, have the style of cabinet picked out. And the wood, of course. That'll save time."

So we go to the kitchen, and I describe what I have in mind as far as the L-shape and then an island. "And I want it to look contemporary but not cheap or flimsy," I finally say. "And light. I don't want any dark stain."

He nods. "I suggest you keep it simple and maybe consider a pretty wood like maple. It'll cost a little more, but since your design is simple, the total for the cabinets should even out."

"Yeah," I agree. "That sounds nice."

"And how about the floors in the kitchen?"

"I'm not sure. On one hand, I just checked out some ceramic tile that might look nice here. And it was on sale too, but I also like the idea of hardwood throughout. Do you think that would be too much wood?" I'm surprised I'm asking for this much advice, especially after insisting this was my flip house. But it seems like after working with Noah these past several days, I've started to trust his judgment more. Probably even more than my own.

He studies the floors. "And you still want to take out these walls and open it up through here, right?"

"Definitely. Dad's already secured a building permit so we can change the footprint. Don't you think that would make it nicer?"

"Absolutely. But it will also take more time and cost more."

"You have to spend money to make money," I remind him.

"The problem will be matching the new wood to the original."

I consider this. "Oh yeah, I hadn't thought about that. Is it even possible?"

"All things are possible."

"Oh, and I was thinking maybe I'd do carpets in the bedrooms," I add. "At least the one with the really bad wood floors."

He nods but looks unconvinced.

"You think I should leave the wood floors?"

"It's your call, Gretchen. But it might save you a few bucks. And the floors in the other two bedrooms are in great shape."

"And saving money is a good thing. I'll only carpet the room with the questionable wood." I don't admit to him that the budget is already feeling strained or that I plan to put the appliances on my Home Depot project card because the Lowe's card is already maxed out. And that will allow me to cover the added cost of the cabinets and roof.

"Did you get that wood I needed?" he asks now.

"It's in the truck."

"And your paint?"

"All ready to go." I don't tell him that I didn't only get exterior paint but also a couple of gallons of interior paint, which I will use in the bedroom with the messed-up floors. The first part of my plan was to test if I like the looks of the exterior color, a nice sage. But the second part was to get the bedroom fixed up enough so I can have a place to camp while working on the house. I figure that once Dad goes home tomorrow afternoon, I will be torn between two houses, and since this place is closer to Dad's than my apartment, I might as well spend nights here. That way I can work whenever I want to…or whenever I have the energy. And I'm sure Riley will like it too. He thinks it's great having a big backyard all to himself.

Together, Noah and I unload the wood and paint and supplies from the back of the pickup. Then he asks me about the power washer, and I explain that I reserved it but needed to unload the wood and stuff to have room for it. "I'm heading back to the rental place to pick it up right now."

"Maybe you should wait until tomorrow," he suggests, "since today is mostly used up anyway."

"Nope," I tell him as I pull out my keys. "I'm going to wash the house until it's too dark to see, and then I'll start again first thing in the morning. I'll return the power washer around noon and then pick up Dad. My goal is to have the house all ready to paint, or almost, before I bring Dad home from the hospital."

Noah just shakes his head. "You're one hard-working woman, Gretchen Hanover."

"Or maybe I'm just desperate."

"Hey, you could start a new TV series called *Desperate House Flippers.*"

I laugh and wave at him as I hop in the cab of the pickup and start it up. I can guess what he's thinking. He's said it already a couple of times when I've rejected offers to get a bite to eat or take any other kind of a break. "All work and no play makes Gretchen a dull girl." What Noah doesn't realize is that I'm keeping this distance between us on purpose. We have a good working relationship, and I don't want to mess with it. And if I was being honest, I'd have to admit that he makes me uncomfortable too. Not that he does anything wrong exactly. Maybe that's the problem; he does too many things right. He's the kind of guy that a girl like me could fall for. Well, other than the divorced thing...and having a ready-made family. That's a scenario I have always wanted to avoid.

But despite what I try to convince myself are his "handicaps," I have a feeling I could fall for a guy like Noah. And the problem is that I feel ninety-nine point nine percent certain that he is the kind of guy who could never fall for a girl like me. Sure, he can pal around with me, joke with me, work with me, and share a soda and a few laughs. I'm sure I could be just like a kid sister to him. But that's where it stops. Because I suddenly feel that Noah is way out of my league, and if it weren't for Dad, he wouldn't be involved in this remodel at all. If anything, it's simply an act of mercy and goodwill. And for those reasons—call it preservation of the heart or just plain cowardice—I am keeping a safe distance.

*You cannot afford a broken heart right now,* I tell myself as I drive back to the rental store. And this is true on so many levels. For starters, I need to stay focused on the house renovation. No distractions. But besides that, I know how derailed I could get with a broken heart. Good grief, it took me more than a year to recover from Collin, and some people think it took longer than that. And he wasn't even the first to break my heart. Normally I don't allow myself to dwell on these previous and completely depressing episodes of my life. But if it helps me avoid another mistake, it might be worth the agony.

So as I drive down Main Street, my mind meanders back to my college days. That might be more than ten years ago, but the pain is still fairly vivid. I'd been dating Brian since the beginning of my sophomore year, and I honestly thought he was the one—the God-chosen one—and I was fairly certain he felt the same way about me. In fact, he even said as much. But then, midway through our senior year, he met a girl named Amy. Shortly after that, Brian and I became history. Just like that. To distract myself from my aching heart, I put what energy I had left into my classes, which resulted in nearly straight A's. But my social life, from the breakup until graduation, was pretty much nonexistent. I would attend class, then return to my dorm room. Study, sleep, and eat—that was my bleak little life. I attended church randomly, but I totally gave up the college group since I felt pretty sure that Brian and Amy would be there.

"Is that enough self-torture?" I ask myself as I pull into the rental place. "Just get over it, Gretchen. Move on. Focus on your house. And quit talking to yourself!" As I get out of the pickup, I notice a woman sitting in the passenger side of the car next to me, and she's staring. I think she even locked her doors, but as I get out, I simply smile at her and act like it's perfectly normal to converse with myself like this. Too bad I'm not wearing a headset.

I sign the paperwork for the power washer, get talked into purchasing some protective eyewear, then listen to some safety tips and general instructions as the guys load the machine into the back of the pickup. This time, as I drive through town, I crank up the radio. It's still tuned to Dad's favorite country-western station, and I'm wondering if I might not become a serious fan by the time the remodel is complete. Already I'm starting to recognize the artists and their songs. But it's preferable to babbling at myself or dwelling on my less-than-illustrious romantic history.

When I get to the house, I go directly to the backyard for the hose but am surprised to see that little Kirsten is back there, casually tossing a tennis ball for Riley, who totally ignores me as he takes off to chase it.

"Hey," I say to her. "What are you doing here?"

"My mom dumped me," she says as she pries the soggy brown tennis ball from Riley's mouth and throws it again. As always, she's dressed impeccably, looking like Little Miss Fashion in a pale blue denim vest and matching ruffled skirt. And I can see by the emblem on the sleeve of the white T-shirt underneath that it's actually a Ralph Lauren outfit and, I'm guessing, fairly expensive. And it figures that she has on what were probably once white canvas shoes but which now look more like the color of this backyard: dirt brown. But I don't mention this fact, because I can tell she's having fun with Riley. And he's certainly enjoying her company.

"I hope you don't mind," Noah calls from the opened laundry-room window. "I had no idea Kirsten was coming to visit today. Camille called on her way to, well, somewhere and then just, uh... dropped her off here."

I can tell he was about to say "dumped" too but stopped himself. "No, that's fine," I assure him. "She's more than welcome."

He grins at his daughter now. "Not that I mind having you around, princess. I'm always happy to see my best girl."

"I'm going to start power washing the house," I tell him as I flick a dry piece of paint off the siding with my fingernail. "I guess I'll start in front so Kirsten and Riley can keep playing back here."

"Or they can come inside and hang with me," offers Noah. I'm thankful the stink that permeated this house has now completely lifted.

"No, that's okay." I gather up the hose, attempting to gracefully coil it, but it's like wrestling with a stubborn snake. "I think I'd rather start in the front anyway."

"Camille promised it would only be a couple of hours."

"No problem." I wink at Kirsten, who seems to be enjoying my little hose-wrestling act. "You're making that dog one happy camper."

She nods as if she knows this, then turns and throws the ball again.

By the time I'm out front, Noah is already unloading the power washer. "Hey, let me help you," I call as I run over to assist. Then together we hoist the heavy machine down onto the driveway.

"Have you ever done this before?" he asks.

"No, but it looks simple enough."

He nods, but I can tell by his eyes that he thinks otherwise.

"What?" I demand.

"Nothing." He turns and walks toward the house, and I'm feeling almost proud of him for holding back what I'm sure is a lecture. "I'll be inside if you need anything."

"Thanks." I turn my full attention to this somewhat formidable machine. The rental-store guys warned me that, although it's only water, the force is powerful, so I should take it seriously. I carefully attach the hose to the machine and turn on the water. Then I put on my safety goggles, and with the wand safely in hand, I cautiously turn on the machine. It's fairly loud, a reminder of its power, but after a couple of practice tries where I spray the foundation and am surprised to see how the darkened cement instantly lightens, I feel I am ready to start.

My plan is to begin at the top and work my way down, but as I aim the wand at the overhead soffits, I realize this is one messy job. Wet paint chips and dirt and debris fly everywhere, and within minutes I am soaked and covered with chunks of gunky paint and dead bugs. Nasty stuff. But as I move down to the top plank of lap siding, I know it'll be well worth the mess. I will be saving myself lots of time in prep work, and as I move slowly across the front of the house, my confidence grows. Although the house looks uglier than ever with various coats of old paint exposed and even some bare wood in places, I imagine that final coat of sage green paint and neat taupe trim. And I know that it's going to be gorgeous.

The only problem is some of the overgrown shrubbery around the house. I wish I'd thought to remove some of it before I started this. It's not easy working around it, and as I fight with it, trying to pull it back as I wash the siding, I feel like the bushes might be winning the battle. I'm in a particularly precarious position, standing with one foot on the stepladder and the other balancing myself against the house as I pull back a boxwood and attempt to spray behind it, when I hear Kirsten yelling.

"Help, Gretchen!" she screams.

Alarmed, I turn just in time to see Riley darting across the front yard, headed for the street, with Kirsten trailing behind him.

# 19

Stop!" I yell at both of them. But as I say this, the stepladder tips away from the house, and to avoid doing the splits over shrubbery and having a painful landing, I toss the wand aside and make a giant leap backward, which lands me on my rump on the ground. That's when I realize that the wand has a branch of shrubbery wedged in the trigger. And it starts flipping around like a wounded snake as it sprays its powerful jet of water in all directions.

Miraculously, both Riley and Kirsten obeyed my command to stop and are standing frozen in the front yard, just a few feet away, watching this strange spectacle. Before I can warn them to run for safety, the wand flips over and shoots into the dirt, deflecting grimy water like a mud shower all over the two of them. Riley takes off toward the house, and Kirsten, holding her hands over her face, lets out a loud shriek as I jump between the wand and her, using my body to shield her from the onslaught of more dirty water. "Run!" I yell at Kirsten as I leap for the wildly flipping wand. I finally manage to snag it and aim it back at the siding of the house as I pry out the branch that's stuck in the trigger. But before I get it free, the noisy engine stops, and I turn to see that Noah has flipped the switch.

I drop the wand and go over to Kirsten, who is standing with Riley near the front door, to assess the damage. Riley, who is naturally brown, doesn't look too bad, although he needs a good bath. But Kirsten is a mess.

"I'm so sorry," I tell her as I kneel down and use the moderately clean underside hem of my soggy T-shirt to wipe her face and around her eyes. To my relief, she's not crying, but she's looking at her ruined outfit with dismay.

"Mom told me not to get dirty."

Noah is actually chuckling now, which I find slightly insensitive, and I give him a look to suggest as much. Then I turn back to Kirsten. "I know it won't help much, but let's get you inside and see if we can clean you up some."

She just nods and allows me to lead her into the bathroom that still has a functioning bathtub. There I do what I can, which isn't much, to clean her up. We wash her face and hands and hair as best we can. But when we come out, she is still a mess…and wet.

"Maybe if you sit in the sun," I suggest as we go outside to find Noah digging through his truck.

"I thought I might have a clean shirt in here that Kirsten could wear," he says as he comes back empty handed, "but no such luck. Sorry, princess."

"I could run to town and buy her something," I offer, but then I see him looking past me with a deep frown.

"Too late," he says, nodding to a white convertible sports car coming down the street toward us.

"Here comes Mom," says Kirsten with worried eyes.

And before we can say or do anything, the sleek white car pulls in front of the house, and a tall, gorgeous blonde gets out and then stares at the three of us as if she's witnessing the remains of a train wreck.

"What happened?" she demands as she hurries to Kirsten. Camille has on a short white skirt that makes her legs seem to go forever and a pale pink polo shirt that's rather formfitting. Her hair, tied with a pink and white scarf, is in a long, perfect ponytail that slides over her shoulder as she leans forward to examine her daughter more closely, although it's obvious she's being careful not to get too close.

"There was a little accident with the spray gun," explains Noah.

Now Camille stands up straight, looking directly at Noah, and I notice they're about the same height. And, with perfectly made-up eyes, she glares at him without saying a word. But I know she is seething.

"There's no reason to get upset, Camille." He calmly folds his arms across his chest.

"I should've known you'd ruin my day," she says evenly. "I cannot even leave Kirsten with you for a few minutes without having all—"

"This is a construction site," he points out. "And that was more than a few minutes. Plus, if you want me to have Kirsten here with me, you need to send her in the appropriate clothes."

"Appropriate clothes for what?" she demands haughtily. "What did you do to her? Roll her in the mud? Or perhaps you sent her out to play with the pigs? Or to clean out the—"

"It's really my fault," I interrupt. "I was power washing the house, and I—"

"This is not your problem." She turns as if just noticing I'm here and peers at me with a narrow-eyed look that's either pity or disgust—I'm not sure I even want to know. "But thank you anyway."

"This is Gretchen," says Noah, ignoring his ex's bad manners. "She's the homeowner, and her dad is a friend, and we—"

"Whatever." Camille turns back to Kirsten now. "Let's go!" She starts to take her daughter by the hand, then pulls her own hand back as if she's afraid to even touch her. Halfway to the car, Camille abruptly stops. "Wait, Kirsten. Don't get in yet." Now Camille turns and looks at Noah with what seems like disgust. "Good grief, Noah, you could at least give us something for her to sit on so she doesn't ruin the leather upholstery of my Mercedes."

"I was just looking for a T-shirt," he says, "but I don't seem to have any—"

"There's a towel in the bathroom," I suggest, then remember that I used it on Kirsten, so it's pretty muddy now too. "Or how about a nice clean drop cloth?" I suggest, trying to be cheerful for Kirsten's sake. Right now her big blue eyes remind me of a scolded puppy that got caught rolling in the dirt. "I just got some at the paint store, and I could—"

"Just get it, *please,*" she commands. I sense Noah's eyes on me as I hurry to the pickup, and I suspect he feels somewhat responsible for his ex's deplorable lack of manners. I dig around the backseat where the drop cloths are stowed along with paintbrushes, masking tape, and various other supplies. I finally find a package, which I open and shake out as I walk back to where Camille is standing by the car with a very impatient expression. "Here you—"

"Thank you very much!" She snatches the white cloth and wraps it like a robe around Kirsten. Then she helps her into the passenger seat, carefully buckling the seat belt around the folds of the drop cloth, I'm sure more to protect the seat belt than to protect her daughter. I make a little wave to Kirsten, smiling apologetically. I won't blame the poor thing if she never speaks to me again. And, okay, I know I'm staring as Camille struts around to the other side, gets in her fancy car, slams the door, and without even glancing back at us, noisily guns her engine, then shoots off down the street. I watch in stunned silence as she drives much too fast in the twenty-five-mile-per-hour zone, past sidewalks where children often skateboard or ride bikes. A word, beginning with the letter *b,* pops into my head as I watch that white convertible zip away.

"I'm sorry," says Noah.

I turn and see his disappointed expression. "I'm sorry too." To be honest, I'm not sure what I'm most sorry about. But I am definitely sorry.

"She's not always that bad," he says sadly.

"Well, I pretty much trashed her daughter," I admit. "I'm really sorry about that, Noah."

"It wasn't your fault," he says. "I told Kirsten to stay out of the front yard."

"She said Riley got out the front door, and she was trying to stop him," I say, replaying the explanation that Kirsten gave me as I attempted to clean her off in the bathtub. "She was sorry too."

"Even so…" He shoves his hands into the pockets of his jeans, then just shakes his head hopelessly.

Now, despite everything, I begin to see the humor in this, and although I try not to, I start to giggle.

"What?" He looks curiously at me.

"Oh, I'm sorry… I just keep seeing the shock on Camille's face, like she was about to faint when she saw Kirsten. I thought she was literally going to blow up, you know, like a cartoon character that splatters all over the TV screen…or maybe we were going to see steam shooting out of her nostrils and ears." I burst out laughing now. "I don't think I've ever seen someone so angry and yet attempting to remain somewhat cool and controlled at the same time."

Noah starts to chuckle now. "And when she looked at you, Gretchen—" A loud snort of laughter explodes from him. "She just had this totally appalled expression, like some prissy old lady who stepped in a pile of—"

"You can't really blame her," I gasp, laughing even harder as I look down at my soggy, sodden overalls and realize how truly disgusting I must look. I point my finger at Noah. "Your ex probably thinks you've really gone to the dogs, Noah."

He reaches over and gently pulls a twig from my hair, his blue eyes twinkling. "Well, that figures. Camille never was a very good judge of character."

Feeling flushed, I don't know how to respond…so I don't. "Well, umm, I better go finish up my mess," I say, turning away and returning to the wand with the stuck trigger. I finally manage to dislodge the branch, and before long I'm back at it again. I still plan to work until dark. As long as I'm already a mess, I might as well get as much done as possible.

After a while Noah comes out and waves good-bye. It's hard to hear his voice over the noise of the power washer, but I think he's saying that he'll see me tomorrow. I just nod, then turn my attention back to the siding. I actually think I'm getting pretty good at this. But by seven, I'm tired. I'm also concerned that the noisy engine might be disturbing the neighbors, so I decide to call it a day.

Riley is in the backyard, and to my surprise he's clean. I run my hand over his damp coat and realize that he, unlike me, has been recently bathed. I figure this must be Noah's doing, and I am very appreciative. So I give Riley fresh water and a bowl of food and promise to be back in an hour or so. I hurry home, where I take a long, warm shower, put on a clean set of work clothes, and then lug several loads of things, including an air bed that's still in its box, down to the pickup. My plan is to get that one bedroom set up so I can spend the night. It'll be very campy, but at least I'll be at the house and ready to get back to power washing in the morning.

Although I've been trying to eat more healthfully, I'm starving, so I pick up fast food along the way and eat most of it before I even get there. And maybe it was a smart choice, because by the time I've unloaded the pickup, I feel like I've gotten a second wind. So I decide to try out the new paint color in the bedroom. I put a Norah Jones CD into the player and begin to paint. I have always liked to paint. Dad taught me the right way to do it when I was fourteen and tired of living in a bedroom with ballerina pink walls. I changed those walls from pink to bright orange, which was awful, and finally to a soft periwinkle blue, which remained there until Dad sold the house while I was in college. But whenever anyone needs help with painting, I'm always quick to volunteer. I love cutting in around baseboards and then filling the roller with paint and evenly rolling it on. I find the whole process soothing. It's like I'm in control.

But by 1:30 a.m., when I finally finish the room, I am beat, and although I had originally planned to set up my bed in there, I decide that sleeping in those paint fumes might not be the best idea. In fact, I begin to wonder if it was a very good idea to spend the night here in the first place. For one thing there are no window coverings, so it's like I'm walking around in a fishbowl. Also, there is no shower. Only a very dirty tub. But I'm too tired to pack it up and go home. So I set up the air bed in a different bedroom and nail a drop cloth over the window for a curtain. Then I bring in Riley and his bed, and before long we are tucked in. And thanks to complete and utter exhaustion, I quickly fall asleep.

~ ~ ~

I awake to the sound of my dog barking. It takes me a couple of minutes to get my bearings, and when I check my watch, I see it's not even six, and yet Riley seems ready to go. Still wearing my sleeping shorts and a flimsy camisole, I slip on my flip-flops and go to the bathroom, where to my surprise I find Noah just strapping on his tool belt, like he's all ready to go to work.

"Whoa!" I literally jump, then turn around and dash back to the bedroom, where I quickly dress in my work clothes.

"Sorry to startle you," Noah calls from the hallway. "But I told you I was coming early today, and I'll be leaving early this afternoon too."

"It's okay," I call back. That's probably what he said when I couldn't hear him over the power-washer noise. Now fully clothed, I take a quick inventory of all that needs to be done. Is it even possible to make the six-week deadline? With only three weeks left until the loan comes due, I wonder if I should check on some kind of extension. I also wonder why I didn't bring my coffee maker last night. How am I supposed to function with no caffeine? I'll have to make a list of must-haves if I'm going to be camping here the next three weeks.

"Hey, you did a great job on that bedroom," Noah says as he

steps into the living room, where I'm still standing and gazing blankly out the front window.

"Thanks," I tell him. "Made for a late night."

"I assume you slept here."

"Yeah. I decided now that I'll be helping with Dad, I can save myself some commute time by kind of camping here. I brought a few things over last night, but unfortunately I didn't think of coffee."

"Wish I'd known," he says. "I could've brought you a cup. Some people say I make the best joe in town. But you know there's a kiosk over on Eighteenth Avenue, not that far from here."

"Good idea," I say, suppressing a yawn. "Without caffeine I might not ever get moving again. And I really want to finish up the power washing."

"It's looking really good out there too," he says. "You'll be ready to start priming as soon as it dries out."

"Thanks. Once I got the hang of that machine, it was kind of fun…in a messy sort of way." I don't admit to him that I was the kind of kid who loved getting dirty and making mud pies, the kind of girl that someone like Camille would've looked straight down at.

"Have you noticed that this house has really good light?"

I nod absently. "Yeah, although this is the first time I've been here early in the morning. With the trees and the angles of the sun, it really is pretty. I can't wait to see how it looks in here when those walls are gone."

"When did you want them to go?"

I turn and look hopefully at him. "As soon as possible?"

He smiles and salutes. "You're the boss."

After a large coffee with two extra shots, I feel wired enough to finish the power washing. I work fast and hard and am surprised to find that I'm finished by eleven, which gives me plenty of time to clean up and head for the hospital. Noah emerges from the house just in time to help me reload the power washer.

"Are you heading over to get your dad now?"

"After I return this and clean up," I explain as I wipe off the safety goggles and toss them into the backseat. "Dad told me yesterday that his ETD is one o'clock sharp and that I better be there or be square."

"Sounds like him. And sounds like he's ready to go home. Tell him hey for me."

"According to him, he's been ready for days now."

"Will you be back to work this afternoon?"

"Probably not until this evening. I thought I'd stick around long enough to get him really settled, make him some dinner, buy a few groceries, and make sure he's got everything he needs."

"Good for you."

"So would you mind locking up when you go? Riley is all right in the backyard on his own for an hour or two. I'd take him with me, but I'm not sure how long I'll be tied up in the hospital."

"I'll make sure Riley's got food and water before I leave."

"Thanks," I say as I get into the truck cab. "See you tomorrow."

"Oh, hey," he calls out. "I forgot to tell you I'm going out of town this weekend, so I won't be back to work until Monday."

I feel a frown crease my forehead but remind myself that I don't own this guy or his time. Also, I remember his tale about being a recovering workaholic. "Okay, see you on Monday then."

"Hope you don't mind."

"I understand," I say. "And, hey, somebody needs to have a life."

He nods. "And you should too, Gretchen."

I try not to roll my eyes. "Yeah, well, hopefully I will…in about three weeks."

Now he frowns. "Three weeks? Is that the actual deadline?"

"The drop-dead deadline."

"Wow…" I can tell by his face that he does not think this is even close to possible. "Then what happens? Does the house turn into a pumpkin?"

"No, but it's a short-term loan. So penalties incur. Dad's credit rating, and probably mine too, goes down. Profits get eaten."

"Can you renegotiate it?"

I consider this. "I'm not sure. Dad set it up. I just signed on the line." The truth is, I don't want to let Dad down. I don't want to renegotiate. I don't want to fail. "Is it hopeless?" I ask weakly.

"All things are possible with God."

"Meaning it'll take a miracle?"

His brows lift like I just nailed it. And I'm afraid he might be right. Still, it's not like I can give up.

"Have a good weekend," I say as I start the truck. Forcing what I hope is a brave smile, I wave. I cannot believe how disappointed I feel, knowing that Noah won't be working on my house this weekend. But then why should I have assumed that he would? Just because I'm obsessed with getting this done doesn't mean that he is. Still, I wonder, What *is* he doing this weekend? Where is he going? And who is going with him?

# 20

How's Noah?" asks Dad when I finally have him in the passenger seat of his pickup and am driving him home. It's nearly two now, and I can empathize with Dad's frustration at how slow things seem to go at the hospital. I guess that's why they call their "inmates" patients—it takes lots of patience to be there.

"He's fine. He said to tell you hey."

"He hasn't been by to see me since Monday." Dad wipes his finger through the dust on the dashboard. "I'm assuming he's been busy at the house."

I nod and give Dad the latest update on progress, probably painting a cheerier picture than is accurate. And I don't mention that this weekend looks to be fairly unproductive or that the deadline is halfway here.

"Why don't we stop by?" he suggests suddenly.

I glance over at him and chuckle. "Yeah, right, Dad. I just signed you out of the hospital, promising that you were going straight home to rest. Like I'm going to take you over to the house."

He scowls like a little boy and looks down at his lap, picking at the piping of the sweatpants I brought for him to wear home.

"Have you heard from Betty?" I ask, hoping to change to a happier subject.

He brightens. "Yes. She called this morning, and we had a nice chat. She and Louise were in France, some little town down south. They'll be heading for Paris in a few days."

"Aah, that sounds wonderful."

"Maybe for some. It's sure not my cup of tea."

Once we get home, Dad is resistant to taking a nap, but I notice that once he's in his own bed, he falls immediately to sleep. I do a little cleaning and freshening of his apartment and tend to the cats, who seem pleased to have Dad home. I stir up a pitcher of his favorite iced tea, the kind that comes in powder form with lots of sugar. Oh well. I check what's in his freezer and pantry, making a list of what I'll get at the store, including a few things I know my dad likes as well as things I know are good for him. A compromise. Then I get some soup ready to heat, and as soon as I hear him stirring, I pop it into the microwave.

"Here you go," I say as I carry the steaming bowl of hearty chicken and wild rice soup to the table. He still looks groggy, and tufts of white hair stick out on both sides of his head. "A late lunch."

"Thanks," he says, sitting down. Then he smiles, and I think it's the first genuine smile I've seen from him in days. "It really is good to be home."

"I'll bet it is."

"Did this place get bigger while I was gone?" he asks as he glances around the space with wide eyes.

"I'm sure it must feel that way after being cooped up in that hospital room."

"I'll say." Dad glances at me curiously. "Aren't you eating?"

"I already had a bowl of soup while you were sleeping. I thought I'd go to the store while you have lunch."

He nods, then bows his head and says a quick blessing. "Now, will you hand me that remote?" he says. "There's a golf tournament I want to see."

I give him the remote and a kiss on the forehead and promise to be back before five. It's weird how familiar this feels to me—taking care of Dad, grocery shopping for him, fixing him food, cleaning his place. Not that I've done much of it recently, certainly not since he retired and got into cooking and housekeeping himself. But while I was at home after Mom died, caring for Dad was pretty much my routine. I got a break during my college years, but then I came back home and fell right into the same old groove again. Finally, a couple of years ago—when I turned thirty—I got my own apartment. And I suppose I only did that because Holly gave me such a bad time about needing to grow up. Not that I didn't enjoy that freedom, although I sure did seem eager to toss it aside when I agreed to marry Collin. Just look where that got me.

"Enough!" I say to myself as I park in front of Safeway. "No more trips down Memory Lane, Gretchen Hanover." Great, I'm talking to myself again.

It's about seven o'clock when Dad's finally settled for the evening. I've gone over everything that he has to eat, which I think would easily sustain him for about six months if necessary. I've written down when he can take his pain meds and placed a bottle of water on his bedside table. I've programmed my cell phone number as number one on his speed dial and told him, in no uncertain terms, to call me anytime. Although I doubt he will. I also spoke to his neighbor while he was napping. I told her that he's much better but still recovering. Then I gave her my phone number, and she promised to send her husband over in the morning. "They often have coffee together anyway," she assures me. "And I'll have Richard bring Hank his newspaper too."

I can't think of one more thing to do as I stand nearby—hovering, I'm sure it seems, but still not willing to leave. "Dad," I begin, "I could spend the night if—"

"No." He firmly shakes his head. "I'm just fine. Go. Now."

So I bend down to where he's comfortably reclined in his La-Z-Boy, his remote and a fresh glass of iced tea on the end table, and kiss him on the cheek. "I'm so glad you're home, Dad, and feeling better."

"You and me both, sweetheart."

"I'll see you tomorrow around noon then?"

"Yes."

"Remember the coffee maker is all ready to go. Just turn it on. And there's orange juice and—"

"I know, I know. You've already gone over that. Go ahead and leave, Gretchen. I'm sure that dog of yours is getting lonely."

"You're probably right. Maybe I'll bring him over to visit you tomorrow."

"That'd be nice."

"Call me if you—"

"Good night, Gretchen."

"Night, Dad."

I decide to run by my apartment again, while it's still light out, and load up some of my things—like a coffee maker—that will make my flip house a little more homey.

"Are you moving?" asks my neighbor Tom. He's one of those guys I normally try to avoid—the kind who talks too loudly, drinks too much, and is always looking for the next big "par-tay."

"No," I tell him as I lug my Karastan wool area rug down the stairs. My plan is to put this in my makeshift bedroom until the wall-to-wall carpeting is installed. And then I will eventually use the rug for the open house, probably in the dining area.

"Need any help?"

I pause to wipe sweat from my forehead and look up at him, noticing that while he may not be the kind of guy I'd go out with, he does have muscles. "Sure," I tell him. "I'd love a hand."

Naturally this makes him clap his hands like he's applauding.

"Thanks," I say, rolling my eyes and doing a little bow. But then he pops down the stairs and picks up the other end of the rug, and in no time it's loaded into the back of the truck.

"Nice pickup," he says, patting the hood.

"It's my dad's."

Then he offers more help, which I don't reject, and before long we've loaded the pickup bed with even more things than I'd planned. During our trips up and down the stairs, I've told him a little about my house flip, and he seems to think it's a great idea and even offers to help, although I doubt he's serious.

"Thanks," I tell him after the last trip. "I'm sure you'd like to be paid with a six-pack of beer, which I don't have. But how about soda?" I lift up a case of Sierra Mist hopefully.

He makes a face and waves a hand. "Nah. I was just being neighborly."

I smile at him. "Well, I appreciate it."

"And..." He glances over his shoulder like he's uncomfortable. "If you ever, you know, want to go out sometime...that'd be cool."

"Well, thanks again," I say, trying not to act shocked. "I'm pretty busy these days doing this house remodel, but..." I trail off to avoid leading him on.

He seems satisfied with my ambiguity as he nods and says, "Later." Then I make tracks to my pickup and wonder why I didn't just say no. Still, it was nice of him to help. And it was flattering to be asked out.

It's dark by the time I get to the house, and I realize I still have to unload stuff from the pickup. Suddenly I find myself wishing for some more "neighborly" neighbors like Tom. Or maybe it's just that I'm missing Noah. I tell myself that it's his help I'm missing, but I wonder if it's even more than that.

I stand in the driveway for several minutes, trying to decide whether or not it would be safe to leave some of the heavier things in the back of the pickup. That's when I spot my dad's big contractor wheelbarrow over by the side of the house. Perfect. I put Riley in the backyard, and my work begins.

After several wobbly wheelbarrow loads right into the house, including a precarious trip with the rolled-up rug awkwardly balanced in the barrow, I have everything unloaded into the living room. And although I'm exhausted, I suddenly decide to "play house." I drag my beautiful rug down the dusty hallway, reminding myself of the salesman when he assured me these rugs are tough and originally were made for use in nomadic tents and were laid upon dirt floors. Then I unroll the pretty wool rug in the freshly painted bedroom and am so amazed that I almost start crying. The carpet has shades of olive, rust, gold, khaki, and black, and it looks great with the wall color. Then I drag my air bed in, situating it on the rug. I put a bronze lamp next to it; no need for a bedside table since the bed's so close to the floor. I move my drop-cloth "curtain" from the other room, and I think it looks rather cozy. And Riley seems to like it too.

Okay, I'm sure some people would think I'm nuts. Why would anyone in her right mind want to camp here? But I suppose I am a driven woman right now. With three weeks left and the clock steadily ticking, I know I am now dreaming the impossible dream. But I will give it my best shot. So I sit down on my bed, pull my notebook out of my house-flip bag, and begin to make more lists. There are lots of things I still need to order, so I make a list for them. I make a list of things that need to be done and a list of estimates for costs and deadlines, which are some pretty depressing figures. Finally I make a list of the supplies I'll pick up tomorrow. And then I force myself to turn off the light and go to sleep so I can get up at the break of day and go straight to work.

Once again I wake up to the sound of Riley barking and running back and forth across the bedroom, trying to get me up. I'm dismayed to see that I've slept in. It's almost eight, and I can hear someone loudly knocking on the front door. I peek out the window to see Holly's white Subaru parked in the driveway.

"Coming!" I yell as I hurry to let her in.

"Good morning, sunshine!" she says cheerfully, holding out a tray with two Starbucks cups and a little brown bag. "Help is here." And with her paint-splattered jeans and T-shirt, she actually looks like she's dressed for work.

"Come in," I say as I open the door wider.

"Did I wake you?"

"Sort of."

"You mean you slept here?"

"Yeah," I admit. "I'm camping." Then I explain my plan to save on commute time.

Holly looks incredulous as she glances around the grungy living room with various tools and supplies piled here and there. "You really spent the night here?" she says again. "Isn't that kind of creepy?"

I shrug. "I think I've gotten over the creepy factor."

"Can I look around?"

"Of course." I take a sip of the coffee, which is a latte and perfect, and open the bag to see two blueberry muffins. "And thanks for breakfast."

"Oh, man," she says as she looks into the bathroom that's completely gutted. "Where do you bathe and—"

"There's a second bath," I tell her, pointing to the end of the hallway. She takes a peek at that one and shakes her head. "You really *use* that bathroom?"

"The toilet works. The tub's kind of gross, but you know—"

"Gross? This place is like a third-world country, Gretch. How can you stand it?"

"Hey, did you come here to help or criticize?"

"Sorry." She turns and looks at me with a seriously concerned expression, like she's trying to determine the level of my insanity. "It's just that I had no idea it was so…so *bad*."

"That's because you only saw the house from the outside. And if you think this is bad, you should've seen it before the cleanup crew came."

"This place has been cleaned?" She makes a face as she points to the grimy wall in the hallway where it looks like animals or children wiped…well, something…all along the walls.

"I took photos," I tell her, "to document how bad it was."

"Yes…but I thought… Well, never mind."

"So, do you really want to help?" I ask.

She presses her lips tightly together as if she's reconsidering, then finally nods. "Yes. A friend in need is a friend indeed, right?"

"I guess."

She peeks in my makeshift bedroom now, then laughs. "This must be where you're sleeping."

"Where else?" I check out my "cozy" room in stark daylight and see how shabby it really looks with the beat-up wood floor, missing closet doors, and a drop cloth nailed over the window. Charming.

"Nice rug."

"Thanks."

We go into the kitchen area, where I have set up a couple of camp chairs. "Care to join me?" I ask as I set the coffees and muffins on the small outdoor table.

"Delighted," she says in an affected tone as she sits down and picks up her coffee. "Lovely little place you have here, Gretchen. You've done so much with it."

"Thank you," I say with a mock snobbish tone. "I call it contemporary grunge with an artistic touch of minimalism." I wave my hand to where the cabinets used to be. "Note the sparse lines of the kitchen."

"Very cutting edge." She plays along. "And I like this filthy patina you've achieved on the walls. Sort of an urban-grime look, but perhaps you could use a little graffiti to set it off better."

"Yes, I think there's a can of orange spray paint in the pickup."

"That should do the trick."

We continue this senseless banter while we dine on muffins and lattes, but finally I tell her it's time to get to work.

"Where do I begin?" she asks.

"Do you like to paint?"

"Inside or outside?"

"Which would you prefer?"

"Outside."

"Perfect." Actually I'm relieved since I really wanted to do the interior painting myself. "The exterior is mostly ready to go, but you might need to do a little sanding in spots."

So we gather up the supplies and a ladder, and I take her out to one side of the house and show her how and where to sand the lap siding, pointing out the spots where the old paint needs to be smoothed out some. Then I open up a five-gallon bucket of primer.

"White?" she says, peering down at the paint with dismay. "You're painting it white? And it's kind of a mucky-looking white at that."

"No, this is the primer coat. After that we'll paint it a nice sage green."

She nods in relief. "Oh good. How about the trim?"

"That'll be taupe, but I don't want to do it until the new windows and doors are in."

"New windows and doors?" She seems to consider this, then nods. "Maybe there's hope for this place after all. How much time do you have left to fix it now?"

I let out a groan. "Three weeks."

I see her eyes open wide. "Wow."

"Tell me about it."

"Well, I'll help you when I can," she says. "Maybe I can come by after work sometimes."

"That would be fantastic."

"And maybe Justin will want to help too."

"Great."

"But don't forget that next Saturday is Tina's wedding. I really hope you'll be there. Tina can't stand unfulfilled RSVPs. Plus I could really use the moral support of a woman, someone who can make fun of Bridezilla with me."

"Of course I'll be there," I promise, although I wish I could get out of it. Then again, it might be nice to do something social for a change.

"So, anyway, I just start?" asks Holly. "Do I use a brush or this little roller?"

"Whichever you like best—probably both."

"What if I make a mess?"

I laugh. "Look around," I say as I point to big flakes of paint still littering the beat-up shrubbery and dead grass. "I don't think you can make it look any worse than this."

"Good point."

"And don't worry about the windows since they're coming out."

"This should be a breeze."

Seeing that Holly has things under control outside, I go inside to work. My plan is to paint both bedrooms and the hallway before this day is done. Of course, I know that I need to check on Dad at noon, as well as make a supply run, but I think this is a doable plan.

As I'm painting the largest bedroom, I become more and more aware that the ceiling treatment, a nasty substance known as "popcorn," has to go. Not only is it gray and creepy looking with old cobwebs still adhered to its bumpy surface, but it's not paintable either.

So I put down the roller and get out a broad knife. I attempt to scrape off some of the crud, which naturally creates an even bigger mess as the chalky, powdery junk coats both me and the floor. Even so, I can see there's no going back now. Still, there must be a smarter way to do this. For starters I need to cover the wood floors so this white muck doesn't get engrained in them.

As I'm spreading the drop cloths, I notice Dad's big Shop-Vac and wonder if that might not come in handy. Finally I've got the Shop-Vac hose in hand and am ready to go. I'm sure I must look like something from a sci-fi or horror movie as I go to work, but it seems my popcorn removal plan is working...somewhat. I have wrapped myself, almost mummylike, in a drop cloth that's secured with duct tape. And I'm wearing my faithful bandanna over my nose and mouth and safety goggles over my eyes. I securely duct-taped the broad knife to the end of the Shop-Vac hose so that as I scrape, much of the debris goes directly into the vacuum. Pretty smart, if you ask me.

Of course, I'm only about half finished when the air is so thick with dust that I can barely see, and breathing is getting to be a challenge too. I have a sneaking suspicion that I never should've started this "little" project.

"What is going on in here?" yells Holly over the sound of the vacuum. I turn to barely see her at the door.

"Close the door!" I yell, not wanting this creepy crud to escape. Then I climb down, turn off the vacuum, peel off my strange getup, and finally emerge to see Holly standing in the hallway looking at me with a stunned expression.

"What are you doing in there?"

I brush dust from my hands as I patiently explain about the popcorn ceiling and how it needs to go, and she suddenly looks very concerned.

"Have you had that checked for asbestos?"

*"Asbestos?"* I repeat weakly.

"Yes." She grabs me by the arm now, holding her hand over her nose, and literally drags me out of the house and stands me in the center of the yard.

"Gretchen Hanover!" She shrieks at me in a slightly hysterical tone. "Are you insane?"

I stand in the center of the yard feeling like I'm about five years old and just shake my head. "I-I don't think so."

"Well, don't move."

I don't.

Then Holly gets the hose, turns it on, and comes over and proceeds to aim the nozzle directly at me. Before I can ask what she's doing, she pulls the trigger, and I am being doused with cold water.

"What are—"

"Do you remember that my parents had *popcorn ceilings* in their house?" she yells as she continues to soak me from head to toe. "And do you remember that it was full of asbestos!"

I sputter and shriek from the cold, but I stand there taking my punishment as she continues to scold me.

"And everyone in our family had to be evacuated from that house for a full week," she yells, "while that toxic stuff was removed by experts who wore hazmat suits and respirators!"

I try to say something in response to this, but a blast of water literally goes into my mouth. I lean over to spit it out, and she continues to hose me down on the backside. Finally she seems satisfied and stops, and I just stand there, dripping wet and staring at her in shock.

"Do you know what asbestos can do to your lungs?" she demands.

I shrug as I blink back tears. What she's saying is beginning to sink in. Have I endangered my life? "Do you think that ceiling has asbestos in it?" I ask weakly.

"When was this house built?"

I tell her the year, and she nods grimly. Then she picks up an unused drop cloth and tells me to go into the backyard and to remove my clothes, which I assume she will bury or burn. Riley looks on with interest as I peel off my soggy, contaminated clothes and Holly wraps me in the drop cloth.

"Now we'll go to your apartment where you can change. And before anyone goes back into that house, you must have it tested for asbestos."

"But I—"

"No buts!"

I wrap the multipurpose drop cloth more tightly around me as I slump down in the passenger seat of her Subaru. Part of me thinks that Holly has totally overreacted to this, and part of me is scared stiff that I will develop lung cancer before the sun sets.

# 21

In my apartment, which Holly thankfully still has a key for, I take a very long and thorough shower and get dressed. Then Holly offers to take me to Dad's since it's nearly noon by now. But she continues to scold me as she drives. "I called some experts while you were in the shower," she informs me. "They say there's a high chance that ceiling has asbestos. Anywhere from five to forty percent of the material may be asbestos. And removing it the way you did, without wetting it or using proper equipment, was the most dangerous way possible. And they said that according to the description I gave them, it's quite likely no certified contractor will want to come in and work there now, and no inspector will set foot in there. You might even be sued."

"Really?" Okay, now I really do feel like crying. How could I mess up this badly? All in one short morning. I wonder what Noah will say. Or my dad.

"Not only that, the guy told me that if you can get someone in there, it will cost up to thirty dollars a square foot to have it removed. Do you have any idea how much money we're talking about here, Gretchen?"

"Ummm..." I do the math in my head. "Like forty thousand dollars."

"What are you going to do?" demands Holly when she turns in at Dad's condo.

"For starters..." I sit up straighter. "We are not going to tell Dad what I did today. He doesn't need something like this to worry him right now."

I paste a smile on my face as I knock on his door, then use my key to let myself in. "Hey, Dad," I say as we find him sitting in his recliner, a newspaper spread over his lap, and a basketball game blaring on the TV. He turns down the sound, then smiles up at us. "Two gorgeous women coming to visit."

Holly bends down and gives him a peck on the cheek. "I'm glad to see you're looking much better, Hank."

I kiss his other cheek and, hoping to avoid any discussion of my morning's work, head straight for the kitchen where I start making a salad. I can hear Holly making small talk with him, and I feel relatively certain she will not let the cat out of the bag. But all I can think of is that dollar figure. $40,000. $40,000. $40,000. It's like that number has been indelibly printed into my brain so it's all I can think about. For all I know I might actually say the figure out loud.

Finally I've done all I can to delay sitting down at the table with my dad. Lunch is ready, and I will myself to be calm as Dad bows his head and says the blessing. Holly says, "amen," and it's all I can do not to blurt out, "Forty thousand dollars!" Fortunately I don't.

"I talked to the roofers today," says Dad. "They expect to be at the house by Tuesday."

"Really?" I consider this. If we have to pay for asbestos, how can we possibly pay for a new roof or the cabinets or anything else for that matter? I take a small bite of salad and chew for a long time but feel unable to swallow. Actually, I feel as if I might need to throw up. Could it be the asbestos? Am I already getting sick from it? I wonder if Holly asked the expert about that. I glance at her, and she's looking at me with a worried expression, and I wonder if my skin has turned some horrible shade of gray or green. Maybe I'm about to expire right here at the kitchen table.

Then, cool and calm as can be, Holly turns to Dad and says, "Say, Hank, I noticed that Gretchen's flip house has popcorn ceilings."

He nods as he takes a whole-wheat roll and slathers some no-cholesterol spread on it, not even complaining that it's not real butter, which I consider real progress.

"My parents had ceilings like that," she continues, and I just stare at her, wondering if I can possibly kick her under the table from here. But this is a wide table, and I'd probably end up whacking Dad's shin first.

"Yes, your parents' house is about the same age as this one, isn't it?"

"Yeah. Gretchen and I were discussing this."

Okay, I am feeling seriously ill now. I'm about to excuse myself to run to the bathroom to either throw up or die from having inhaled about a gallon of asbestos—or maybe both.

"Anyway," continues Holly, "my parents found out their ceiling had asbestos in it, and they—"

"Excuse me!" Then I jump up from the table and dash to the powder room. I stand over the toilet for a full minute but finally realize I'm not going to throw up. The door is open behind me, and I can hear Holly and Dad laughing now. Laughing! I'm in here, possibly dying from asbestos poisoning, and they are in there telling jokes? Finally I can't take it. I go back to where they're still laughing and demand to know what's so funny.

"Holly was just telling me about...about...about h-hosing you down," says Dad. He's laughing so hard he has tears in the corners of his eyes, and I'm actually worried about his heart.

"So she told you about the asbestos?"

He nods, using his paper napkin to wipe his eyes and then blow his nose.

"And then, Hank," gasps Holly, who is hysterical too, "I made her go into the backyard and strip...buck naked."

"She wrapped me in a drop cloth," I add. But they're both laughing so hard I don't think they even heard me. So I just sit here thinking that if my own dad and my very best friend don't care about the possibility that I might be dying, well, maybe I should find myself some new people to hang with. Maybe muggers or thugs or ax murderers.

Finally they quiet down, and Dad looks at me. "I guess I forgot to tell you that I had the house checked for asbestos right after I saw the place."

"You did?"

"The test came back negative." He chuckles. "One of the few positive things about this whole crazy house flip."

I let out a huge sigh. "So I'm not dying?"

"Is that what you thought?" asks Holly.

I nod. "Despite my bandanna, I must've breathed in about a gallon of that nasty dust." I take a long swig of iced tea now, hoping to get rid of that powdery taste.

Dad shakes his finger at me now. "Asbestos or no asbestos, you need to use a proper respirator when you do projects like that, Gretchen. And at least a fiber mask for sanding regular surfaces. Your lungs are supposed to last a lifetime." Then he tells me the basics for the proper way to remove sprayed-on ceiling, which doesn't include a Shop-Vac. "Of course, you'll have to put some kind of texture up there once you're done."

"Like what?"

"Well, you could probably slap some Sheetrock mud up there, use the broad knife, and move it around to make it look like plaster, then give it a good coat of paint."

"Right…" I wonder why I even bothered with the stupid ceiling to start with.

"And if you need advice, Gretchen, you know my number."

"Next time I'll call you, Dad, I promise."

"That'd be good." He glances at Holly and chuckles again. "You really hosed her down like that? Right there in the front yard with God and the whole world watching?"

Fine. I am relieved to know I'm not dying—at least not today. But their jokes at my expense begin to grate. So I quickly finish my lunch and start putting things away in the kitchen as well as straightening the house and watering the plants and checking on the cats. Finally I tell Dad I'll change his bandage and then I need to get back to the house to clean up my unfortunate mess. The nurse at the hospital showed me how to do the bandage, and although it's not easy seeing a big incision like that on Dad's chest, I'm reassured that it looks clean and healthy, with no signs of infection.

"Looks good," I tell Dad as I gently tape the fresh bandage on.

"Still hurts sometimes," he admits as he buttons up his Hawaiian shirt.

"Take your pain meds if you need to," I remind him. "The doctor said you'll heal more quickly if you're not in pain." I reach for the ones that I set by his bed last night and hand them to him along with the water bottle. "And then you should take a nap."

He kicks off his slippers now. "Maybe I will."

"Because you are still recuperating," I say as I help him lie down. "And you promised the doctor you'd follow her instructions if she let you go home." Then I pull the cover over him and kiss him on the cheek. "I'm sure glad you thought to check for asbestos," I say, and he chuckles. "I'll see you at dinnertime, okay?"

He nods slightly, closing his eyes. "You be careful, Gretchen Girl. You're all I've got, you know."

"Same back at you, Dad."

"Tell Holly thanks for coming."

I find Holly putting the last of the dishes in the dishwasher and tell her that Dad's going to rest now. Then she drives me back to the house and actually apologizes for my cold morning shower.

Now I have to laugh. "Under the circumstances, I guess I can't blame you. You must think I'm an idiot."

"I actually think you're very smart. And taking on this whole house-flipping project is very brave."

"You think?"

"Yeah, as I was painting outside, I started to get a vision for this place. I mean the trees in the backyard are great. I can imagine a family really enjoying this place. If Justin and I hadn't just bought that condo, I would consider something like this for us."

"Really?" I begin to feel hopeful again.

"Well, if it was fixed up. I don't think I'd try to do it myself. But then we both have to work full-time. You're lucky to have summer vacation."

Summer vacation? I wonder, what is that?

Holly goes back to work on the primer, and I head to the building-supply store to get the things on my list as well as the items Dad said I need to continue to safely and efficiently remove the gunk from the ceilings. When I get back, I see that Justin's car is now parked in front of my house, and I worry that something's wrong. Hopefully Holly hasn't fallen off the ladder. I hurry around to the side of the house to see that they're both painting now.

"Wow," I say as Justin swipes on a fresh swath of white primer. "More help!"

Holly winks at me. "I figured at the rate you're going, well, maybe we should call in the troops."

"The troops?"

"Well, this is it for now. But what about our Bible study group?" Holly makes a face. "Even though someone—we won't mention names—doesn't go anymore."

"Yeah," says Justin. "How about a work party sometime?"

"When?" I say eagerly.

"Not next weekend," says Holly. "That's Tina's wedding."

"How about the one after that?" suggests Justin.

"That'll be one week before my supposed open house," I say, feeling even more desperate than I felt last night.

"And you'll probably need help, won't you?"

"Or a straitjacket."

"We'll talk to them about it this week," says Justin as he dips his brush again.

"Thanks," I tell them. "I'll owe you guys big time."

"We'll know who to call when we need to repaint," says Holly.

"No problem." Then I go inside, and equipped with spray bottles, a respirator, coveralls, lots of disposable plastic drop cloths and tape, and goggles, I attack my mess in a much more strategic manner. At first it seems hopeless, but after a while I figure out a few things. And finally I have the messed-up bedroom and hallway fairly clean, as well as not one piece of popcorn on the ceiling. I've just tossed the nasty, goopy drop cloth, along with my coveralls, out the window when Justin and Holly come to check on my progress.

"Wow," says Holly, looking at the scraped-clean ceiling. "You did that?"

I nod proudly as I remove the safety eye gear. "Yep."

"But it looks kind of rough," observes Justin.

"I'm not *finished* with it," I explain somewhat impatiently.

"Speaking of finished," says Holly lightly. "We have to go. Tina's in-laws-to-be are having a barbecue, and the family is expected to be there."

"Thanks so much for helping," I tell them both. "I really, really appreciate it."

"It was fun," says Justin. "And we'll be back."

I want to ask him *when* but think that might be a little presumptuous. It's already five, but I think I have enough time to get the next bedroom set up for scraping the ceiling tomorrow. Or maybe even tonight after I check on Dad.

~ ~ ~

As it turns out, I'm still scraping that ceiling at midnight. After taking Riley to visit Dad at dinnertime, at which I surprised Dad with takeout buffalo burgers from Henry's, I came back and painted the room where I'd already scraped the ceiling. I just wanted to have one room that felt close to being done…although it still needs a new window, closet doors, baseboard, and trim, not to mention the floor being refinished… But oh well.

Then I was so pleased with my progress and since it was only ten o'clock, I attacked the ceiling in the second bedroom. Probably a mistake. Anyway, it's two in the morning, so I decide to stop, and I quickly realize I'll be forced to shower in the nasty bathtub with no shower curtain. So I tape up one of the plastic drop cloths, and as I clean myself up for the second time today, I consider writing a handyman's guide titled *150 Ways to Use Drop Cloths.*

I feel slightly guilty for missing church the next morning, but besides not having any clean or proper clothes at this house, I didn't wake up in time. I make a pot of coffee in the bathroom, which is admittedly a gross place to make coffee, then walk around my sorry-looking house sipping coffee as I assess what seems like an impossible mountain to climb. To make myself feel better, I go out in the backyard with Riley, but unfortunately it's not terribly encouraging either. Not that he minds as I toss his ball for him. I'm sure he'd be happy to spend the rest of his days here. Not only does he have a big backyard to romp in, he gets to sleep with me every night. What dog can beat this setup?

I move the rug and furnishings from my makeshift boudoir to the most finished room, complete with a clean ceiling and painted walls. I consider attacking the ceiling in the last bedroom and actually get the room all draped and ready to go, but for some reason I cannot force myself to take it on. Maybe it's because my coveralls are still outside drying from last night, and anyway it'll soon be time to go check on Dad and make his lunch.

So, feeling somewhat useless, I pick up a sledgehammer and start whacking on the living room wall that I want removed. Admittedly, I'm not sure this is the wisest thing to do, but it does relieve some stress, and I've seen people do this countless times on TV. The main thing is to avoid hitting the studs since this is a load-bearing wall, and I don't want the whole house falling down on my head. Or do I?

I'm swinging hard and wishing I was more comfortable using swearwords since the idea of being stuck in this flip house for three more weeks, if not the entire summer, is making me seriously angry. Suddenly I hit something that makes a loud pop, and the electricity cuts out. I know this because my CD player stops playing Corrine Bailey Rae, and the work light that's been illuminating this wall goes dark. I peek into the hole that I just smacked open to see that I've managed to hit some wiring. Great. Call in the electricians. While we're at it, why not call in the wrecking ball or the guys with dynamite? I am hopeless. I drop the sledgehammer with a thud, whistle for Riley, get my purse, and leave. What in the world made me think I could take on something like this? Am I losing it?

Dad and I are both quiet as we sit down to eat the lunch I fixed. He doesn't inquire how the work is going, and I don't bring it up.

Maybe this is our new don't-ask-don't-tell policy. Whatever. It works for me.

Then, as I'm cleaning up, I realize how selfish I'm being. I haven't even asked how he's feeling. For all I know he could be having heart pains and doesn't want me to know. What kind of nurse am I?

"So, Dad," I say as I set a fresh glass of lemonade on the end table next to his recliner, "how are you feeling?"

"Useless."

I sit down across from him on the sofa now. "Dad, you are not useless."

He shakes his head. "I was thinking about the Eskimos."

"Eskimos?"

"The way they put their elders out on an iceberg when they're too old to work. I was thinking you ought to do that with me."

I actually laugh at this. "Well, admittedly, it is pretty hot out there, and an iceberg sounds kind of refreshing. But they're a little hard to come by around here, Dad."

"You know what I mean."

"Dad," I give him a stern look. "You are useful. Good grief, it's just one week since you had heart surgery, and you're home and—"

"And being nursed by you." He sighs. "And I know you need to be at that house. Confounded house. I wish we'd never done this."

"Me too."

Now Dad looks up at me with surprise. "You too?"

I nod sadly. "I think it's hopeless."

"Oh, now, well, okay, I'm sorry… It's not hopeless, Gretchen."

Tears are starting to come now. "Yes, it is, Dad." Then I confess how I just knocked out the electricity.

"Oh, that's nothing." Then he gets a concerned look. "But you did turn off the circuit breakers, didn't you?"

"Circuit breakers?"

"Well, shoot."

"What?"

"If you've got broken wiring in the wall, you better get back over there and turn the power off."

"Turn the power off?" I frown. "How?"

"Switch…off…the…breakers." His expression and slowly enunciated words might make one think he was addressing the village idiot. Maybe he is.

"I don't even know where the breakers are. Or what they are." I'm imagining waves breaking on the ocean now. The ocean… Wouldn't that be nice?

"In the laundry room, Gretchen. By the back door. There's a metal panel with switches inside. You might as well turn them all off until an electrician can come take a look."

"Okay."

"Better hurry."

"Why?"

"We don't want the place burning down, now do we?"

I consider this. My Karastan carpet is still in there. And Dad's tools. Okay, maybe I don't want it to burn to the ground. Not yet anyway. Of course, I do feel a little nervous when I hear the sound of sirens as I drive through town. It doesn't help when I begin to imagine several fire engines parked along Lilac Lane, hoses spraying as they put out the inferno. Consequently I do drive a little faster. But when I get to the house, I'm relieved to see that it's still standing. At least I think I'm relieved. Then I wonder if we have any sort of insurance on it. Of course, I'm not actually considering torching the place; that would be illegal. But accidents do happen. My decision to become a house flipper is proof enough of that.

# 22

I turn off the breakers like Dad has suggested, then attack that third bedroom ceiling. No electricity needed to scrape popcorn. After it's done and the debris tossed out the window, I go ahead and paint the walls. And although I realize there's still a lot of work left to complete these bedrooms, I think this is at least a start. I'm feeling a tiny bit more hopeful. Then, after a trip to the "usable" bathroom, I notice that the partially torn-out wall—the one that's been damaged due to dry rot—actually abuts the largest bedroom. Suddenly I wonder if there's any way to open that bathroom to the bedroom and create a master suite. I know from watching *House Flippers* that a master suite always increases the value of a home.

I walk back and forth from the bedroom to the bath, trying to figure this out, and finally I think it makes perfect sense. Instead of being a shared bath, like it's been for decades, it could be closed off where the current door is, perhaps with room for a storage closet there, and then it could be opened up to the bedroom. Why not?

Since the electricity is already off, I wonder, what could it hurt to open that wall up a little? So I go for the sledgehammer. True, there's a little voice in my head warning me to be careful…perhaps even call Dad. But he might be resting. And he could get all worried if he thinks I'm tearing the place down. Really, what could it hurt?

This isn't even a load-bearing wall. The electricity is out. I look at where the sink used to be, the exposed pipes, and where the replacement sink will go. This bathroom did have double sinks with a long vanity. My plan is to replace this with a space-saving pedestal sink. That, combined with the extra storage where the door used to be, should provide plenty of space. Besides, I saw a gorgeous pedestal sink at Home Depot last week. And with the travertine tile that I plan to lay in here, it will be sleek and beautiful.

With this in mind, I take a swing up high, around where I think the top of the doorway should go. The Sheetrock breaks apart fairly easily, and to my relief nothing goes wrong. I swing again, making the hole go all the way through this time. Feeling more confident, I take a few more swings, and my excitement builds as I begin to see the bedroom through the opening. This is going to be great. I take another big swing and realize that something stopped the sledgehammer from going all the way through the wall. Then, as I pull it back, I see a squirt of water. I reach down to pull off the Sheetrock that's hanging there, and suddenly that squirt of water becomes a spray.

I grab the dirty towel and shove it against a pipe I hadn't noticed before, a now broken pipe, but the towel doesn't help. Water is coming out fast. There must be a way to shut this off, but I don't know how. I see some knobs and attempt to turn one of them, but this results in water coming out from a different pipe, so I quickly turn it the other way. Then I run outside, thinking there must be some place to shut all the water off. I'm sure I've seen this on HGTV. But I'm running around the yard, literally looking like a chicken with her head chopped off, when a guy from the yellow house across the street walks toward me.

"Anything wrong?"

"Yes!" I yell at him. "I broke a pipe inside, and I need to shut off the water."

"If it's like our house, it'll be over here." And he jogs over to the side of the house and hunts about in the shrubbery. "Here it is," he calls. "I'll shut it off."

I look over his shoulder as he strains to turn a handle that's in a box underground. "Does that shut off all the water?" I ask as he stands and wipes his hands on his denim shorts.

"Yep." Then he sticks out a hand. "I'm Jeremy Stein."

I wipe my brow, then shake his hand. "I'm Gretchen Hanover."

"I know. My wife, Jenna, said she met you this week."

"Oh yes. In fact, I should give you her plate. I've been meaning to return it, but it's been kind of crazy with this remodel."

"No problem," he says. "We're just so thankful that something's actually being done about this place. The people who lived here before turned the house into a dump, which of course affected the value and even the morale of our neighborhood." He stops there, maybe realizing the pressure he's inadvertently adding to my shoulders. "Anyway, what color are you going to paint the house?"

"A sage green," I say as we go inside. "Hopefully soon."

"Jenna wants to paint ours blue, but I'm trying to talk her out of it. I think an earth tone would be better."

"Earth tones are preferable for resale," I point out, knowing that I sound like the narrator for *House Flippers.*

"Wow," he says, looking around. "You've made some progress in here," he says. Then he points at the wall that I beat up this morning. "Are you taking this out?"

"Yes. I want to open it up into the kitchen...like a great room."

"That's a good idea. I'd like to do that too. But aren't you worried about this being a—what do you call it—a supporting wall?"

"You mean a load-bearing wall? Actually, it is. We're going to support the house with beams." I hand him the cookie plate. "Sorry. I would've washed the plate..." I wave to the barren kitchen. "But no dishwasher."

"No kitchen," he points out.

"Yes. New cabinets and appliances are coming soon."

"Well, anyway, I hope that broken pipe isn't too serious."

"It'll be okay," I say, mostly to assure myself.

"I'm interested to see how the house looks when it's done."

"Come to our open house," I offer. "Hopefully in about three weeks..."

"That soon?"

I sort of laugh as I walk him to the door. "That's the plan, but it seems more like the impossible dream right now."

"Well, good luck."

"Thanks for helping me locate that shutoff."

"No problem. I'm sure we'll be running to you for some remodeling advice before long."

I decide not to tell him that I won't be around here by then. At least I hope not. But on the other hand, it's kind of fun imagining what it would be like to live in a neighborhood like this, getting to know your neighbors, sharing cups of coffee, helping them fix up their houses. Maybe someday.

It's time to go back to Dad's now. And I'll admit I'm feeling like a yo-yo. The possibility that I'd be caring for Dad *and* working on the house never crossed my mind when I decided to do this flip. Of course, I should simply be thankful that Dad's okay. Still, taking care of him requires time…and time seems to be getting scarcer and scarcer.

Since I won't be returning to the house because of the pipe incident, I bring Riley with me. After fixing Dad dinner and cleaning up, I take Riley back to the apartment. I can tell he's not too pleased with this arrangement. But I promise him that it'll only be for a few days. "Just until we have water and electricity again." I try not to beat myself up too much. I did what I thought was smart, and everyone makes mistakes, right? I decide the least I can do is make use of the evening by heading to Lowe's to pick up a few things for tomorrow.

On my way to Lowe's, I'm thinking about Noah. I don't want to be thinking about him, but the fact is I have been missing him a lot this weekend. And I've been thinking about him more than I want to admit. Then I remember that horrible scene where I blasted his daughter with mud. That's when I decide I must attempt to make it up to her. So I stop by Old Navy, where I pick up an adorable pair of overalls, a couple of T-shirts, and some flip-flops for her. Now if she ever comes to my house again, which I suppose is unlikely, she will at least have some "work" clothes to wear so we can protect her expensive designer clothes from further destruction. I also pick up a few things for myself. Work-type clothes, but with a little bit of style. And a new pair of lime green flip-flops that are on sale. Okay, it's not exactly haute couture, but for work clothes…I think even Holly might approve.

Then I go to Lowe's and do some serious shopping, picking out plumbing fixtures and faucets and even some carpeting for the one bedroom with the bad wood floor, and I arrange to have it all delivered and installed by the end of the week. Then I go home to my stuffy little apartment and am relieved to sleep in my own bed.

The next morning Riley wakes me up bright and early. It's as if he knows that we need to get out of here and over to the house. Or maybe his canine sense informed him that I want to beat Noah there this morning. I know I have some explaining to do about the lack of electricity and water, and I'm not looking forward to it.

Unfortunately, I discover that I'll need to get up a lot earlier to beat Noah to work in the morning. His truck is already there. Feeling sheepish and in need of caffeine, I attempt to sneak into the house, but Riley races straight to where Noah is surveying the damage in the bathroom and gives me away.

"Looks like someone had fun this weekend," Noah says as he emerges with a curious look.

"Yes. I sort of broke a pipe."

"And the electricity?"

I jerk my thumb over my shoulder toward the living room. "I hit some wiring on that wall. Dad told me to shut the electricity off."

"How is Hank?"

"Better every day." Then I frown. "Well, except that he feels useless."

"Useless?"

"He said I should put him on an iceberg."

Noah laughs. "I'm sure it's normal to feel like that after such a serious surgery. Maybe we can do something to make him feel useful."

"What?"

"Oh, you know, just involve him more. Let him keep track of the subcontractors. Like when are the roofers—"

"Tomorrow."

"Then you can ask him to track down a plumber and electrician."

"Because of me?"

"Because you'll *need* them soon. You need an electrician to install lights and move some of the wiring and a plumber to move some pipes and put in the plumbing fixtures."

"What about the things I messed up? Do we need them to come out today?"

"I can temporarily fix that pipe. And show me the wiring. Maybe I can do something about that too."

"Good," I say, "because I'd really like to make some coffee."

Noah takes a look at the damaged wiring and decides it can be temporarily fixed as well. "But call Hank and ask him to get the pros lined up to come in here and do these things right."

Before long, Noah, true to his word, has both the water and electricity running, and feeling like I just won the lottery, I am making a pot of fresh, hot coffee. I take my coffee and a camp chair out to the back deck to sit in the dappled sun and watch Riley happily romping in the backyard like he just won the doggy lottery.

Then when Noah comes out, toting a camp chair and a cup of coffee, and asks if he can join me, I find myself thinking, *This is good. This is really, really good.*

# 23

I spend most of Monday morning running from tile stores to home improvement stores to lighting stores and finally to my dad's to check on him and fix him lunch. Afterward, as I'm cleaning the kitchen, I begin to list things he can do to help me with the house. He sits at the kitchen table and writes it all down on a yellow legal pad. Mostly the list is just the subcontractors he can call, but it also includes finding a good deal on hardwood flooring since he "knows people," and we need matching hardwood so that the kitchen and dining areas can seamlessly connect to the living room in my new open floor plan. As I'm getting ready to leave, he seems pleased and already has out his Rolodex and is flipping through it, which makes me think Noah was right. Dad does need something like this to keep him busy.

"And you need to order some turf too," he says as I'm heading for the door.

"I know."

"Have you done it yet?"

"No."

"I'll take care of that too."

"I planned on it going in right before the open house," I say.

"Why?"

I shrug. "Why not?" The truth is, that's how I've seen it done on *House Flippers.* They always seem to wait until the last minute to put in the yard, and it's always a dramatic improvement just in the nick of time. I guess I just figured that's how it's done.

Dad frowns. "I can think of lots of reasons."

"Like?"

"Like the lawn needs time to establish. It keeps the dust and dirt down when you're doing the exterior painting. It's a—"

"Fine, fine," I say impatiently. "Go ahead and order it then."

"Not if you don't—"

"No, really," I say more gently. "It's fine. I'm sure you're right."

"But it's your house, sweetie. I don't want to—"

"Really, Dad, it's okay. I guess I'm just a little overwhelmed. Did you know that our time is more than half gone? And it seems there's still so much to do…"

"Sometimes it just looks like that, Gretchen. Sort of like being darkest before the dawn."

"I hope you're right."

He grins now. "Of course I'm right. I'm your dad."

I get back to the house just in time to see a white Mercedes convertible pull up. Fortunately I beat her into the driveway, and she parks along the street. I'm tempted to dart into the house without speaking to Camille since she's obviously not here to see me, but then I realize that Noah's truck is gone.

"Where's Noah?" she demands as she clicks up the driveway in what I swear must be five-inch heels, making her look like an Amazon. Okay, a gorgeous Amazon.

"I don't know," I admit.

"I thought he was working for you."

"He is." I force a smile, trying to be nice for Kirsten's sake. "And he was here when I left this morning. My guess is he's picking something up."

"Well, I need to leave Kirsten with him today." She glances over her shoulder to where Kirsten, once again dressed in an adorable outfit, is standing near the car as if she's afraid to make a move.

I consider this. It would be very easy to say "Too bad, tough luck." But I can see that Kirsten is the one caught in the middle here. And then I remember the work duds I got her at Old Navy and think it might be fun to have her here. Also I know Riley would love someone to play with. "Why don't you just leave her with me?" I suggest in what I think is a cheerful tone.

Now Camille grimaces, folding her thin, tan arms across her front as she looks down on me like she thinks I might be some degenerate loser lady who enjoys hosing down children with power washers before she rolls them in the mud. "I, uh, I don't know… Do you think Noah will be back soon?"

"I'm sure he'll be back soon," I say, sounding more patient than I feel. "Don't worry; Kirsten will be fine. If it makes you feel better, I'm a kindergarten teacher, so I'm technically licensed to hang out with young children."

She looks surprised. "*You're* a teacher?"

I nod. "I have been for eight years."

"Well, okay then…" She turns to Kirsten. "Come on; it's all right. Greta is going to baby-sit you until Daddy gets here."

Kirsten chimes in, "It's Gretchen, Mom, not Greta."

I want to hug her, but I simply stand straighter and wait.

"Sorry." Camille tosses a long strand of glistening blond hair over her shoulder in an impatient way. "*Gretchen* is going to baby-sit you, Kirsten." Then she kneels, looking her daughter in the eyes as if she thinks Kirsten is uneasy with this. "You'll be okay, Kirsten," she says in a babyish way, like Kirsten is two and a half. "Gretchen is a kindergarten teacher."

"I know," says Kirsten in her wonderfully no-nonsense voice.

"Well, good then." Camille stands up and smiles down on me. "Perfect."

"Do you know when you'll be back?" I call out as Camille clicks back toward her car.

She turns and frowns. "Tell Noah I'll give him a call."

Then Kirsten and I watch as Camille starts her car, waves, and drives away. Fortunately a little slower this time.

"I'll stay out of your way," Kirsten says in a serious tone. "I know you've got a lot of work to do."

I sort of laugh. "You don't need to stay out of my way. In fact, I might put you to work."

"I get to work?" Kirsten's face brightens.

"Do you like to paint?"

"Paint?" Her eyes light up, then suddenly darken as she looks down at her cute yellow and white sundress. "I'm not supposed to get dirty."

"Well, you're in luck because I bought you some work clothes."

"Really?" she looks up eagerly at me. "You got work clothes in my size?"

"I think so. I sort of had to guess, but they should be close. Let's go inside and check them out." I take her to my makeshift bedroom, find the Old Navy bag, and pull out the things I got last night.

"Wow," she says, "these are cool."

"I felt really bad for ruining your other outfit," I explain. "So I thought maybe you could keep a set of work clothes here...you know, in case you dropped in again, like today." I go to the door now. "You can change in here if you want."

Then as she's changing, I hear someone at the front door and go out to find that the refrigerator is being delivered. "Oh yeah," I say, slapping my forehead. "I totally forgot."

"Where do you want it?" asks the guy.

"In the kitchen," I say, like, *Duh.* Then I realize I don't really have a kitchen. But before long, they've set it up in the spot where I think it should go.

"Most people get their appliances delivered *after* the cabinets are in," says the guy as I sign the delivery paperwork.

"Yeah, well, I guess I'm not most people."

"Can I go say hi to Riley now?" asks Kirsten when she emerges, looking adorable in her overalls, T-shirt, and flip-flops.

"Sure," I tell her. "By the way, I like your outfit."

"Me too." She grins now. "Thanks, Gretchen."

I smile as she walks out the door. I transfer drinks and a few cold snacks from the cooler into the new stainless-steel fridge, then unload some stuff from the pickup, and do some sweeping in the house. Finally I am ready to begin painting where Holly and Justin left off on the front of the house.

"It's really okay for me to do this?" asks Kirsten after I've given her a quick painting lesson.

"Sure, why not?"

"What if I make a mess?"

I laugh. "You know, that's just what my best friend, Holly, asked. I'll tell you what I told her. You can't possibly make more of a mess than what's here already. Just do your best, and don't worry about it."

"This is fun," says Kirsten as she swipes some white primer on a board below the window.

"And if you get tired, just stop," I tell her. I don't want to be accused of breaking any child-labor laws. To make sure I don't drip on her, I go to the other end of the house to paint. After a few minutes I hear Kirsten talking to someone and turn to see that the boy from across the street is watching her.

"It's easy," Kirsten is telling him. "You just dip the brush in the paint like this and then go like this." She swishes it across a plank like an old pro.

"Can I do it too?" he asks eagerly.

"I don't know." She frowns at him. "How old are you?"

"Almost seven."

"Well, I'm already seven," she tells him. "What's your name?"

"Cory."

"Hey, Gretchen," she calls. "Can Cory paint your house too?"

I come over and look down at Cory, like I'm doing an inventory. "Well, he looks strong enough."

He stands straighter. "I am."

"But you would need to get your mom's permission. And you'd need to wear painting clothes."

"I can do that," he says eagerly, and I start feeling like Tom Sawyer.

"Tell your mom to come talk to me," I say. "If she's okay with it, I'm okay."

"Cool!" Then he heads back to his house, carefully looking both ways, I observe, before he crosses the street. Then I notice his mom out front, working on her flower beds. She waves, and I wave, and I once again think, *This is nice.*

Before long, both Cory and Kirsten are hard at work. And although there's a lot of dripping going on and it takes them awhile to cover much territory, I think it's better than nothing. Plus, they are having fun, and Kirsten is acting like a regular girl instead of a little dress-up doll.

"You got quite a paint crew going on here," says Noah after he pulls up and comes over to check out my laborers.

"Daddy!" says Kirsten eagerly. "Gretchen said I can help her paint." She holds out her arms to show off her new outfit. "And she got me work clothes."

Noah tosses me a surprised but appreciative look. "And who's this?" he asks, nodding to Cory.

"That's Cory," says Kirsten. "He's almost seven, and he lives in the yellow house across the street. His mom is Jenna, and she said he can work too."

"I'll be seven in July," proclaims Cory. "And I'll be in second grade next year."

"The same as me," points out Kirsten.

"Well, it's nice to meet you, Cory," says Noah. "You two keep up the good work." And they do keep it up for about another half hour, but then they need a break, so they go into the backyard, where Kirsten introduces Cory to Riley. Meanwhile, I continue priming.

I'm intently painting around a bedroom window when it suddenly opens, and Noah sticks his head out. I jump and nearly smack him across the face with my brush.

"Sorry," he says. "Didn't mean to startle you."

"That's okay." I continue painting now.

"I was surprised to find Kirsten here. Sorry I wasn't around when Camille dropped her off."

"You mean you didn't know she was coming?"

"No…and it's not that I mind her being here. I just hope you don't mind. I didn't really plan that Kirsten would be around this much, and I don't want to take advantage of—"

"I've already told you. I *like* Kirsten," I say as I dip the brush again. "I don't mind her being here."

"Okay…I just thought I should check."

I nod as I swipe the brush beneath the windowsill. "Seriously. She can come here any time." He smiles, and I smile back, and then I return to my work. Of course, I'm wondering what that exchange was really about. Did he seriously think I don't like Kirsten? Or that I'm irritated about having her around? Or was he simply being thoughtful? I think I know the answers to my questions. And although those answers make me feel good about Noah, I'm not sure I'm comfortable with that feeling.

My goal is to focus here. I need to get the rest of the house primed today. It'd be helpful to have it done before the roofers get here, which I hope will be tomorrow, like Dad promised. Thinking of Dad makes me check my paint-splattered watch. In a couple of hours, I'll need to head over there. I'll fix us a quick dinner, make small talk, then hurry back here to finish the priming before dark. It almost seems possible.

Being a normal kid, Kirsten gets antsy about midafternoon. Cory's gone home, and she's bored with painting and tired of Riley. I suggest she go inside and take a break. But, of course, there's nothing in there to entertain her. Still, as I paint furiously, racing the clock, I tell myself that's not my problem. As I continue to paint, I also begin to create a mental list of things I might keep here for times like this: picture books and crayons, felt pens, paper, scissors, art supplies—things I already have at home. And maybe some sidewalk chalk to use in the driveway. I also make a mental list of supplies I can bring to make the kitchen more user-friendly. I'll borrow Dad's card table and bring my microwave and get more paperware, like cups, plates, napkins, paper towels. It's amazing how much you can think about while painting. But finally it's time for me to call it quits and go check on Dad. Noah and Kirsten have already left, apparently to drop Kirsten at her mom's in time for dinner.

When I get to Dad's, he happily reports on the contacts he's made while I fix a dinner of broiled salmon filets and a mixed-greens salad. I can tell that it's been good medicine for him to be on the phone today, setting things up and probably having some friendly chats with his old subcontractor buddies.

"Don't plan on doing anything outside tomorrow," he tells me as I slice a tomato, "because the roofing crew will be there early in the morning, and they plan to have the old shingles stripped off by noon. It'll be pretty messy."

"And the new roof?"

"Hopefully by the next day...or maybe Thursday at the latest."

"How about the cabinet guy?" I ask. "Any news from him?"

"I've left two messages asking him for a delivery date."

"That'd be good." I set the salad dressing on the table and look around to see if I forgot anything. Then we sit down, Dad says a blessing, and I give him today's progress report, even telling him about my young paint crew.

"That Kirsten's a pistol."

"She's a sharp little girl."

"But that mother..." He shakes his head with disapproval.

"You've met Camille?"

"She's dropped Kirsten off before when Noah was working with me."

"She's very beautiful," I point out, as if he hadn't noticed.

"Well, looks aren't everything." He dips his sourdough roll into the balsamic vinegar dressing around his salad.

"Mom was beautiful," I say quietly.

He sighs. "She surely was...both inside and out."

"I'm sure there's more to Camille than meets the eye, Dad." Okay, I'm not even sure why I said this. I guess I just want to keep the conversation going.

"You're probably right. But it's hard to see past the veneer sometimes." He smiles. "It's a good thing God can."

"Yes," I agree, "it is."

"As for me, I'll take my women with both inward and outward beauty. Like you and your mom."

"Oh, Dad," I say, "I'm not that kind of a beauty."

He sets his fork on his salad plate with a clink and frowns at me. "What are you saying?"

I shrug. "Just that I'm not a beauty...not like Mom."

He looks at me like I've lost my senses. "You don't look like your mother, but you are most certainly a beauty, Gretchen."

"Well, thanks, Dad. I wasn't really fishing for compliments." I don't remind him that all parents think their children are beautiful.

I try not to be too obvious about being in a rush as I clean up the kitchen, but finally I admit that I want to finish priming the house before the roofers come.

"That's good thinking, Gretchen Girl." Dad slaps me on the back. "You get back over there and get 'er done." So that's just what I do. But as it's getting dark and I'm finishing the last bit of priming with the help of the builder's light I've situated out on the back deck, with Riley lying nearby and watching me curiously, I think about what Dad said tonight. I think about how he likes his women beautiful on the inside and the outside, and I realize that's what I want to be too. I just don't know if it's even possible.

# 24

This, the fourth week of renovating, is a killer. Unfortunately, I don't think the next two weeks will be any better. But slowly, slowly, things are getting done. By Thursday the roofers have ripped off the old roof and are now putting on the new one. Noah has removed the wall in the living room, opening up that whole area into one big great room, which everyone thinks is a huge improvement. Dad has located wood flooring for a good price, and both the plumber and electrician are scheduled to come next week. Still no word from our mysterious cabinetmaker.

Today, after taking a tile-laying workshop at the flooring store, I am beginning to install twelve-inch squares of travertine in what will be the master-suite bathroom. Fortunately, Noah, who knows the basics of plumbing, finished putting in the new doorway and closing up the old one, as well as removing the old toilet. Since I've decided on a pedestal sink, the kind with a wooden base that looks very contemporary but classic, I will be laying the tile from wall to wall and right up to the tub, which I have scheduled to be refinished a week from now. Then I will run the same travertine tiles up the sides of the freshly refinished white tub, which I think will be quite handsome. I've also picked out new bronze plumbing fixtures and bathroom accessories, also in a classic contemporary style. The final effect should be very nice. Already, with only a dozen tiles laid, I am happy with how things are looking.

"Gretchen!" It's Cory, and he sounds frantic. "Come here! Hurry!"

I drop my trowel in the adhesive bucket and leap to my feet to see what's wrong. Just like every other day this week, Kirsten is here today, and the last time I looked, she and Cory were doing chalk art on the sidewalk. My heart pounds furiously as I imagine Kirsten hit by a car that has driven recklessly up over the curb. But when I find Kirsten and Cory, she's sitting on the front stoop with her foot in her lap.

"She stepped on a nail!" Cory tells me as he places one hand on her shoulder.

"Where's your dad?" I ask as I sit down beside her to see that the nail has gone through her Old Navy rubber flip-flop and into her foot. It looks like a roofing nail, so hopefully it's not too long. Still I know it hurts, and she has tears coming down her cheeks right now.

"He went to get us some lunch," she explains.

"Oh yeah," I say, remembering that he mentioned this while I was putting down tile. But I was so absorbed I barely registered it.

"Do you want me to pull it out?" I ask, unsure whether this is the best remedy or not.

"I don't know," she cries. "Will it hurt?"

"Probably," I admit, wondering if it also might cause it to bleed more.

"You'll probably need to go to the doctor," I say. "I'm sure you've had a tetanus shot, right?"

"What's that?" asks Kirsten.

"Never mind," I tell her as I pull my cell phone out of my overalls pocket and dial Noah's number.

"Hey," he says.

I quickly explain the situation, and he tells me that he ran across town to pick up the hardwood flooring Dad located. "I'll be right there," he says without hesitation.

"No no. I'll take her to the doctor. She'll be fine, and I don't want to make you come all the way back here after driving across town."

"Are you sure?"

"Of course. Do you know if she's had a DPT shot?"

"What's that?"

"Tetanus," I explain. "It's required for school kids."

"In that case, she must've had it."

Now Kirsten is crying harder. I slip an arm around her shoulders and ask Noah where her doctor's office is located and if he can call ahead and say that we're coming. Then I hang up, and as I carry Kirsten to the pickup, I tell Cory that she needs to go to the doctor and that we'll see him later. I buckle her up in the front seat and prop her wounded foot on a cooler, reassuring her that she's going to be just fine. I even pause to wrap yet another soft cotton, multipurpose drop cloth around her, lest she go into shock, which I think is unlikely. I continue to chatter cheerfully, telling her about the time I stepped on a nail barefoot. I'm trying to conceal my own anxiety as I drive her to the doctor's office, which is located at the opposite end of town from where Noah is picking up wood. Once we're in the examining room, I call him.

"I really appreciate this," he says. "Do you need me to come?"

"No," I explain, "the doctor is seeing her right now, and it doesn't look serious."

"What about Hank?" he asks. "Don't you usually check on him around now?"

"Oh yeah, I totally forgot about his lunch."

"How about if I take him something?"

"He'd love that."

"And I know, low cholesterol, low fat."

"You got it. And I'll get something for Kirsten and me."

"Thanks, Gretchen."

And when he says my name, I hear such warmth in his voice that my voice cracks ever so slightly. "No problem."

"I think she's going to be fine," proclaims the doctor as the nurse bandages Kirsten's foot. "Doesn't appear to have any nerve or muscle damage. Just keep her off it for a day or two or until it doesn't hurt. Keep the wound clean, a little Neosporin and bandage. No swimming for a few days, and a baby aspirin if she needs it."

As we're driving home, I commend Kirsten on her bravery and ask her what she'd like for lunch.

"Can I have a corn dog?" she asks timidly.

I laugh. "You like corn dogs?"

She nods, looking slightly embarrassed, like it's rather uncouth to like corn dogs.

"Well, so do I, and I happen to know of a little kiosk that has the absolute best ones around."

"Really? Do you like corn dogs too?"

"I do."

"Cool."

Within minutes we're sitting outside the Corny Canine kiosk at a slightly grubby picnic table, with Kirsten's foot propped up on the bench, still wearing our paint-splotched overalls and eating our corn dogs with mustard and drinking root beer. Suddenly Kirsten tells me that she wishes she could live with her dad all the time. And since she's opened this door, I decide to walk on through.

"I'm curious about something," I say to her.

"What?"

"Well, I know you were supposed to spend the summer with your dad, but then your mom changed her mind, and yet it seems like you spend most of your time with him anyway. Why do you suppose that is?"

"Mom thinks I'll drown."

I blink. "You'll drown?"

"Because Dad's house is on the beach, and Mom thinks I'll run out there like a little baby and drown in the ocean."

"Oh..."

"And his house is really small too," adds Kirsten. "I think it's really cool, but Mom says it's not big enough for him to have me. She says he needs to get rid of it and grow up."

I laugh. "Grow up?"

"Yeah. Mom says that Dad's a little boy. But I love him. I think he's a cool dad."

"He is a cool dad," I agree. "You're lucky."

"Are you my dad's girlfriend?" asks Kristen, and it's all I can do not to blast root beer straight out my nostrils.

"No-no," I sputter.

"Why?"

I frown at her. "Well, because I'm just not. Why do you ask?"

"Because it would be okay with me...I mean, if you were."

I want to ask her whether or not her dad has other girlfriends but feel this would be out of line. "Well, thank you," I tell her. "I feel honored that you'd think that."

She just nods, then ceremoniously dips her corn dog into the little mustard cup and takes a big bite. Okay, I really, really hate to admit it, but this is a girl after my own heart.

When we get back to the house, I'm relieved to see that the roofing crew has arrived and is hard at work. I was starting to get worried that with my house-flipping luck the rain predicted for the weekend might come before the shingles were on. Of course, Riley's not too sure about this intrusion and is running back and forth in the backyard and barking like a mad dog.

I help Kirsten into the house, and while she's using the bathroom that had been completely gutted but that Noah just set the toilet into yesterday, I let my crazy dog inside, reassuring him the workers are here to fix and not destroy. Even so, he's running from room to room, acting like we're under siege and he's the only protection we have. Then I get Kirsten set up in my makeshift bedroom with a bag of kids' books I brought over just in case she needed some quiet time.

"You'd make a good mom, Gretchen," she tells me after I set a water bottle nearby, just in case she gets thirsty.

I hardly know what to say at this point; the girlfriend comment was shocker enough. "Well, umm, thanks, Kirsten. I'm sure you're a very good daughter."

She nods somberly, as if she's carefully considering this. "Yes, I am."

"I'll be working in the bathroom, okay? Putting down tiles. Just call if you need anything."

But as I work, all I hear are the sounds of power tools and hammers banging and occasional yells from the roofing crew. When I peek in on Kirsten, she is fast asleep with Riley right next to her. Without disturbing them, although that seems doubtful in light of the noise, I slip out my camera from the hall closet and snap a couple of pictures. It's not the first time I've caught these two on film. I've also got what I hope will be some adorable shots of them in the back of Noah's pickup and playing ball in the backyard as well as some of Kirsten and Cory painting on the house. My plan is to get these photos printed in black and white and enlarged. Then I'll mat and frame them to use for decoration when it's time for the open house.

I go back to work in the bathroom and am almost done with the floor when my cell phone rings. Thinking it might be Noah checking on his daughter, I quickly answer it, but it's Holly.

"Hey, I'm just calling to remind you that Saturday is Tina's wedding." She chuckles. "Not that you'd forget."

"Oh, Holly..." I sigh. "Do you think Tina would even notice if I didn't show?"

"I'd notice! And my parents would notice. Please don't do that, Gretch."

"It's just that—"

"I know, I know...you have a ton of work to do. But I already have the answer for that. Last night Justin told our Bible study group about your little project, and they're all willing to give you the entire day next Saturday. So I figure you should be able to give up a few hours in exchange for like twenty slaves at your service next week."

"Twenty?"

"That's right. Maybe more."

I'm imagining a landscaping party, a painting party, and who knows what other kind of party. "I can provide pizza and drinks," I offer, thinking of the invaluable help they could provide.

"So you'll be there Saturday, right?"

"I guess."

"Good."

Of course I feel totally bummed when I hang up. I'd managed to blank Tina's wedding out of my head, and maybe I actually thought I could convince Holly I'd completely forgotten. I guess not.

I continue to lay the tile, but instead of enjoying the work and imagining how great this bathroom is going to look in a couple of weeks, all I can think about is how lame I will look as the pathetic single girl at Tina's wedding. And it doesn't help that there's a slight chance Collin, a friend of Tina's fiancé, might be there. With his wife, Selena, of course.

"I just checked on our patient," says Noah.

I look up from where I'm crouched in the bathtub laying the last several pieces of travertine. "Hi! How is she?"

"Happily reading *Curious George*."

I nod. "Oh, good. She was asleep a little while ago."

"Glad to hear she's resting her foot. Hey, you're doing a great job. But you've kind of worked yourself into a corner, don't you think?"

"Yes…" I look at how I've trapped myself in the tub. "I sort of got distracted and forgot my original plan to work my way out the door."

"I'm sorry," he says. "That's my fault. I shouldn't have left

Kirsten here, but she and Cory were having such a good time with their sidewalk art, and I—"

"No no," I say quickly. "That's not why I got bummed. I didn't mind taking Kirsten to the doctor, and we had lunch. Really, that didn't take as much time as it does to check on Dad."

"He's fine, by the way. And he's busily getting your ducks in a row."

"That's good."

"So why are you bummed?" asks Noah as he kneels in the doorway, bringing himself down to my level.

"Oh, it's nothing. Just something stupid." I focus my attention on the last piece of travertine as I apply the adhesive.

"What?" he persists.

I roll my eyes. "My best friend just called to remind me to come to her sister's wedding on Saturday, and I wish there was some way to get out of it."

"Why?"

"Why?" I lean my head back and moan. "Well, you're not a single woman, so you probably wouldn't get why. Let's just say that the night won't end without an older woman saying to me, 'And now, dear, when are we coming to your wedding?' And I can guarantee I'll be stuck sitting alone at a table set for couples with an empty chair next to me that screams, 'She's single!' And to top off the evening, I'll likely run into an ex, who is now happily married, maybe even expecting his first baby. Oh, let me count the reasons why." I have just said way too much; I can tell by the stunned look on his face.

"Why don't you just take a date?" he recovers.

"Why?" I feel myself about to jump into my little why routine again, and I definitely don't want to go there. Instead, I press the tile to the floor, give it a little twist, then let out a sigh. "I don't know."

"Why don't you take me?"

I look up at him. "What?"

"Why not? Wouldn't I pass for a date?"

I nod with wide eyes. "You'd really do that? For me?"

"Of course."

Okay, I have the distinct impression he feels guilty for leaving me with Kirsten and that whole nail thing, but if this is a payback, I think I'm ready to cash in. "Sure," I tell him a little too eagerly. "If that's a genuine offer, I'll take it. I mean, it'd be a whole lot easier doing this with a fake date than by myself."

"A fake date?" His brow creases. "Does that make me a gigolo?"

"I think I'd have to pay a gigolo." I chuckle. "Do you want me to pay you?"

He laughs. "Not with money."

Okay, I'm not even going to ask him what that's supposed to mean as I stand up and give my legs a stretch. I smile shyly, then change the subject. "So how do I get out of here? Or maybe you could bring me a pillow, and I'll just take a nap."

"Hang on," he tells me. Then he disappears and returns with a two-by-eight, which he suspends like a diagonal bridge from the edge of the tub to the bedroom. He steadies it with his foot, and I gingerly climb on board.

"I feel like I'm walking the plank," I say as I hold my arms out for balance.

As I get closer, he reaches out and takes my hand, and I relax a little. But then I look at his face and see that he's gazing intently into my eyes, and I suddenly feel awkward and self-conscious—like I'm about to lose my balance and tumble gracelessly, ruining my beautiful but still wet tile work. He has clearly picked up on my anxiety and says, "It's okay, Gretchen. I've got you." And then I'm on solid ground, and he's still holding my hand.

"Thanks," I mutter, turning away. "Umm, I'm going to check on the roofers."

For the rest of the afternoon, I keep a safe distance from Noah. Not only that, but I have second thoughts about accepting his offer to escort me to Tina's wedding. Why did I let myself fall into that one? What happened to my self-preservation plan?

Finally, I check one last time on Kirsten. She and Cory are in the living room with art materials spread all about the floor.

"Look what I made for you," she says, holding up a colorful collage-type picture in shades of red, orange, and yellow.

"That's beautiful," I tell her. "I'll frame it and hang it in the dining room."

"Really?"

"Of course!" I promise as I look at it more closely, imagining it with a white mat and dark frame, sort of like modern art. "The colors in it are perfect. I love it. Now you just need to sign your name down here." I pick up a black felt pen. "Use this."

"Cool," says Cory as she carefully writes her name on it. "You're like a real artist now, Kirsten."

"Maybe your mom will frame yours too," says Kirsten, "and hang it in your dining room."

"Nah," he says. "She already has a bunch of her fancy pictures in there. She always hangs my stuff on the refrigerator."

"I have to go," I tell Kirsten. "Can you let your dad know I had to leave early to pick up some lights and ask him to lock up for me?" I notice Riley's still in the house. "And if the roofers are done, can you guys put Riley outside?"

"And give him food and water?" suggests Kirsten.

I grin at her. "You know the routine. But since you need to stay off your foot, I'll take care of that, okay?"

"Okay."

"See you."

"I'll be here tomorrow too," she calls cheerfully.

I'm not so sure she'll be coming tomorrow. For all I know Camille might have a fit when she sees that Kirsten's been injured. Maybe she'll want to sue me. Although I'll leave that to Noah to explain and sort out. Still, I have to wonder about Camille. Why does she give Noah such a bad time about custody, refusing to let Kirsten spend the summer with him, and yet she's left her with him almost every single day since school let out? *Baggage,* I say to myself as I start the pickup. Major baggage...and something I don't need any more of in my life. But something about this "line" I've drawn is starting to wear thin. And my little game of denial—pretending I don't have feelings for a certain someone—is getting old.

# 25

Betty's worried about you," Dad tells me at dinnertime.

"About me?" I look up as I pass him the soy sauce. Tonight it's stir-fry and rice, and although I told him to go easy on it, I realize Dad cannot eat that many vegetables without some soy sauce.

"Yes, she thinks you're working yourself to death."

I feign a laugh...although Betty's not too far from the truth. But I would never admit that to Dad.

"Really, she said she wants you to take a break tomorrow."

"A break?" I look at Dad like he's nuts. "How am I supposed to take a break?"

"She booked you an afternoon at Amari."

"Amari? That new day spa at the resort?"

"That's the one."

I consider this. "That does sound good, but she doesn't need to do that, Dad."

"She wants to."

Then I turn the subject to the house. I tell him about my tile project and how I plan to get the tub refinished.

"How about the other bath?" he asks as he takes a second helping of stir-fry.

"I'm going to do just a shower in there. It was pretty crowded with that bathtub, and most people don't use bathtubs that much anyway."

"You're going to do the tile work for the whole shower stall yourself?" Dad looks skeptical.

"Like I said, I took the workshop. If you follow the directions, it's not that hard."

"How about cutting? You don't have a tile saw, do you?"

"The tile store does the cutting. I just mark the tiles and take them in, and the next day they're ready to lay."

Dad nods with a look of approval. "Well, that sounds good. I can't wait to see it."

"Maybe next week," I tell him. "The doctor said you could get out after a week of rest at home."

"That sounds good to me. I thought my condo unit was a castle when I first got home from the hospital, but now it's starting to feel like a prison cell."

So I change the subject back to the house and what he can do, by phone, to help. Then he actually helps me clear the table. "It's good for me to move around," he assures me. "The physical therapist said so during my session today." Then he shows me the list of exercises she gave him to do.

"You'll be playing golf before long," I tell him.

"It won't be too soon for me."

I feel sorry for my dad as I leave. I know it must be hard to be cooped up. Still, it's just a matter of time. Time, time, time…for some it's like a turtle race, for others it's a wild horse that can never be caught.

The next day, Friday, I am moving as fast as I can. My goal, after grouting the bathroom floor, is to remove the popcorn from the ceiling in the great room and retexture it since Noah wants to start laying the hardwood floor in the kitchen and dining room this afternoon. Our hope is that the kitchen cabinets will be here by early next week, and it would be nice to have this mess out of the way before they arrive. By noon I at least have the kitchen ceiling scraped clean and textured.

"You look like a mud monster," says Kirsten when she and Cory see me dragging the mucky plastic drop cloth out to the Dumpster.

I hold up my hands and walk toward them like Frankenstein, and they scream in mock horror. Then I peel off the grungy coveralls and remove my eyewear and clean up as best I can with the hose. No way am I going to clean up in my freshly grouted bathroom before the grout is sealed. But I must still look pretty bad when I'm getting ready to go to Dad's, because Jenna gives me a funny look as she comes over to call Cory home for lunch.

"Remodeling is a messy business," I tell her as I head for the pickup. She smiles warmly and walks away, Cory in tow. I take a peek at myself in the visor mirror and laugh. "I do look like the mud monster," I say as I start the engine.

I'm barely in the door at Dad's house when he announces that I need to get going.

"Go where?" I demand.

"Your appointment."

"What appointment?"

"I've been calling your cell phone." He hands me a piece of paper with the word *Amari,* a phone number and address, and one o'clock written on it. "Just get going. You should get there in time."

"I can't go to Amari like this," I say.

"Betty has already scheduled it, Gretchen. She prepaid for the whole package. You said you'd go, and you... Just go, Gretchen. This is Betty's way of showing she cares for you. Don't spoil it, sweetie."

"But what about your lunch?"

"I'm warming some soup now."

"Okay...I guess I'll see you at dinnertime?"

He smiles. "Yes. See you then. Just get going."

It's a couple of minutes past one when I walk into the lobby of a very swanky spa where everything is Asian style and peaceful and, I'm thinking, very Zen. The fountain, the music, the décor—all seem designed for relaxation.

"Can I help you?" asks the receptionist, an impeccably groomed woman dressed in black. I can tell by her face that she thinks I must be lost.

"I'm sorry," I begin, "but a friend, Betty Schwartz, called—"

"Oh, you must be Gretchen." The woman smiles. "Betty is one of our favorite customers. She called from Paris to make your appointment. Have you been to Amari before?"

"No, and I was working on a remodel and didn't have time to—"

"Don't worry," she says calmly. "All you need to do now is complete this paperwork." She slides a clipboard and pen toward me, and I hurriedly fill out a form that makes me feel like I'm at the doctor's office.

"There," I say, sliding it back.

"Now, let us take care of you. Betty has booked you for a European facial and a mani/pedi," she informs me. "You're going to feel like a queen."

"That sounds great." And I must admit, it really does sound great.

Another woman dressed in black greets me. "I'm Mara," she says. "I will take you back."

Mara leads me to a dressing room and shows me to a wooden locker bay, handing me a key. She explains that I'm to undress, shower, and put on the robe she hands me. "Slippers are there." She points to a shelf that's filled with varying sizes of black rubber sandals. "And towels are here."

"I'm supposed to shower?" I repeat, feeling like an idiot.

She looks at me like she can't believe I'd even question this, then simply nods. "After that, you may relax in the soaking tub while you wait for Fiona." She points to a door labeled "hot tub," then leaves.

There's no one else in the dressing room, but I still disrobe quickly, shoving my messy work clothes and things into the locker. The key is on an elastic band which I assume is to put on my wrist. And I have to admit that the shower is very nice and equipped with a luxurious selection of shower gels, shampoos, and conditioners—many that I take advantage of so that I emerge feeling almost like a new woman. Maybe this spa thing is better than I thought. I pour myself a glass of lemon-infused water and take a long, cool sip as I look at the door to the soaking tub. Come on, I urge myself, you can do this.

I go into the soaking-tub room and see that no one is there. I've heard that it's no big deal for complete strangers to sit naked in a hot tub together in Japan, and even though I'm certain this area is only for women, I'm still not too sure about this concept. And yet the bubbling water looks tempting, and the atmosphere in here with dimmed lights and a massive rock fountain is very inviting. Finally I decide why not, and standing near the entrance to the large tub, which is more like a small swimming pool, I quickly peel off my robe and plunge down the stone steps into the water.

*Aah...this is heavenly.* The very warm water, which is supposed to contain minerals, feels like silk against my skin, and I think I could get used to this. I lean back and allow the jet to massage my sore neck and shoulders. Then I hear the sound of female voices and suddenly am not so sure I can do this. I'm about to make a leap for my robe, but it's too late. Three women in white robes identical to mine are coming into the room. I go back to a corner where I won't have to look at them as they remove their robes. It's one thing to be naked in front of strangers, but something else altogether to have to *see* them.

But I'm surprised they're taking so long to get in as they talk and joke and pour themselves glasses of water. Finally I peek up and see that these women are not naked. They're all wearing swimsuits. Okay, pretty skimpy suits but not as skimpy as my birthday suit. And then, as they're getting into the pool, I realize with gut-wrenching horror that one of these women is actually Camille! I consider submerging but know I can't hold my breath that long.

The three women seem oblivious to me, and I'm hoping that maybe they will ignore me completely, and I'll just sit here, even if I shrivel to a prune, until they leave. But after a few minutes, one of the women speaks to me.

"I'm sorry," she says to me. "Are we talking too much? I know we're supposed to use spa voices."

"It's okay," I say woodenly.

"Greta?" says Camille with surprise.

"Gretchen," I answer.

"What are you doing here?"

"The same as you, I suppose…" I glance away as Camille explains to her friends who I am in a Camille-like, rather unflattering way.

"Are you naked?" asks one of the women.

I cross my hands over my chest now and just nod. "I didn't know you were supposed to—"

"No way," says Camille. "You came in here naked?"

Now they're all laughing, and Camille points to a sign by the door that says swimsuits are required.

I feel my face turning hot, and I don't know what to say…or what to do.

"Don't you know this is coed?" says Camille.

"Coed?" I repeat in a high, strained voice. "I came through the women's dressing room and—"

"And that's the men's dressing room." She points to a door on the opposite end. "This is a coed spa."

The harder they try to subdue their laughter, the more they crack up. They are laughing so hard that I expect the management to show up and shush them, but I don't know what to do.

"Do you want to get out?" asks one of Camille's friends. "I can stand guard for you if you want." Bless her.

I nod silently as I make my way toward the stone steps, staying low in the water and as far as possible from these three equally gorgeous women—who could easily be posing for a *Sports Illustrated* swimsuit edition if they were on a beach. I wait as the dark-skinned woman gets out and positions herself in front of the men's dressing-room door, and I try not to stare at her perfect proportions and long sleek legs. The other two friends are laughing as I take a deep breath and emerge, feeling about as graceful as a beached whale, and make a leap for my robe, then struggle to slip it on over my soaking wet, naked body. I mutter a humiliated "thank you" as I make a beeline for the women's dressing-room door.

"Oh, there you are," says Mara. "Are you ready for your treatment?"

I want to scream, "No, let me outta here!" But I don't. She takes me to a private room where a nice woman named Fiona gives me a relaxing European facial, which also includes a neck and shoulder massage. This is followed by a pedicure and manicure, and I feel so pampered I could almost forget about that embarrassing hot-tub episode. Almost. Unfortunately, I feel certain that Camille will repeat the humiliating story to Noah and probably Kirsten as well. And I cannot, for the life of me, imagine explaining how it was that I came to be naked in a coed soaking tub where a sign clearly stated that swimsuits were required.

To my relief, Noah and Kirsten are gone when I return to the house. Of course, they should be gone since it's past seven and I've already had an early dinner with Dad. But I discover that Noah has left me a little note asking me to call him regarding tomorrow's "date" for Tina's wedding. Almost hoping that Camille has told him about my streaking at the spa and that he wants to cancel, I brace myself and call.

"I just wanted to find out what time I should pick you up," he says. "And where."

"I thought maybe you changed your mind," I say uncomfortably.

"No, why would I do that?"

I clear my throat. "I thought perhaps Camille mentioned something to you..."

He laughs now. "About the spa?"

"She told you?"

He laughs even louder, and I want to dig a big hole and jump in. The only reason I can even carry on this conversation is because it's not face to face. "I'm sorry," he says, "but you have to admit it's pretty funny."

"What did she tell you anyway?"

"Just that it must've been your first time at a spa and that you were confused and thought the soaking tub was for women only and decided to go skinny-dipping."

So I quickly explain how Betty set the whole thing up, how I was caught off guard and thought I was being brave, and that I've never been so embarrassed in my whole life. "Well, at least not since junior high," I admit. "But don't ask me about that."

"Hey, I don't blame you for going in," he says. "I'd have done the same thing myself under similar circumstances."

"Really?"

"Oh yeah. I go skinny-dipping in the ocean occasionally. Only at night. And only by myself."

"Seriously?"

"Don't tell anyone."

"Well…"

"So I'm still on for tomorrow, Gretchen. Just tell me when and where, and, oh yeah, is this a formal wedding or maybe something more beachy?"

I roll my eyes as I remember Holly saying it is a very formal wedding. "I wish it were beachy, but unfortunately it's formal."

"No problem."

"It's at four with a dinner following. I guess you should pick me up at the apartment, probably around three fifteen…so we can get there in time?"

"It's a date— I mean, it's a deal."

"I assume you're not working tomorrow then."

"No, I have Kirsten for the weekend, and I—"

"I'm sorry. I didn't mean to take time from your weekend—"

"It's okay. She's going to spend the evening with my mom."

So we agree on the details, and I hang up and realize this means I need to call Holly about my RSVP. I manage to catch her between the wedding rehearsal and the rehearsal dinner, and she's pleased as punch that I'm bringing a date. "No problem," she assures me. "I'll take care of it. By the way, what are you wearing?" I admit that I don't know, and she reminds me that it's formal…like I didn't know that.

I tell her not to worry and good-bye, then I close my phone and just stand in the partially torn-up "great" room of the flip house. I begin wondering how on earth I'm going to finish this stupid thing.

But then something hits me, and suddenly I know what I need to do. There's a very insecure part of me that would rather stay by myself in this house, put on my overalls, and hide out here, working my fingers to the bone. And I absolutely know that part of me would like to forget all about Tina's wedding. But I know that's not going to happen. And I know that kind of thinking is wrong.

It's as if something inside me has reared its head and said, "Enough!" I'm going to handle this differently. I'm going to handle my life differently. I'm not even sure why or how. Only that I will. With God's help, I will.

I look down at my freshly manicured nails and realize that working on my house, either tonight or tomorrow, will ruin both my manicure and pedicure And, okay, it's not just about the nails. It's something much, much deeper. I think about what Noah said—that being a workaholic means not trusting God. I also remember what Dad said today about Betty being worried that I was working myself to death. I have no doubt anymore that I am out of balance. I know I have let this house flip become an obsession. I haven't been trusting God with any of it. The truth is, I've been carrying most of the load on my own two shoulders, thinking it's entirely up to me to make this thing work. And it's killing me. And I'm sick and tired of it. In fact, I am just plain tired.

"It's time for a break," I tell Riley. Of course, I doubt he'll think a night spent in our cramped apartment is much of a break. But I'll bring him back here tomorrow, and he can have the run of the place while I'm at the wedding.

As I drive to the apartment, I create a plan. I will spend a comfortable night in my own bed. Sleep in as late as I like. Shower as long as I like. And then I'll take time to do my hair and makeup—carefully, the way Holly has shown me it's supposed to be done.

Then I'll go through my closet, and if I can't find the perfect dress, which is what I expect, I'll drop Riley at the house and head over to Nordstrom and do a little shopping. After that, I'll return to the apartment for some more time of relaxing and primping. Maybe I'll even clean the place up a little, sort some things out. And when Noah picks me up, I will be like Cinderella—magically transformed into a princess. Well, something like that. And, like Cinderella, I will return to my raggedy clothes and housework the next day. But I will go about it with a new attitude. Instead of taking full responsibility for the house flip, I will put it in God's hands, and I will trust him for the outcome.

# 26

"Wow," says Noah when I open the door to my apartment. "You look fantastic."

I smile at him, feeling confident in the aquatic blue-green silk dress that the salesgirl assured me made my eyes look more blue than gray. "Thank you," I tell him. "You look very nice too." And he does look nice in what I know can't be a rented tux, because it is perfectly tailored—it's classic and very handsome. "Want to come in?"

"Sure, if we have time."

"We do."

"You've cleaned up your apartment," he comments.

"Yes. I decided I might as well make the most of it. I mean, if the house gets done and put on the market, I'll have to move back."

"I like your music," he says. "Is that Coltrane?"

"It is." I go to the fridge, where I have a small cheese platter and a bottle of sparkling cider chilling. "I made us snacks," I say as I pull it out, trying not to feel self-conscious.

"That looks delicious," he says. I can feel him looking over my bare shoulder as I set the wooden tray on my recently cleared dining room table, which I even decorated with a vase of fresh flowers. Isn't this how people were meant to live?

I fill a champagne goblet for each of us, then hold up my glass. "I want to make a toast," I tell him.

He grins. "Go for it."

"Here's to your advice and to me finally getting it," I say. "I'm letting go of my house-flipping obsession, and I'm trusting God to carry it for me."

Noah looks genuinely surprised and hugely relieved. And I wonder if he thought I was going to propose marriage or something.

"Here's to trust," he says as he taps his glass against mine. Then we both sit down at the table, and I try to explain my revelation.

"It was weird," I say. "It's like it just hit me. I was standing in the flip house last night after I'd fixed dinner for Dad and everything. I was about to go to work on that ceiling again, and I just stopped. It's like I suddenly realized that I was obsessed and that it was crazy. And I remembered what you said...and some things my dad said...and what the Bible says, and I just decided to offer it all back to God." I sigh and lean back in the chair.

"Good for you."

Then we talk a little more, and I realize we need to go. "It's not that I wouldn't like to be fashionably late," I tell him as we walk to Noah's truck. "But not to Tina's wedding."

"Hey, your dress goes with my pickup," he says as he helps me inside.

I laugh as I smooth the iridescent folds of my tea-length skirt—a length the salesgirl, who I think may have been an angel, said was perfect for my legs and trim ankles. She actually called my ankles "trim." And when I picked out the sandals to go with the dress, I made sure to get strappy ones that showed off my "trim" ankles. But with heels that weren't so high I'd be limping before the reception.

It's about ten minutes before four when we get in line for the wedding. Naturally, as fate or God would have it, Collin and Selena are only one couple away from us. I nudge Noah, then nod at Collin and cross my two forefingers together to form an *X*. He nods like he gets it. And when Collin just happens to look back and spot us, Noah steps a little closer to me, like he's being protective. Although I know he's doing it for Collin's sake, I like it. And I wish we weren't playacting.

The wedding ceremony goes smoothly, and I can't imagine that Tina has anything to complain about...well, except that her matron of honor, Holly, is entirely too beautiful.

I can feel Collin looking at me during the reception dinner, and although I'm over him, I don't think I'm ready to speak to him just yet. "I'm so glad you came with me," I tell Noah as the entrée is being served. "You have no idea how miserable I'd be right now if I was alone."

"I don't know," he says. "I think something in you has changed, Gretchen. I have a feeling you could handle this on your own."

"Really?"

He nods, then smiles. "Still, I'm glad I came."

And then, as if something inside me has been unhinged, I begin to tell Noah my story. Not that there is much to tell, not really. I think the more you keep something inside, the bigger it seems. Even as I tell my story—filling in the dramatic details like how shocked and devastated I was when Collin broke off our engagement, how angry and jealous I got when I discovered it was because he was in love with his old flame, and finally how totally humiliating it was to notify everyone (including vendors who didn't return deposits) that the wedding was off—it all seems to feel kind of flat and anticlimactic.

"I know it seems like I should have fully recovered by now," I finally admit. "But I think it changed who I was—like something in me got broken—and I still don't know how to function completely normally." I think that's the truest thing I've ever said about my situation.

At that, he puts his hand over mine. "I think I know how you feel."

At first I'm not sure what he means. Surely he was never abandoned at the altar. And then, of course, I realize how stupid I am. His pain was much worse than a canceled wedding; he has survived a canceled marriage.

Just then I see Holly making her way toward us, looking like a real princess in her pale pink gown. It's a relief to have her interrupt my true confessions.

"Hi, Noah," she says, shaking his hand.

Noah looks totally blank on her name, so I jump in to save him.

"This is Holly," I tell him. "You met her last year at Dad's annual Christmas party."

He nods. "Yes, of course I recognize you."

Holly looks at me now. "You look fantastic, Gretchen." Then she hugs me and whispers in my ear. "And you are absolutely glowing. Is it love?"

"No," I say with a cool smile but cheeks that are flushing, "I don't think so."

"Well, we need to talk."

"What else is new?"

As the evening progresses and the real champagne, not sparkling cider, flows, I feel even more relaxed, and when Noah asks me to dance, I accept. For some reason I assume that he will be an expert dancer, and I must admit I'm relieved to discover that he, like me, isn't totally graceful on his feet. Somehow we stumble through a few songs.

Finally I feel that we've put in enough time at the wedding. We've congratulated the happy couple, and I feel exhausted. I suggest to Noah that we could probably go.

"Are you sure?" he asks, almost as if he's reluctant to leave.

"Yes," I tell him. "I don't think that even Tina can fault me with tonight's performance."

"Performance?" he says as we leave.

"I guess that's not exactly right. But I was so reluctant to come... I guess I felt like I was simply doing it to make others happy."

"So did you have *any* fun?" he asks as we walk through the hotel lobby.

"Sure," I admit. "I had more fun today than I've had..." I pause to consider this. "In a long, long time."

Noah nods and seems relieved. And then he does something totally unexpected: he takes my hand. And as we stand outside the hotel, waiting for the parking valet to bring his pickup, he continues to hold it. And despite all my previous judgments and misgivings and concerns about too-attractive men and their baggage, I wish he would hold my hand forever. And although that scares me, I know it's just one more thing I will have to trust God with.

Noah tips the valet and then helps me into his pickup, carefully closing the door without trapping my skirt in it. But I feel a little nervous as he slowly walks around to the other side. I'm worried that I misread the little hand-holding gesture. But I decide not to obsess over it. And I don't obsess over what I confessed to him about my broken engagement or over how quiet he is as he drives me back to the apartment complex. Then, like a perfect gentleman, Noah walks me to my door.

"Thanks for being my escort," I tell him.

"Still just an escort?" he queries. "A gigolo?"

"Well, as I mentioned, a gigolo gets paid."

"And as I mentioned, I might insist on a payment."

Okay, I'm not sure how to respond to this, so I just smile and hold up my little beaded purse. "Okay, how much do I owe you?"

"One kiss."

Well, I'm thankful my door is solidly behind me, or I might fall over just now. "A kiss?" I echo quietly.

"I'm sorry," he says quickly. "I shouldn't have said that." And before I can stop him, he tips his head politely, says a quick good-night, and takes off. And I just stand there and wonder why I am such an idiot.

Thirty minutes later, feeling very much like Cinderella—Cinderella after midnight, that is—I am wearing my old work clothes, and with Riley in the back of my dad's red pickup, I am driving across town and listening to country-western music again. Most of all I am wondering what exactly happened tonight. My head is spinning. And while part of me is excited at the prospects, part of me is screaming, "Watch out! Danger! Danger! Lock up your heart, you silly girl!"

I distract myself with all that must be done to the house—and the list is truly overwhelming. My plan is to spend the night here and get an early start tomorrow. Travel time is valuable time. And the deadline on the loan looms like a death sentence before me. Every minute is precious.

As I work Sunday, I have all day to process the events of the previous evening and to convince myself it was nothing. By Monday, I feel almost certain that Noah and I were both under the influence of the wedding, the champagne, and the moonlight. Maybe whatever it was that happened at the door of my apartment is best forgotten.

And it's just as well because the next few days are hectic-crazy. It's like everyone my dad's been calling this past week has suddenly kicked it into high gear. Both Noah and I are running as fast as we can to keep up with plumbers, electricians, and window installers. Even the sod for the yard arrives on Friday. I cannot help but be incredibly glad Noah's here with me. His calmness in the midst of chaos feels like a safe port in the storm. And yet he's not just sitting around. I'm amazed at what he's able to accomplish—and how much the other workers seem to respect and rely on him. I'm becoming more and more aware that there is no way I could pull this off on my own. And it's humbling.

Later on Friday afternoon Kirsten joins me on a shopping run to purchase bedding plants at a nursery that's having a half-price sale. I can't wait to perk up the flower beds alongside the new green lawn.

"I thought you said you weren't my dad's girlfriend," Kirsten abruptly says after we've loaded the pickup bed so full of plants that it looks like a garden on wheels.

"What?" I turn and stare at her. She has a smudge of dirt on the tip of her nose, and I use my bandanna to wipe it off.

"You said you *weren't* Dad's girlfriend," she says.

"I'm not." Okay, I'm blushing now, and I hope she's too young to know what that means.

"But he got all dressed up and took you to that wedding. And my grandma says she wants to meet you now."

"Why?"

"Because you're Dad's girlfriend." She states this as if she's questioning my ability to understand English just now.

"I think that's an overstatement," I say.

"What's that mean? Don't you want to be his girlfriend? Don't you like him?"

"Of course, I like him."

"Don't you like me?"

"Yes, of course I like you!"

Now she looks disappointed. "Then what's wrong?"

I have to laugh. "You're so sweet to want me to be your dad's girlfriend, Kirsten. But what if your dad doesn't like me as a girlfriend?"

"But he does," she insists. "I know he does."

I decide to change the subject now. No way am I going to allow a seven-year-old to be the middleman between Noah and me. This is getting too crazy. "So, do you think you and Cory can plant some of those petunias for me?" I ask as I point at a big flat of red blooms.

"Yeah!" she says. "Where?"

"In front," I say, "out by the walk."

As we continue to talk about flowers, all I can think about is Noah. Well, Noah and the fact that there is only one week before my so-called open house, and the cabinets still haven't shown up. Dad had practically promised they'd be here this week, but Miguel, the cabinet guy, has not been answering his phone lately. Not a good sign. Still, I'm not going to freak out. Instead of worrying I'm trying to rely on God. And somehow that relieves much of my anxiety.

"There you are," says Noah as I help Kirsten down from the pickup. Her sore foot makes it hard for her to climb in and out.

"What's up?" I ask, trying to act nonchalant.

"Not much...except that the floor is down."

"I can't wait to see it!" I exclaim. I don't know why I feel so excited, because it was nearly finished when we left. But something about seeing completed projects is very fulfilling these days. And the idea of the new wood floor meeting the old one—making it into one complete space—is encouraging.

"I'd join you," he glances at his watch, "but Kirsten and I need to get going."

"Already?" complains Kirsten. "I wanted to plant flowers."

"Sorry, princess," he says. "But we've got places to go and people to see." He turns to me. "I wish I could be more help this weekend, but I've got to—"

"It's okay," I say quickly. Noah made his position clear from the start. As a recovering workaholic, he has determined that weekends weren't made for working. I know he has a life beyond Lilac Lane. Maybe someday I will too. "Have a great weekend," I tell them.

"I'll see you on Monday." He pauses after helping Kirsten into his pickup. Then he looks directly into my eyes with a gaze so intense that my knees turn to mush. And I think he's about to say something... well, romantic. But all he says is, "Too bad about those cabinets."

"I know..." I swallow hard and take a steadying breath. "I'm trying not to freak out. I'm trying to pray and have faith..."

"Do you have a backup plan?" His eyes are still fixed on me, and the air between us seems to crackle with electricity. Even as we discuss what now feels like the most mundane of details, it feels more like we are talking about us—our future together—and that makes me wonder if I'm becoming delusional.

I push a strand of hair away from my face, then look away. "Not really...other than delaying the open house."

"That'd be bad."

I look back at him now, and my chest tightens...like I'm on the verge of tears or something else altogether. "I know...but I haven't given up yet."

"No..." He smiles now, and his eyes sort of twinkle. "Neither have I."

If we were in a movie and I was directing this scene, I'd have these two characters fall into each other's arms...kiss passionately... fade out...and live happily ever after. But in this real-life scenario, I stand in the cracked driveway and wave as I watch his old turquoise pickup drive away. Then I go into the house and admire Noah's craftsmanship. The floor looks amazing. He has seamlessly matched old to new. And other than the color variation, which will disappear once the new wood is stained and the old wood is refinished, it is perfect. I can't wait to get to work on it, and I've already reserved the floor sander for the weekend—and I didn't scrimp. I got the big machine that you simply push like a vacuum over the floor. And I have the baseboard and window-trim pieces laid out over sawhorses in the garage, ready for their final coat of paint.

I walk through the house, admiring the progress made this week. Dad was right; once things start falling into place, it happens quickly. The windows are in, and except for the missing trim, they look fantastic. The new light fixtures are in and working. Most of the interior painting is done. The doors have all arrived, and Noah will install them next week. The bathrooms and my tile work are nearly completed, and all the plumbing fixtures are in and functioning. The only thing missing is the kitchen—only the most important selling feature of any house. Other than that small glitch, everything looks pretty good. Even the kitchen appliances are here, still in their boxes, waiting for the missing cabinets to join them. Of course, I still have the exterior painting to do…and the landscaping…and a dozen other "final touch" chores. But even if all that's completed, without a kitchen, what's the point? I decide this is a good time to mentally hand these concerns over to God. And while I'm at it, I also give God my turbulent feelings toward Noah.

After a brief but quiet moment, I go out and unload the plants and flowers to the garage, where I apply the final coat of paint to the baseboard and window trim. I check on Riley, who is happy as a clam out on the cool green grass in the backyard. I fill his food and water dishes and sit down on the deck, which still needs refinishing. Although it's not too high on my priority list right now, if enough helpers show for Holly and Justin's work party, I might want to have the materials ready to go. I look around the backyard and imagine how great it's going to look once the house is painted and the flowers and shrubs are planted. All it needs is some outdoor furniture.

And this gives me an idea. Just this week Dad asked me to see if a particular set of teak outdoor furniture was still at one of the home-improvement stores. And it was. What could be better for Father's Day? And then I can bring his old set back here.

So I tell Riley to be a good dog and I'll be back later, and I head back to Home Depot, where I purchase the teak set along with some deck sealer and planters, putting all these on my project card, which is close to maxed out now. Then I head over to Dad's and surprise him. Of course, this poses a problem, because now I have to unload the heavy pieces, and I cannot allow him to help. Fortunately, as I'm lugging the second chair out of the pickup, which is backed up as close to the condo as possible, I notice a couple of teenage boys and offer to pay them for some help. They seem glad to make a few bucks, and in no time we have switched the outdoor furniture sets, and my dad is happily sitting on his patio in a teak chair.

"Let's order takeout," suggests Dad as he sips his iced tea and admires the finish on the table. And so we do. Then as I'm cleaning up, Dad reminds me that his physical therapist told him it's okay to venture out now and that he'd like to see the house.

"How about after the weekend?" I suggest. Then I explain about tomorrow's work party. "And on Sunday, Father's Day, I thought I'd come over and fix you a special lunch. We can celebrate out here with your fancy new furniture."

He smiles. "Sounds perfect. But on Monday, I want to see the house."

"Speaking of the house…," I begin slowly, not sure I want to broach this subject, "any word from the cabinet guy?"

Dad brightens. "Yes!"

"Really? Good news?"

"I think so. I spoke to him this afternoon, and he assured me the cabinets are done."

"They're done?"

"Not only that, but he said his brother can give you a great deal on a slab of granite."

"No way!" I practically spill my iced tea I'm so excited.

Dad laughs. "But what about your budget? You said we've already put a huge dent in the reserves."

I frown now. The truth is, the reserves are almost completely gone. There's just enough left to pay for the cabinets and countertops. "But he said a great deal?"

"Yes...but it's granite, sweetie. You know that's pretty spendy."

I do some mental calculations now. I still have a Visa card that I've been holding on to for emergencies. Is this an emergency? Maybe I can get the rest of the building materials on my credit card and use the remaining reserves to buy the granite. Mostly, I'm so happy to hear the cabinets are coming that I feel slightly euphoric.

"What's Noah doing this weekend?" asks Dad.

"Huh?" I pull myself back into the present. "I don't know," I admit. "Something with Kirsten."

Dad nods with a curious expression. "So...have you changed your opinion of him? I mean, working with him and all...do you still—"

"What is it with everyone?" I say quickly. "Noah's a nice guy, okay. And he's a fantastic carpenter, but that's where it ends. We have one week—no, make that five working days since he won't be back until Monday—to work together, and then I expect Noah will move on with his life. End of story." Okay, I don't know where that outburst came from; I think I'm just tired. Or maybe I'm just sick of everyone—well, except for Noah and me—being very certain about our so-called relationship. Or maybe I just need a nice long vacation on some deserted island in the South Pacific.

"Me thinks thou dost protest too much."

*"Dad!"* I decide to humor him with a smile as I walk out toward the pickup.

But as I drive back to the house, all I can think about is the fact that there are only *five* days left to spend with Noah and Kirsten. And that is killing me.

# 27

Saturday's work party is larger than expected, and although I had planned to sand the floors today, I find myself directing traffic and playing gofer instead. But the amount of work that is completed by the end of the day is nothing short of astonishing. Even the kitchen cabinets arrive and are much nicer than I could've imagined—well worth the wait. Miguel and Justin put them in place, and I'm so pleased that it's all I can do not to just stand in the kitchen and stare. The finish on the maple is like silk, and the sleek, contemporary styling is absolutely perfect. I can't wait to see them with the nickel hardware I picked out. And when Miguel shows me a sample of the slab that his brother can use for the counters, I gladly agree. When I hear the cost, I know it will stretch me, but I am convinced it will be worth it.

"Wow," says Holly at the end of the day. She and I are walking around now, both inside and outside, observing what looks like a brand-new house. The work crew, tired and paint splattered and full of pizza, has dispersed, and Justin is just finishing the last of the baseboard in the great room. Tyler Barrett, the handiest guy of the bunch, was in charge of cutting and fitting the baseboard and window trim, and I think that even Noah will be satisfied with his work. It turned out that Maureen McCulley knew how to use a floor sander, and she and her sister Megan took over the floors, which are now ready to be stained and sealed. I plan to do this tonight so they can have a good long time to dry before Monday. Riley and I will spend the night at the apartment.

Other than the exterior window and door trim, which still isn't in place, the outside painting is almost completely done, and the soft, dusty shade of green is perfect. Also, the landscaping is finished except for the two flats of petunias I'm saving for Kirsten and Cory. Kelly Majors took charge of this, and we all decided that she may need to give up her nurse's job to take up landscaping. The deck is repaired and sealed, and before long I will be placing the beautifully arranged flowerpots and deck furniture around. I can hardly wait.

"I think we're going to make it," I say to Holly as we stand in the kitchen and admire the most amazingly transformed area of the house.

"I can't believe what you've done with this place," she admits. "You might want to take this up professionally."

"Oh, I don't know…" I think of the sacrifices…the stress…the work…the sleep deprivation.

"Noah's going to be surprised, isn't he?"

I shrug. "I guess."

"What is it with you, Gretch? Every time I mention his name, you just freeze. What's going on?"

"Nothing."

"Come on, spill the beans. I know you, and I know something is going on. Out with it."

"Really," I say, "there's nothing going on, Holly. If there were, you'd be the first one I'd tell." But the fact is, I can't bring myself to tell her the truth. I can't even admit the truth to myself. I don't want to think about it. I don't want to get my hopes up. Most of all I don't want to get hurt...not again. I know I'm making assumptions...getting my hopes up. And I'm afraid before long I'll be sorry.

It's around one on Sunday when I take Riley and several bags of groceries over to Dad's house to fix us a late lunch. For Dad's sake, I primped some and dressed nicely, even putting on a flowery sundress that I was surprised actually fit. And Dad seems genuinely pleased with everything. As I wash and clean the seafood I just picked up, I give him a full progress report. I even get out my digital camera and try to show him some shots I took yesterday, but as usual he complains they're too small to really see.

"Someone's at the door," I call outside to Dad. "I'd get it, but I've got shrimp gunk all over my hands." So he and Riley go to the door.

"Betty!" exclaims Dad joyfully. I put down the shrimp I'm cleaning, quickly rinse my hands, and rush out to greet her, only to discover that I have to wait for Dad to let go of her first. I cannot believe how happy he is to see her. He's beaming like a sixteen-year-old boy after his first kiss!

"I came home a week early," she explains as she hugs me. "I enticed Louise's husband to join her in Paris for the last week, and I changed my flight, and, well, here I am." She hugs Dad again. "Boy, did I miss you, darling." Soon they're sitting together outside, catching up and celebrating her homecoming with a glass of Pinot Noir that she brought all the way home from France. I'm back in the kitchen as I continue to fix one of Dad's favorite meals—seafood linguine—but I'm starting to feel like the best thing would be to serve it and leave. Maybe Dad and Betty would like to be alone. If I could just come up with a graceful way to do this. As I'm draining the pasta and getting an impromptu steam facial, I hear Dad calling me.

"Another guest," he says, and I go to see that Noah is standing by the door with a slightly sheepish expression.

I use the back of my hand to push a damp strand of hair from my eyes and stare at him curiously. "What's up?"

He holds out another bottle of red wine to Dad. "Happy Father's Day."

"You're just in time for a late lunch," says Dad. "And Betty's here too!"

"I don't mean to intrude," says Noah, looking cautiously at me. Does he think I don't want him here? That I might throw him out?

"Where's Kirsten?" I ask.

"With Camille and Peter."

"Oh..." I want to ask why but then decide not to. I have a feeling it's not a happy subject. "Well, there's plenty of food. Do you like seafood linguine?"

"Love it. Need any help?"

I consider this and then decline. My confidence level in the kitchen is usually high, but I have a feeling Noah could rattle me today. So I encourage him to join Betty and Dad and to check out the new patio set. Soon we're all seated together, enjoying the meal, and the conversation is lively. Betty tells great stories about her trip, and Noah and I update her on the house, telling her it might actually be ready to go on the market in a few days. And she offers to act as my real-estate agent—without charging a fee. I can almost safely say that things are coming together.

We're just finishing up when Dad asks Noah about his boat.

Noah grins. "As a matter of fact, Kirsten and I took her out on her maiden voyage yesterday."

"How was she?" Dad asks.

"Very nice." Noah's look of humble pride shakes me a little.

"Well, you'll have to take me out sometime," says Dad. "I'm pretty sure it'd be good for my heart."

"Not for several more weeks," I point out.

"How about you then?" asks Noah.

I blink. "Me?"

"You're not working today, are you?"

"That's a great idea," says Dad. "You kids take off and enjoy yourselves."

"Perfect," agrees Betty a little too quickly. "Be on your way, kids, and I'll clean things up in the kitchen." She pats me on the back. "That was a fantastic lunch, Gretchen, and you need a break."

So it is that I find myself sitting on a boat out in the San Diego harbor and wondering if life can get any better than this. It's amazing how thoughts of house flips and remodels totally evaporate with the smell of the fresh sea air and the clean blue water to focus on. And the sailboat is incredible. I can hardly believe that Noah actually built it, well, except that I've seen his work. The man is an artist when it comes to wood.

"This boat is absolutely beautiful," I tell him as I run my hand over the sleek mahogany surface of the deck. It's as smooth as satin. "You are a master."

"Thank you." He smiles, and his eyes crinkle at the edges. "It was very satisfying to complete."

I nod and think about the house and how it might feel to

complete it. I lean back and look up at a cloud that's floating across the sky, moving north as we move south. Then I take in a long, deep breath and just feel thankful to be alive—and to be out here with him on a day like this.

"You really handle the boat well," I say. He's turning now. Or is that keeling? I try not to look too anxious as I cling to the rail and the boat changes directions. Fortunately I remember to duck as that big thing that looks like it could knock me out moves across the boat. I think it's called a boom, but I hate to keep asking. I should've been taking notes as Noah told me the names of various parts of this magnificent vessel. Between the sheets and the shrouds and the jib and the jibe, I don't really know leeward from starboard. Still, I wouldn't mind learning.

He steers the boat back toward the docks. "I never felt the least bit seasick out there," I tell him. "You must be a good driver, rather captain."

"Thanks. You're a pretty good first mate." He looks down, almost embarrassed, clearly aware of his cheesy line. Still, I can't help but giggle a little.

Once we're back at the docks, I offer to help. He gives me simple chores, like coiling the rope as he ties down the sails, but I get the impression that he can handle this by himself just fine. Even so, I try to appear useful.

As he drives me back to Dad's, I chatter about how fantastic that was, what a great boat builder he is, and how much fun I had.

"I take it you enjoyed yourself," he says as he turns down the street toward Dad's condo.

The sun is just setting now, and I am incredibly happy. "You mean I didn't gush enough?" I ask. I sigh and relax back into the seat. I feel completely refreshed. And to my surprise, I feel hopeful that life can actually be fun again.

He chuckles. "No, you gushed plenty."

"I wasn't exaggerating either," I remind him as he turns in to the condo. "That boat is fantastic. And now I can see why you love sailing so much."

"There's nothing quite like it." He pulls up near Dad's unit, but all the spaces are full, and I notice that Betty's car is still here, so I tell him I'll just grab Riley and head out.

"That sailboat trip made me sleepy," I admit as I reach for my bag.

He nods. "I know what you mean. Tell Hank and Betty good night for me, will you?"

"No problem." I get out now, but to my surprise he gets out too.

"See you tomorrow," he says just like always. But he just stands there. And suddenly it seems he's giving me that same look again, staring deep into my eyes as if he's trying to see what I'm thinking. What am I thinking? We both just stand like we're frozen, and then before I have time to second-guess or question anything, he leans toward me. And we are kissing. Although I'm no longer on the boat, I feel myself keeling, as if the earth is rocking and I'm about to tip over.

Then he steps back and looks uncomfortable. "I, uh, I hope that was okay."

I just smile, and without saying a word, I nod. I'm actually hoping he'll kiss me again. I am ready…waiting.

Instead, he takes my hand in his and just looks into my eyes with that same sweet intensity that renders me speechless. "I've wanted to do that for weeks, Gretchen."

I blink in surprise.

"And there's so much I want to say—"

Just then Riley comes bounding toward me, and I look up to see Dad and Betty waving from the front door of Dad's condo.

"Sorry about Riley's interruption!" calls Dad. "He was whining to get out. He must've known you were here."

"It's fine," I say as I reach for Riley's collar. Okay, so Dad's and Riley's timing were a little off. But at least Dad didn't see what happened between Noah and me. If he had, he would have surely held Riley back. Or he might've dashed over here to shake Noah's hand and tease me.

"Anyway," says Noah quickly, "we can talk later."

"Thanks for the boat ride," I say. Suddenly I feel a pull to get away…although I want to stay too. Mostly I want the moment to repeat itself. Without interruptions.

After I hoist Riley into Dad's pickup, I replay that amazing kiss. And I replay what Noah said about wanting to do that for weeks. As I drive across town to the house, I wonder what it means. Is he saying that he's in love? Am I in love? Or am I just hoping…just imagining things?

~ ~ ~

The next three days are spent completing all the finish work. Although everything looks so close to being done, it all takes longer than I expect. But we don't give up. We stay focused, and one by one the list of tasks shortens. And when I'm tempted to take a shortcut, like not sealing the grout lines properly, Noah reminds me that if we're going to do this, we might as well do it right.

The granite countertop is in place by Wednesday morning, and later that day Noah hooks up the plumbing to the countersunk sink himself. It all looks wonderful.

"Nice work," I say as I admire the faucet, which actually works.

"Nice choice of materials," he says to me. And once again we are pausing to look at each other, and I wonder if he's about to take me in his arms again. I think I may simply leap toward him. And maybe I would...except my confidence is just not there yet.

"We make a good house-flipping team," I finally say, then I wish I hadn't. Maybe it sounds too presumptuous. Or maybe it sounds too final.

"I never would've guessed this house could turn out so well," he admits. "When I first saw it, I honestly thought you were crazy."

"You're not alone there."

"And if I could afford it, I'd buy this place myself."

"You mean you can't afford it?"

He laughs. "Did you think I was rich?"

I shrug and glance away uncomfortably.

"Well, as you know, I used to be," he admits. "But life and Camille and my mom... It all continues to take a toll on my savings, and working as a carpenter is not exactly lucrative." Then he smiles. "Although that was my goal—to live a simpler life. So I'm not complaining." And that's it. The moment has passed, and we're both back working against the clock to finish this thing.

By Thursday the last of the work is complete. In my mind the house is perfect, and I am ready to stage the rooms. Dad thinks staging is a waste of time and energy, but Betty is all for it, and Noah, fellow HGTV fan, understands too. He helps me move some of the larger pieces from my apartment to the house. I also borrow a few things from Dad, and Betty even loans me some nice pieces. It's an all-day task, and Noah has to leave to pick up Kirsten before I'm done. But I am driven. All I can think about is getting things in place, being ready for the open house, selling this place…and then what? I can't think that far ahead anymore. I'm too tired.

"This looks awesome," says Holly on Friday night. It's almost ten o'clock now, and tomorrow is the open house. She's helped me with the final cleaning and tweaking, and now we're hanging pictures.

"You've been a great help," I tell her as I straighten a black-and-white photo of Kirsten and Riley sitting on the tailgate of Noah's pickup.

"I assume you took these photos, Gretch."

"I did."

"They're amazing. Everything is truly fantastic."

"I hope the buyers think so." I frown as I consider the price I'm putting on it. "Betty said that it might be a challenge."

"Why?"

"Because of the price."

"I'd buy it if I could," she says.

"Me too. But Betty's worried that we might be overpriced for this neighborhood."

"Oh…"

But the open house seems to go wonderfully. Everyone appears to be very impressed. With everything but the price, that is. As it turns out, Betty was right. While they all agree the house is absolutely fantastic, which I admit is almost enough for me, the consensus seems to be that the neighborhood is not so hot. Consequently, the price is too high.

By the end of the weekend, Betty strongly suggests that we reduce the price.

"After only two days?" I plead with her. I'm having dinner with her and Dad tonight. She cooked this time, and I'm probably acting like a baby. "Can't we wait a week or two?"

"You can wait as long as you like, Gretchen, but it's doubtful anything will change. Other than you'll be sending the wrong message to Realtors; they'll think you're not serious about selling."

"But the house is so nice," I point out. A fact that no one has denied.

"Yes, but all the Realtors insist it's overpriced," she tells me. "Even if a buyer wanted to purchase it, a conventional loan wouldn't be approved for that much—not without a substantial down payment, which a first-time buyer probably won't have."

"Why wouldn't it be approved?"

"Because the house's appraisal won't equal the amount of the loan."

"Oh."

"Unless you had a buyer come in with lots of cash and a burning desire to buy the house despite the lower values of neighboring homes, no one would want to pay that much." Betty sadly shakes her head. "I hate to be the bearer of bad news."

"But the facts are the facts, Gretchen." Dad pats my hand. "It is what it is."

"In other words my flip is a flop."

"No, not at all. You'll still make a little bit of money," Betty points out.

"And we'll be able to pay back the loan." Dad looks hopeful now, like maybe he really was worried about losing his condo.

"And you've learned a lot," says Betty.

I nod. Obviously, I have no choice but to agree. And I know I should be thankful, but I feel really deflated. Naturally, Dad and Betty assume that my less than cheerful demeanor is because of the reduced price, but the truth is, I think I am grieving. I cannot believe I won't be going to work on the house tomorrow. I won't be spending the next week with Noah and Kirsten. Add to that the fact that Noah hasn't even called. I know that it's over. Not that it had ever begun…not really. But, besides that, I feel lost. Like there's nothing left to do. Nothing to distract myself with. And every time I think of Noah, I feel a great big stab of pain in my heart, and I wonder if I might be the next one to undergo coronary bypass surgery. Hadn't I known it would come down to this? Why did I allow myself to be taken in?

Finally I can't stand it anymore. It was sweet of Dad and Betty to invite me over, and they're trying to be kind, but I know I'm being a party pooper. I hate to spoil their time together since I know for a fact that any day now my dad is going to pop the big question—maybe even tonight. So I tell them good-bye, and I get into my little Bug and go home to my little apartment where my big dog is also in deep grief. He misses that backyard and green grass and freedom. And maybe he misses Kirsten too. I don't want to think about it.

I spend the next couple of days in serious grief. I won't even go to the house—it hurts too much to see it. Plus, it adds insult to injury that the price is being reduced so much that, once the loan is repaid, I won't have enough for a down payment for anything bigger than a travel trailer, which means I'll be stuck in this apartment for another year.

Although I am beginning to toy with the idea of flipping another house. Part of me thinks it's crazy, and I can't believe I would dare to entertain such a thought. But Betty told me it's probably like childbirth: it's painful, and you swear you'll never do it again, but in time you sort of forget, and you go through it again. Maybe next summer. Who knows? And maybe Noah would help me again…or would that be asking for trouble? Not that it matters. I can't stop thinking about him anyway. Why doesn't he call?

On Wednesday afternoon Betty calls, and there is genuine excitement in her voice. She has a full, "unconditional" offer for my reduced price and wants to know if I will accept. Of course I know I must accept. So I tell her it sounds fine. And I know I should be happy—and greatly relieved that Dad's condo is no longer on the chopping block—but I am still grieving. I hate to let it go.

"Oh, there is *one* condition," she says as I'm about to hang up and indulge in a good long cry.

"I thought you said it was *unconditional*."

"Well, it's not a *written* condition, but the buyer has requested that you show the house yourself. Apparently there are some questions, some concerns about how things were done during the remodel, and you need to discuss—"

"Maybe Noah should talk to the buy—"

"No, Gretchen," she says firmly. *"It has to be you."*

"Well, fine," I almost snap at her. "When am I supposed to meet with them?"

"Tonight at six."

*"At six?"*

"Maybe the buyer can't get time off work during the day. Do you want to sell the house or not?"

"Fine," I say again. Then I hang up and feel guilty for being such a grouch to her. Poor Betty. She thought she was giving me good news, and I bit her head off. I know I'll have to apologize later. Maybe I'll even take her flowers. I'm thankful she's a forgiving person.

As I get dressed, thinking it might not be too impressive to show up in my grungy old sweats that I've worn for two days straight, I decide it's time, once again, to give this whole thing to God. Really, why am I being such a baby? Here I thought I had grown up, and suddenly I'm going backward again. So I pray, and my attitude improves.

It's nearly six now, and Riley is running around the apartment like he can read my mind. Like he knows I'm going somewhere he wants to go. So I think, what the heck? Why not just take him with me? I mean, the house is still officially mine, and the backyard is still officially mine. What can it hurt to let him run around a bit…one last time?

~ ~ ~

When I arrive at the house, I'm surprised to see Noah's pickup in the driveway, but I decide Betty must have taken my suggestion. After all, if the buyer has serious questions, Noah is the man to answer them. I'm halfway tempted to keep on driving and let him deal with it. But I go ahead and park behind his pickup. I lead Riley to the side gate and let him loose in the backyard. He is in doggy heaven once again.

But as I walk around to the front door, I begin to feel nervous, and my heart is pounding. I know this is not related to showing the house to my perspective buyer. This is about Noah. I am all aflutter to see him again.

The door's not locked, so I assume he's inside. Taking a steadying breath, I slowly open the door. But as I enter the great room, I feel a huge lump in my throat. Why should it hurt so much to let go of this place? You'd think I'd be glad and proud of the work I've done. Suddenly I notice there's soft jazz music playing—a nice touch. And there are candles burning—another nice touch. Why has Noah gone to so much trouble for a buyer who's already sold on the house?

"Welcome," says Noah. He smiles as he motions me into the kitchen, where it seems that someone has actually prepared dinner. Okay, I know that scents reminiscent of home, like cooking spices, are supposed to help sell houses, but isn't this going a bit far? Then I notice that my dining room table is completely set. And I see there are even *more* candles, as well as what looks like a bottle of champagne chilling in a silver bucket that doesn't belong to me.

"What's going on?" I ask, feeling like I'm in a dream. "Where is the buyer?"

Noah looks sheepish as he points his thumb to his chest.

I blink and reach for the back of a dining chair to balance myself because it feels like the world is suddenly tipping sideways.

"*You* are the buyer?" I finally manage to say.

"I am...but there is one condition."

I feel weak, like maybe I should sit down or faint or something. "Betty said it was an unconditional offer." Okay, I know how lame that sounds, but it's the best I can do at the moment. I'm having trouble breathing.

That's when Noah goes down on one knee, and he takes my hand in his, and I seriously think I am going to faint now—or throw up or something equally humiliating.

"Gretchen Hanover, will you please marry me and share this house with me and help me raise Kirsten and—"

"What?" I stare at him in disbelief.

"I know I haven't done it all right," he says quickly. Then he stands, and I suddenly worry he's about to take it back. Or maybe I've misunderstood. But then I look around—the candles, the champagne… I get the picture.

"I wanted to tell you after we went sailing that I love you. I wanted to take things slowly, but then I needed to tell all this to Kirsten… I needed to get things in order. I'm sorry if I'm catching you off guard."

"No no," I say quickly. "That's okay."

"Do you love me?" he asks.

I take a deep breath…then I nod. "Yes, Noah, I do love you." I can't believe I just said that, and yet I am so glad to have it out in the open.

Now he goes back down on one knee. "So, I repeat, Gretchen Hanover—"

"Yes!" I shout out. I don't even let him finish. I don't even hesitate. I don't want to think about it anymore. I absolutely know that this is what I want. What I've wanted for some time but couldn't admit—even to myself. And now he's standing and laughing, and I'm laughing too, although I have tears streaming down my cheeks. And the next thing I know, I am in his arms again, and once again he is kissing me—passionately!

Just like that scene in my make-believe movie, we are fading out...and it's clear this happy couple will live happily ever after, right here in this house. Or perhaps we will sail out into the sunset on Noah's beautiful boat.

But I soon discover that's not to be the case. At least not the part about sailing off into the sunset. As Noah serves me dinner, a meal that's actually quite good, we talk about everything—replaying all that's gone on these amazing past six weeks and how God's been at work in both of us and how miraculous it is that we found each other and all sorts of sappy, wonderful, romantic things.

"But how can you afford this house?" I finally ask. Dinner is done, and we're standing outside on the deck, wrapped in each other's arms. I hate to bring up a subject like finances in the midst of romance, but it's been in the back of my mind since we finished dessert.

"Promise you won't get mad?"

I laugh. "I've been engaged to you for like maybe ninety minutes. Do you seriously think I could get mad at you now or anytime soon?"

"I sold the sailboat."

I can't even speak as I consider this. Did I hear him right?

"Are you okay?"

*"You sold the sailboat?"* I echo.

"You promised you wouldn't get mad."

"I-I'm not mad. Just confused. You love that boat, Noah. You put your heart and soul into it."

"I put my head and my hands into it. My heart has better things to do."

I cannot believe this incredible sacrifice, and I feel tears welling up again. "I just can't believe it," I finally mutter. "You sold your boat…"

"I wanted to sell it, Gretchen. Honestly, it was worth it. And if it makes you feel any better, I got an incredibly good price for it, enough to pay off most of the house. And I can build another boat. Maybe a little smaller this time, a little easier to handle. And your dad can help me, and—"

But I stifle his explanation with a kiss. A sweet, long kiss. And then, as I run my hands over his face and stare deep into his eyes, I say, "And, hey, if all else fails, we can take on this house-flipping business professionally."

Looking directly into my eyes, he nods. "The thought has crossed my mind too."

"And to think…I thought this flip was going to flop."

# About the Author

MELODY CARLSON is the award-winning author of more than one hundred books for adults, children, and teens. She is the mother of two grown sons and lives near the Cascade Mountains in central Oregon with her husband and a chocolate Lab retriever. She is a full-time writer and an avid gardener, biker, hiker, and home remodeler.

## Other Books by Melody Carlson

*These Boots Weren't Made for Walking*

*On This Day*

*Finding Alice*

*Crystal Lies*

Notes from a Spinning Planet series

Diary of a Teenage Girl series

The Secret Life of Samantha McGregor series